Se... the H...rt

Lori Stratton

//
F
Stratton
T56909

Seasons of the Heart

Lori Stratton

Parson Place Press
Mobile, Alabama

Hesston Public Library
P.O. Box 640
110 East Smith
Hesston, KS 67062

Copyright © 2008 by Lori Stratton

All rights reserved. No part of this book may be used or reproduced in any manner whatsoever without written permission from the publisher, except in the case of brief quotations embodied in reviews. For information contact:

Parson Place Press
10701 Tanner Williams Road
Mobile, Alabama 36608

Cover Design by Just Ink

ISBN 10: 0-9786567-2-5
ISBN 13: 978-0-9786567-2-0

Library of Congress Control Number: 2007941441

For my mother, Joy, who always believed I could,
and for Marc, who always knew I would.

Chapter One

Anna Svensen brushed aside the wisps of hair that had blown loose from the coiled braids at the nape of her neck. Placing her hands at her waist, she arched back, straightening her shoulders against the muscle tightness she felt. Sweat ran in rivulets under her dress and beaded across her upper lip and forehead. Just when she thought she had grown accustomed to the hot, heavy, stillness of Kansas in July, the wind had begun to blow. It had gusted heavily now for two days, and still only a few thin clouds drifted across the sky. She wondered if it would ever rain again and calm down the dust that seemed to be everywhere in the air.

"Anna! Daughter, hurry back!"

Sighing at the sound of her mother's voice, Anna lifted her flour-bag apron and wiped her forehead with its edge, hoping to avoid the stinging sensation of sweat entering her eyes. She turned back to the pump and gingerly grasped it, being careful to touch only the part of the handle that had been shaded by her body. She filled both buckets before beginning the short walk back to the family's shanty.

Elsie, Anna's five-year-old sister, smiled and waved as Anna passed. The youngster had been helping their mother clear the table when Anna had left to get water, but Christina could never seem to resist Elsie's pleadings for play time. Now she sat with her rag doll near a patch of wildflowers growing in the shade of the shanty.

"Did you fill both?" Christina asked as Anna stepped into the room. Her mother spoke Swedish, as she was prone to do unless reminded by her husband.

"Yes, Mama."

Stopping for a moment, the teenager let her eyes grow accustomed to the dim light inside the home. With only three rooms and two windows, the shanty was often in darkness unless the day was fair enough to leave the door open. At least the darkness helped somewhat to keep the heat out.

"Bring the water here, then. We will warm it, and I will wash and you can dry," Christina directed. "I let Elsie play outside. She wanted to be in the fresh air so badly, and we are almost done here, anyway."

Anna nodded, wondering how her mother could think of the blasts of hot air outside as fresh.

Soon the pair stood side by side next to the small basin in the largest room of the house, the room that served as a kitchen, living room, and Anna's bedroom. As the youngest, Elsie still slept in the trundle bed pulled out at night from under her parents' larger bed. Her brothers, Aaron, Joseph, and Bjorn, shared the lean-to behind the kitchen. Although the family had been in America for nearly two years, they had only lived on the homestead since the end of February, purchasing it inexpensively from a man who had decided to give up homesteading and return to the more civilized East.

As her mother washed, Anna carefully dried the dishes and cooking pots and stacked them on the rough hewn shelves attached to the wall. They had accumulated such few possessions since arriving in Kansas. The dishes would soon be used again when Anna and Christina prepared the evening meal. Anna sighed as she rubbed the plates dry with the rough dish towel.

"What is it, daughter?" Christina asked. "Are you not feeling well?"

"Oh, Mama," Anna murmured, the unexpected tears pressing against her eyes. "I feel fine. It is just so . . . so hard here. It is hot day and night, and our house is so small, and Papa and the boys have to work in the fields . . . all the time in the fields. There is so much work . . . the chickens, the garden. I sometimes wish . . . I wish we could just go home!"

The teenager burst into tears, covering her face with the towel.

"Oh, Anna," Christina said, dropping the dishcloth and embracing her daughter. Anna breathed in the smell of her mother – an outdoorsy smell, but more like spring than summer – and she sobbed uncontrollably.

"It is so hard here, Mama," she repeated between sobs. "I feel hot and dirty all of the time, and we barely have room in this house to turn around. Why did we have to come here, anyway? I want to be at home, in our house, and I want to see the river and the hills and feel cool breezes, not wind that is so hot it feels like it comes from the oven!"

"I know, my love, I know," Christina said, holding her daughter for several more minutes until the teenager's sobs began to slow down. Finally, Christina brushed back Anna's hair and looked into eyes that mirrored her own in their bright intensity.

"We must talk," she said, wiping Anna's tear-stained cheeks with her thumbs, and carefully breaking away. "Come. Let us sit."

Christina led Anna to one of the three benches that encircled the family's table. She waited until Anna sat and wiped her eyes again, and then she reached over and took her daughter's hand. Silently, Christina prayed to find words that might be comforting.

"You remember the day that your father and I told you that we would be coming to America?"

Anna nodded. It had been the middle of winter when her parents had called their three eldest children into the great room of their home in Sweden. Oscar had begun the conversation with prayer, asking for guidance while explaining a change in the family's circumstances to his children. Anna remembered how rapidly her heart had pounded in reaction to the news that the family would soon be leaving the only home she had known to start over in a new land among strangers.

"Good." Christina's voice brought Anna back to the present. "And you remember, also, the reasons that your father gave for making this move?"

Anna looked down at the table and ran her finger along its scratched edge. Oscar had spoken with pain in his voice about losing his job. The lumber mill which he had managed for fifteen years was closing. The owner was leaving the country. She nodded again.

"All right, then," Christina said. "Do you also remember what else your father told you on that day? I don't mean about the mill closing, but the part about why we were really moving?"

Anna looked into her mother's gentle face, an older version of her own.

"Your father felt led by God to come to America," Christina said, almost in a whisper. "He believed God knew there would be opportunity here for him as a Christian, and for us, his family."

Anna looked at the table again.

"We prayed about this move before we decided to come," Christina continued, a faraway look in her eyes. "We never could have bought a farm in Sweden. There wasn't any land we could …" She paused a moment, lifting her hands in the air. "We felt much at peace about the decision."

Christina drew her eyes back to Anna and leaned forward.

"We must continue to trust in God, daughter," she said, an urgency to her voice. "We must trust that we are following the path that God has laid out for us. Our needs are being met. We may not have much, but we are not hungry, and we have shelter. When it becomes difficult, we must trust that God knows our needs and will provide for them."

Anna felt tears threaten again. She searched her mother's face for doubt, but found only peace and even joy.

"Yes, Mama."

"We will make do," Christina said, dropping her daughter's hands and standing. "Now, come, let us get back to work. Please check on Elsie, and then we will work on that pile of mending."

Christina began to bustle around the small room, putting away the final few dishes. Anna watched her for a moment, and then walked out the door to check on her sister. She wished she felt her mother's calm peace about living in America. She envied Christina's ability to trust God and not worry about the luxuries the family was missing. Anna herself often felt angry at God. How could He, after all, ask her and her family to leave the people and places they had known and loved all of their lives?

Why would He bring them to such a desolate place where all that could be seen was rolling prairie and endless, endless sky?

She tried to clear her thoughts as she approached her sister. Elsie still played with the rag doll, seemingly oblivious to the heat and wind.

"Hello," Anna said, sitting down by the child. The earth pushed against her, and Anna knew her skirt would be dusty when she stood.

"Oh, isn't it a beautiful day?" As usual, Elsie spoke with an enthusiasm that shone through her light blue eyes.

"Yes, I suppose so," Anna said, mustering a smile as she gazed lovingly at the child. "I do think it is a little warm, though."

Elsie nodded, and then cocked her head to the left, a perplexed look crossing her face.

"Do you hear that bird? I wonder what kind of bird it is."

Anna smiled again, thinking about Elsie's unending curiosity.

"I believe it is a meadowlark. They are quite common here."

She scanned the field surrounding the homestead until she saw a bird perched on the top branch of a tree growing about six feet from the well. It was the only tree in sight, except for those a few hundred yards away, near the creek.

"Look, Elsie," she said, pointing toward the tree. "There he is. See the yellow on his breast? That is a meadowlark."

As if on cue, the tiny bird warbled again, and Elsie clapped her hands in delight, frightening the bird from its perch.

"Oh, he flew away!"

"Don't worry; I'm sure he'll come back."

Anna placed her arm around her sister and pulled her into a soft hug. "Maybe he has a nest nearby."

"Oh, do you think so?"

Anna stood up and brushed her skirt. She only had two work dresses, and this one had to stay clean until washing day on Monday.

"There might be a nest," she said. "We'll go and check after supper tonight. Right now, I must go in and help Mama."

"All right."

Anna turned toward the house, and then looked back at her sister.

"Elsie, do not go too far from the house. Remember Papa said there might be snakes where the grass gets taller."

Elsie looked up at her sister and smiled. Because she was the youngest, she had grown accustomed to having her siblings as well as her parents fuss over her and issue frequent warnings for her safety.

"I will stay close to the house."

Satisfied that the youngster would do so, Anna turned back toward the shanty, thinking about the mending that awaited her and wondering if she would ever grow accustomed to the desolation of the prairie.

Chapter Two

"Dear Father, bless this food which we are about to eat. Thank you for our home and our good health. If you see fit, Father, please let the rain come to quench the thirsting crops. In Your name we pray, Amen."

As Oscar finished the blessing, seven blonde heads lifted in unison from their bowed positions, and seven pairs of hands began passing the dishes Christina and Anna had prepared. It was a simple meal, made from the few vegetables the family had already harvested from their new garden, and some of the dried beef they seemed to consume three times daily. The kitchen had been hot while they cooked, but Christina had tried to keep Anna's spirits lifted by singing the teenager's favorite hymns. Along with her fair hair and eyes, Anna had inherited her mother's clear, strong voice, and the pair made quite an impression on all who heard them.

Oscar had been unusually quiet after praying, watching his family with a bemused look. He and his three sons had just returned before supper from West Bend. They had taken the wagon in for some supplies, and Anna knew that he might have news to share. He had already given Anna a long-awaited letter from Katerina, her Swedish school friend, and she hungered for any other item he could tell the family that might break the monotony of the long, hot days. Finally, as if on cue, he laid down his fork.

"They say there is to be a new teacher for the school this fall," Oscar said in broken English. In the hopes of encouraging his family to embrace their new culture, Oscar spoke English whenever possible, and always when the family ate together.

"An answer to prayer," Christina said, her eyes shining.

Anna, who had been absentmindedly pushing her food around her plate, had perked up when Oscar had mentioned the word, "school."

"Tell us, Papa, what you have heard," Anna breathed, reverting to her native language in her excitement.

"In English, please," Oscar said, trying to be stern although the twinkle in his eyes gave away his purpose.

"Oh, Papa," Anna said, wringing her hands in frustration. She tried again, this time in slow but careful English. "What do you . . . know . . . about a . . . the . . . new teacher?"

Oscar directed his gaze around the table until he had everyone's attention, and then began:

"It is a woman. She is coming from Missouri. She is young, not too much older than our Anna, and this is her first teaching job. She will be staying with the Allen family, and school will start in September."

He paused, lifted his cup to his mouth, and took a drink of water. It had been difficult for him to make such a long speech in English.

Anna felt her heart beat faster. A teacher for the school! The Svensen children had not been to school since they had boarded the ship that had brought them to America. When they arrived at West Bend in the spring, they had discovered that the school had closed in mid-winter when the teacher, a young man, had broken his leg by slipping on the ice. He left soon after for his parents' home in Topeka. Anna, who loved to read almost more than anything else in the world, had dearly missed attending school. And now there would be a chance to go again . . . .

Suddenly, she had a thought that brought quick tears to her eyes. She stifled a sob. There was so much work to do on the homestead. With water to carry, and cooking, laundry, mending, and the garden – surely her mother could not spare her eldest daughter for something so frivolous as school. After all, Anna could already read, write, and do sums, although she was a little slow at reading in English.

She took a deep breath and looked up, finding six pairs of eyes staring at her.

"You are lost in your own thoughts again, my Anna," Oscar said speaking softly, this time in Swedish. "You did not hear us call your name?"

"Oh, Papa," Anna said, trying not to sound disappointed. "I was thinking of how wonderful it will be for Joseph, Bjorn, and Elsie to go to school. Mama and I will be anxious to hear all about their lessons when they get home."

Christina and Oscar shared a knowing look across the table. They had suspected this might come up.

"Anna," her father said, again pretending to be stern. "I will not hear of it. You have two more years of school to finish, and you will not get out of doing so, no matter how hard you try."

Anna lifted her eyes to her father's face and saw understanding there. Oscar reached out a hand and touched his daughter's cheek.

"Of course you will be going to school, my love. A smart girl like you must finish."

"Oh, Papa," Anna breathed, tears of gratitude threatening to spill from her eyes. "But how will Mama . . . ?"

"I will manage just fine without you," Christina said. "But there will be plenty of work left when you return."

Anna beamed at both of her parents. Maybe Kansas wasn't going to be so bad, after all. She was going to school in September! She sat through the rest of the meal putting food in her mouth, but not really tasting anything.

Floating through the next few weeks, Anna eagerly anticipated the start of classes. The heat emanating from the Kansas sun still made chores difficult and slow, but she managed to keep her spirits high at the thought of returning to books in the fall. The Svensens hadn't room to bring but just a few books with them on their trip across the Atlantic, and Anna yearned to open the pages of a new volume, to discover the mysteries and worlds hidden between the covers.

Daily she practiced speaking English while she carried water, hung out clothes, or milked the family's sole cow. She worried about her speaking skills, but she knew she was a quick learner, and that there would be other immigrant children attending the rural school. After all, the Johannsens had been in Kansas even a shorter time than the Svensens.

Not all of Anna's siblings, however, shared her enthusiasm. At nineteen, Aaron would not be going, staying instead to help his father on the farm. Joseph, age fourteen, and Bjorn, ten, would be attending, although both of them claimed that they needed to help their father and brother much more than they needed an education. Even little Elsie would be going to school for the first time, and her eyes shone every time she spoke of it.

"Tell me again what it will be like, Anna," Elsie said one day, holding her sister's hand and skipping beside her on the walk to the family's well.

Anna smiled at Elsie's excitement, noticing that it was not much different than her own.

"Well, there will be lots of books there, and you will learn how to read and how to write."

Elsie nodded quickly.

"We will sit in rows with the other boys and girls," Anna continued. "It will be very important to mind the teacher. We must be on our best behavior, always."

Elsie nodded again, her expression solemn.

"Will it be different from the school in Sweden?"

Anna had already asked herself that question, and it had caused her more than one moment of fear.

"That I do not know," she said, frowning slightly. "We will just have to wait and see. I know the language will be different. We will be expected to speak English all of the time."

Elsie tightly squeezed her sister's hand. The five-year-old worried a little about school, but she knew that with her sister there, she would always be safe.

About two weeks before classes were scheduled to start, the Svensens met the new teacher. Tina Stevens attended church that morning with Tom and Marjorie Allen, the people with whom she was to board. Anna stared at Miss Stevens in disbelief when, at the end of his sermon, Pastor Heggarty introduced the petite brunette to the congregation.

"It is my pleasure to introduce West Bend's new schoolmistress, Tina Stevens," the elderly pastor had said, extending his hand.

Anna's breath caught in her throat. She wondered how tiny Miss Stevens could possibly command enough respect to teach a schoolroom full of students. After all, the teacher was just a girl who looked to be almost the same age as Anna herself.

But when Anna glanced at her parents, both of them were nodding and smiling, as if they totally accepted the fact that a young girl would attempt to do the job of an adult.

When Christina and Oscar motioned their children forward to meet Miss Stevens after church, Anna hesitated, falling back behind Elsie and her brothers. But the rest of the family did not seem to notice.

"Miss Stevens, these are the Svensens," Tom Allen said, gesturing toward the family, "Oscar and Christina, and their children Aaron, Anna, Joseph, Bjorn, and little Elsie. Let's see, I guess all except Aaron will be attending, right Oscar?"

Anna's father beamed widely and nodded his assent, then bowed slightly before Tina Stevens.

"We are so pleased that you are here, Miss Stevens," Oscar said with his heavy accent. "We have been praying for a teacher since we arrived in West Bend."

Anna flushed at her father's forwardness. She took another step backwards.

"Thank you so much, Mr. Svensen," Miss Steven's voice came out surprisingly confident and warm. "I, too, have been praying for the perfect post for my first job. It may be too early to tell, but I think the Lord has found an answer for me."

She smiled at the whole family, and then turned her gaze to Anna.

"I'm so glad that you'll be coming to school, too, Anna," the teacher said, having to tilt her head slightly to look into the taller girl's face. "I am expecting to have many little ones, and I was hoping some of the older students might serve as tutors."

Anna caught her breath quickly. She had served as a tutor in her school in Sweden, but she hadn't dared to hope that she might fulfill the same role here.

"I would be glad to help if I can," she said, stuttering only a little. "I do not know the language well, but I will try."

Tina Steven clasped Anna's hand.

"You seem to do quite well with English. I'm sure I would have much more trouble speaking Swedish," the teacher chuckled.

The Svensens said their good-byes and made their way to the wagon. It was only after settling in the back with her brothers and sister that Anna realized Aaron was still gazing longingly back at the church. He had never looked quite so moonstruck before.

"Stop staring, Aaron, or you will embarrass all of us," Anna said in a harsh whisper.

"What?"

The tall, lanky, 19-year-old turned his gaze towards his sister.

"People will notice," Anna said, this time a bit more forcefully.

"Did you see her, Anna?" Aaron said, not hearing his sister's words. "She is unlike any teacher we had in the old country."

Anna chuckled as the wagon pulled out of the churchyard.

"That is for sure, brother. But as you say all the time, 'This is not the old country.'"

With his eyes still fastened on the church fading into the distance, Aaron, however, didn't appear to hear his sister's response.

Chapter Three

The first day of school dawned unusually cool and a little damp after a small thundershower passed across the prairie during the night. With thoughts of school weighing heavily on her mind, Anna had lain awake long into the evening hours listening to the wind shake the small shanty and the thunder roll across the sky. She had awoken quickly in the morning, though; tired, yet anxious to begin the day.

"Well, daughter," Oscar said, coming into the house after completing his morning chores. "Are you ready for this first day?"

"Oh, Papa," Anna gushed. "I am so worried. What if I am not as far in my studies as the other students? And what if I cannot remember the correct words? And what if . . . ?"

"Hush, Anna" her father said, gently taking her shaking hands into his calloused ones. "You will be just fine. You are a smart girl, and you have always made me proud."

He planted a kiss on her forehead, and then drew back.

"God will be with you today, Anna, as he is every day. Trust in Him, and He will calm your fears."

Anna looked doubtfully at her father.

"You must have faith, my daughter," Oscar murmured.

"Yes, Papa," Anna obediently replied, yet her doubts still crowded in. How could her parents feel such faith when she never seemed to be able to find peace?

The family soon sat down to a breakfast of warm mush with fresh cream and biscuits hot from the oven, but Anna could barely eat a bite.

"Daughter, you must try to eat something," Christina encouraged in her gentle voice. "It is a long walk for you to school, and there will be much time until lunch. You will need your energy."

Anna smiled uncertainly at her mother and made an effort to swallow a spoonful of mush. When the family finally finished, Anna cleared the dishes in haste and quickly grabbed the water buckets.

"Leave the buckets here, Anna," she heard her father saying. "I will help your mother with the dishes this morning. You take the young ones and leave. It is a long walk to the schoolhouse."

Anna set the buckets down and smiled at her father.

"Thank you, Papa."

Quickly, after donning bonnets and smoothing hair, the four youngest Svensens set out the door and began following the wagon trail that led to both the church and the school. The white clapboard school was not far from the church, but on foot, it would take nearly an hour to get there. Before leaving, Joseph grabbed the tin bucket into which Christina had carefully packed leftover biscuits and dried beef for the children's lunch.

Anna tried to be conscious of Elsie's small legs as they walked, but she found herself pulling the younger girl along. It wasn't until Anna heard her sister gasping for breath as she struggled to keep up that she slowed her stride to accommodate the child. It was a beautiful day for walking. A slight breeze kept away the heat, and the previous night's storm cleared away any haze from the crystalline sky, but Anna hardly noticed. As it was, the children arrived early, anyway, being only the second family to reach the schoolyard.

In anticipation of opening day, the neighboring families had spruced up the school building. A fresh coat of wax had been applied to the hardwood floor, the outside of the building had been whitewashed, and, after being scrubbed with vinegar, the windows lining the two long walls sparkled in the morning sun. Anna's heart beat rapidly in anticipation.

After arriving, the Svensens waited near the steps outside the front of the building and watched the other children. Although two or three families arrived on horseback, most of the children walked. With the exception of Minnie and Edward Johannsen, the rest of the students knew each other from school the year before. Loud greetings rang out as more and more children showed up, scrubbed and excited. Some students glanced curiously at the Svensens, but none approached until a solid girl with freckles sprinkled across her nose came right up to inspect them. She had red hair, wound tightly around her head in braids, and a wide smile.

"I'm Mary Richards," the girl said, standing directly in front of Anna. "You must be the Svensens. My pa told me that you would be coming, and I was so excited to have another girl my age in school."

Mary smiled again, revealing her straight white teeth.

"Last year, I was the only girl over the age of 15 who came to school."

She leaned toward Anna conspiratorially. "I got so tired of listening to the younger ones recite, if you know what I mean." She smiled again.

Anna didn't think she would ever grow tired of working with younger children, but she wanted to make friends, so she nodded her head and smiled back.

"These are your brothers and sister?"

Mary's gaze swept across the younger Svensens who now pressed closely against Anna.

Anna nodded again, and then hesitated. Her voice seemed frozen in her throat.

"Well, do they have names?"

Mary again flashed the smile that Anna would soon come to recognize as a near-permanent feature on the girl's face.

"Oh, yes . . . of course," Anna spoke haltingly, while she felt her cheeks burn. "This is Joseph, this is Bjorn, and my sister . . . she is Elsie."

"Great!" Mary said, clapping her hands together. "Let's see . . . we'll call you Joe, you . . . hmmm . . . Bud? And Elsie . . . hmm . . . I guess there is no way to shorten that, so we'll just leave it as Elsie!"

The redhead smiled again, and all of the Svensens found themselves smiling back at Mary's contagious enthusiasm.

At that moment, the door to the building opened, and all eyes in the schoolyard turned to see Miss Stevens step boldly out. The petite brunette hesitated only slightly before raising her right arm high in the air and ringing the brass bell. Obediently, the children filed into two lines, the boys on one side, and the girls on the other.

Once inside, the room was in virtual silence as Miss Stevens directed each child to a seat. The girls sat on the right side, and the boys on the left. Each group reserved a few spaces on the front row for the smallest children.

Waiting in the back, Anna let her eyes roam around the room. A map of the United States and its territories hung behind the teacher's desk, which sat on a slightly raised platform directly in the center of the room. An American flag stood in the right corner. Although she had never seen one before, Anna assumed the round blue object on Miss Stevens' desk was a globe, and her heart raced. She would love to find Sweden. Two tall bookshelves lined the walls beside the teacher's desk, and Anna was relieved to see that both contained many books. Without being aware of it, she released a contented sigh.

When Elsie's turn came to take a seat, the young blonde held back and grasped her sister's hand. Miss Stevens smiled slightly at Anna, then bent to one knee and looked into Elsie's eyes.

"Would you like your sister to walk you to your seat?" she asked.

Elsie looked at Anna and nodded.

"I think that would be just fine for today." Miss Stevens stood and winked at Anna, then motioned for her to escort the younger child to the front of the classroom.

Anna walked Elsie to the first row and got her settled beside a tiny girl with large brown eyes. She took Elsie's hands into her own, and whispered into the child's ear in Swedish.

"You will be all right today, Elsie. Remember I will be here with you all day, and we can sit together at lunch."

Elsie nodded and released her sister's hands. Anna turned and made her way to the back of the room, sliding into a seat on the last row, the one reserved for the most advanced students.

After all of the students had been assigned a seat, Miss Stevens began questioning each one as to their name, age, and last grade completed. She recorded all the information into a large black book she took from the top of her desk. While she worked, Anna glanced around the room, stealing cautious glimpses of the other students. There were eleven boys and nine girls attending the school, and she and Mary were by far the oldest. Joseph was close to being one of the oldest boys attending, although there were two others taller than him who sat across the aisle from her. Anna guessed that they might be fifteen or sixteen.

Miss Stevens worked quickly, and she soon reached Anna's row. At that moment, the door opened again, and in stomped a hulking boy with shaggy brown hair and small black eyes. He looked around the room, and Anna noticed Mary shifting uncomfortably in her seat.

The boy's eyes came to rest on Miss Stevens, who, taken by surprise, was staring openly at the newcomer.

"Hiya, Teach," the boy said, a grin breaking across his lips that revealed several widely spaced teeth. "I guess I'm a little late today."

Miss Stevens struggled to regain composure. "My name is Miss Stevens, and yes, you are late. Please see that it doesn't happen again. Now, you may take your seat in the last row, over there."

Seeming not to hear her, the boy hitched his thumbs into the waistband of his trousers, and sauntered closer to where the teacher stood. He stuck out one grubby hand.

"I'm pleased to make yore acquaintance," he drawled. "I'm Jed Dennison."

After it became obvious that Miss Stevens was not going to shake his hand, he dropped it.

"We've never had such a purty teacher before. I guess I'll be making a better effort to git here from now on."

Jed leered at Miss Stevens. The teacher took a deep breath and drew herself up to her full height. Even so, she still had to tilt back her head to address Jed.

"I have asked you to take your seat. See that you do so immediately."

He squinted at her and began to mumble something, then turned away.

"Okay, okay. No need to get so mean about it. I'll sit down."

He shuffled over to the seat across the aisle from Anna and slouched nosily onto the bench. Anna pointedly did not meet his gaze.

"Now," said Miss Stevens, drawing in another breath. "Where were we? Oh, yes. Anna Svensen. Age?"

"Seventeen," Anna murmured, acutely aware that the eyes of all the students in the room were upon her.

"Seventeen," Miss Stevens repeated. "Last grade completed?"

Anna hesitated.

"It is different here than . . . our home country," Anna searched for the right words. "I believe it would be the . . . the . . . ten grade."

A slight ripple of laughter snaked around the room, and Anna felt her cheeks flush hotly. Immediately, she realized her grammatical mistake.

The teacher ignored the laugher and gave Anna an encouraging smile.

"The tenth grade. That is wonderful! You will be such a help with the younger students."

She looked warmly into Anna's eyes, and briefly touched her on the shoulder before looking at Mary. After writing down Mary's information, Miss Stevens stiffened slightly, and then turned to Jed Dennison.

"Name?" Miss Stevens asked in a tight voice.

"I already told you my name, Teach, I mean Miss Stevens," he drawled. "Jed Dennison. That's D-E-N-N-I-S-O-N."

She ignored his insolence.

"Age?"

"I'm seventeen," he said, and then leered at her again. "But I'll be eighteen next month."

"Last grade completed?"

"Well, let's see," Jed frowned and scratched his head. "I never seem to make it through the whole year. I always have to stop and help my pa with the crops and stuff."

He paused and grinned at Miss Stevens. "I'd probably say the fifth."

Loud laughter cascaded around the room, and Jed shot up out of his seat.

"Hey, what're you laughing at? I told you I had to help Pa!"

Tightly clenching his fists, Jed turned back to Miss Stevens.

"I come here to learn to read better, but I won't put up with 'em laughin' at me like that," he growled in a low voice.

Anna could see Miss Stevens tremble slightly, but her voice rang out steady as she said, "You will take your seat now, Jed, or you will be asked to leave the building. There will be no more laughing."

The room immediately grew silent. Jed glared at Miss Stevens before slumping back into his seat. Anna hadn't noticed she was holding her breath until she watched Miss Stevens stride purposefully back to the front of the room.

"All right, class. We will begin today with mathematics. Please get out your slates and your chalk."

The students did as Miss Stevens requested. Pushing thoughts of the morning's confrontation aside, Anna soon lost herself in her schoolwork.

Chapter Four

The remainder of the first day passed without incident, but Anna wondered how long it would be before Jed Dennison attempted to disrupt the class or interrupt the teacher again. Miss Stevens had quickly won Anna's respect, not only by the way she handled the overgrown boy, but also by her proficient manner in conducting lessons and gaining the confidence of the youngest students. By the end of the day, Elsie had lost all fear of school, and was her usual outgoing self when Miss Stevens called upon her to recite.

As the students gathered their books at the close of school, Anna heard Miss Stevens call her name and ask her to come to the front after the others had left. Anna waited in anxious anticipation, wondering if she had misjudged her academic ability and really should be in the ninth or even eighth grade studies. However, after spending only a few moments speaking with the teacher, Anna quickly forgot her fears.

"I'm impressed with your ability in math, Anna," Miss Stevens said, flashing one of her frequent smiles.

"Thank you Miss Stevens," Anna replied.

"I don't want to impose on you," the teacher continued, "but I'm feeling a little overwhelmed with all of the different abilities of the children. I really need someone to take over the math primer class, the one Elsie is in. Would you be interested?"

Anna's heart beat faster. She remembered discussing this at church when she met Miss Stevens, but she had no idea that the teacher had meant to have her help so soon.

"I am . . . honored Miss Stevens," Anna said haltingly. "But my English. It is not good yet. I do not know if I could . . . ."

"Oh, I think you speak quite well, Anna. This would really be a big help to me."

Anna thought she detected a small waver in the teacher's speech. She wondered if the confrontation with Jed Dennison, on top of the many other responsibilities Miss Stevens was carrying, had bothered the young teacher more than she had let on.

Miss Stevens handed Anna a worn brown book.

"Here is a book with some exercises in it. I think we'll spend 30 minutes in the morning working on writing numbers, and 30 more in the afternoon learning sums. How does that sound to you?"

"Oh, yes, Miss Stevens," Anna agreed. "When do you want me to start?"

"Would tomorrow be too soon? I really do appreciate this. I have prayed for such help, and I truly believe God has decided to reward me with you."

Miss Stevens smiled, and Anna could see the relief etched in her face. She felt a sudden rush of warmth towards her teacher.

After Anna had turned and left the room, Miss Stevens breathed a long sigh. It had been a difficult day, and the morning's incident had been more trying than she had led the class to believe. She opened her center desk drawer, and took out her beloved Bible, its cover worn from many hours of use, and turned to the thirteenth chapter of Mathew, one of her favorite passages. She spent the next thirty minutes in study and prayer, and then stood and straightened her desk. Tomorrow would come soon, and she had many lessons to prepare.

Anna was tired yet excited as she helped her mother finish the last few supper dishes. While the family ate their simple meal of baked squash, fried potatoes and dried beef, conversation centered on the school and the children's reactions to their new teacher. Joseph and Bjorn spoke mainly about the baseball game that the other boys had invited them to play during the noon recess. Although they had heard of the sport before coming to America, neither had experienced the thrill of hitting the ball with the stick until today.

Elsie, on the other hand, spoke with wonder about the little girl she sat beside, Miranda Lewis, and about the story Miss Stevens had read to the primary class after lunch.

"It had a rabbit in it," Elsie exclaimed, her eyes wide. "And a cat, and a dog, I think. Was it a dog, Anna?"

Anna smiled fondly at her sister.

"I do not know, Elsie. Remember? I was reading out of another book at the time."

"Oh, yes!" Elsie exclaimed. "Miss Stevens read just to the four of us who sit on the front row!"

Anna smiled again, and then thought about how Miss Stevens had found the time during the day to speak to each student individually, even to Jed Dennison despite his rude behavior. Suddenly, she became aware of Aaron staring at her.

"Yes?"

Aaron's ears turned pink on the tips, and Anna had a sudden recollection of him staring out of the wagon at the church a few weeks back.

"I was just wondering," Aaron stammered, "is . . . is . . . Miss Stevens nice? I mean, does . . . she . . . ."

"She is very nice. She is much more capable than I would have thought, considering her age and her size. I think she will be a wonderful teacher."

Aaron nodded his head.

"Are you sad that you are no longer in school, brother?" Anna couldn't resist adding.

Aaron took a quick drink of water and squinted at his sister. She winked at him, and then turned to her father and mother.

"There was one problem today, though."

With Joseph and Bjorn's help, Anna explained the incident with Jed Dennison.

"It does seem that the boy may be looking for some trouble to cause," Oscar said after hearing the story. "I think it best that we all pray for Miss Stevens. We should ask God to give her the wisdom to handle this situation. We should pray for the Dennison boy, also."

"Yes, Papa," Anna said obediently, yet inside she felt frustrated. Why did her father and mother always insist on prayer? Clearly, the boy was too unprepared for school, and he was only there to cause trouble. Anna felt sure that Miss Stevens needed something more than prayer. She needed a few of the students' fathers to talk to Jed Dennison and his parents and tell them he was no longer welcome in school. She kept these thoughts to herself, however, and set about considering how she would introduce numbers to the younger children the next day.

The days soon settled into a comfortable, yet busy routine, with Anna rising early to help her mother prepare breakfast and haul water before walking with her siblings to school. All day she kept occupied practicing her English through her own reading and writing lessons, and working with the younger children on their mathematics. After school, the Svensens hurried home so that the boys could help with the farm chores, and Anna could help her mother prepare the evening meal and finish any chores leftover from the afternoon. In the evenings, Anna would sit as long as she could keep her eyes open, working on her own lessons or preparing lessons for her young charges. Every night when she fell into bed, it was only a few moments before her eyes would close and she would fall into a deep sleep.

But, even though she loved school and the oppressive Kansas summer had given way to a pleasant fall, Anna felt discontented. She still wondered if her parents had made the right choice in coming to America, and she worried about her father as she watched him grow thin and tired from the grueling farm work.

In the middle of October, Anna and Christina were interrupted on a Saturday morning by Pastor Heggarty riding into their yard on a brown mare. The two women had been hanging laundry on the line when the pastor approached.

"Good morning, ladies," Pastor Heggarty said, dismounting from the mare.

"Oh, good morning, Pastor," Christina replied, speaking English with her heavy accent. "Oscar is not here right now. He and the boys is plow the field."

Anna flushed at her mother's mistake, but the preacher did not seem to notice.

"That's quite all right, Mrs. Svensen," Pastor Heggarty replied. "I have come to deliver an invitation, and I can deliver it to you just as easily as to your husband." The man smiled widely.

"Please, come in," Christina said. "Would you like some coffee?"

"That would be wonderful. Thank you, Mrs. Svensen."

Christina pulled Anna aside as they entered the shanty.

"Quick, put the coffee on to boil," she whispered. "And cut some slices of the bread we baked this morning."

"Yes, Mother," Anna replied, feeling embarrassed about the preacher entering her family's modest home. If only he could have seen their comfortable home in Sweden and its parlor with the velvet-covered chairs and small piano, then he would know that the family had not always been poor. However, much to Anna's surprise, Pastor Heggarty did not seem to notice the roughness of the family's dwelling.

"Why, you've made this old place into quite a comfortable home, Mrs. Svensen," the pastor said, his eyes sweeping the small room, taking in the blue gingham curtains and the handful of cut wildflowers in a cup on the table. "I can tell you and your family have worked very hard."

"Thank you, Pastor," Christina replied, smiling with pleasure at the man's compliment. The family had only had a few visitors since arriving in Kansas, and Christina relished the chance to entertain.

Just then, Elsie, who had been working on rocking her rag doll to sleep in her parents' bedroom, entered and sauntered over to the preacher.

"Hello, Pastor Heggarty," she said, in almost perfect English.

"Why, hello, Elsie," the man said, taking the child onto his lap. The pastor was a known soft touch for small children.

"Did you come to give us a sermon?" Elsie asked, looking the pastor straight in the eyes.

The man threw back his head and laughed.

"No, not today, Elsie."

Christina placed a cup of steaming coffee in front of their guest, and Anna followed with thick slices of bread spread with freshly churned butter.

"Thank you."

The pastor smiled at the two women.

"Elsie, I came to invite your family to the barn-raising at the Tom Allens one week from today."

Anna's heart quickened at the news. She had heard enough about prairie traditions to know that a barn-raising meant a lot of work, but also a lot of fun. The Svensen family had definitely been missing social events since they had come to America.

"A barn-raising," Christina said, almost in a whisper. "Why, we would love to help raise the barn, Pastor."

The reverend smiled at Christina, his eyes twinkling. "I'm sure the Allens will be pleased, Mrs. Svensen. Tom planned on coming out to invite you himself, but I saw him in town and told him that I'd be happy to do it. I had wanted to come out and call on your family for some time now, and I was glad of the excuse to make it out this way."

Christina nodded happily, but Anna was not sure that her mother had understood all of what the man said.

"What do we bring to a barn-raising, Pastor?" Anna asked, knowing that in her excitement, her mother might forget to think of asking until after Pastor Heggarty had left.

"Well, if you have any tools such as hammers and saws, those would be helpful."

The pastor took a sip of coffee and continued, "And, of course, all the women folk usually bring some food to share. The men get mighty hungry working on the constructing all day."

"Oh, yes," Christina said, and Anna could tell that her mother had already begun to plan which dishes to bring.

"Who else might be there?" Anna asked.

"Well, most folks from here abouts will make it out for at least part of the day," he replied. "The Allens lost their old barn last winter when lightening struck it, and there hasn't been time yet to build another one, what with the harvesting and butchering and all. Folks around here take every chance they can to get together and socialize."

He finished with a smile.

The two women continued questioning Pastor Heggarty until Oscar and the boys arrived for lunch. The pastor quickly agreed to stay for the noon meal, and Christina and Anna threw together a simple lunch while the pastor filled the men in on the barn-raising details. Anna couldn't help but notice how interested Aaron became in the invitation as soon as Pastor Heggarty mentioned that the event was to take place at the Allens where Tina Stevens boarded.

The pastor left soon after lunch, and Oscar and his sons prepared to return to the field, but not before Aaron quietly pulled Anna aside.

"You must help me with my English," Aaron said in a whisper. "I would like to be able to speak to Miss Stevens at the barn-raising."

If it were not for the urgency in her brother's voice, Anna would have found a way to tease Aaron about his boyish crush. Instead, she found herself promising Aaron that she would help him learn English during the next week whenever they had a chance.

As the week wore on, Anna did not find much time to keep her promise because the unpredictable Kansas weather had turned suddenly cold, and the whole family became involved with winter preparations. Anna even stayed home from school for two days to help harvest the rest of the autumn garden vegetables. After clearing the garden, Anna and Christina diligently canned and preserved the vegetables, stacking the glass jars neatly on the wooden shelves in the lean-to Oscar had built off the back of the kitchen.

Sending word with Bjorn and Elsie that she and Joseph would be gone for two days, Anna hoped that her absence from school would not inconvenience Miss Stevens too much. Anna knew that it was critical to harvest as many of the vegetables as possible to feed the family all winter, yet she hated missing school. She had been making great headway with teaching arithmetic to the younger students, and Miss Stevens had recently let her take over their spelling lessons, also.

"If you wouldn't mind, Anna," Miss Stevens had said, placing a list of carefully printed words on Anna's desk one Friday afternoon. "You seem to be so far ahead in your own studies, and I really could use the help."

Anna had simply beamed at the teacher and nodded her quick agreement. Never had Anna enjoyed school more and she felt that her English skills were increasing rapidly. Anna enjoyed a true bond of friendship with her teacher, one that extended beyond the usual pupil-teacher relationship. In fact, Anna had even been considering teaching as a profession for herself after she finished school. If, that is, her parents could spare her from the farm.

Anna's heart grew heavy, then, when she heard the news that Bjorn and Elsie brought home the second day of their sister's absence.

"Jed Dennison is going to marry Miss Stevens," Elsie said, bursting through the shanty door.

Anna turned from her post by the stove where she had been stewing tomatoes.

"What did you say?"

In her excitement, Anna addressed Elsie in Swedish.

Momentarily confused by the language change, Elsie wrinkled her brow and repeated herself. "I said Jed Dennison is going to marry Miss Stevens."

Christina took the spoon from Anna's hand, and they both walked over and sat at the table. Just then, Bjorn came in, set down his books, and took a cookie from the plate Christina had just filled.

"Hello Mother, Anna," he said, his mouth full of crumbs, nodding to both women.

"Bjorn, what is this that Elsie is saying?" Anna demanded. "Is Miss Stevens really going to marry that . . . that . . . person?"

Bjorn almost choked in surprise. "Oh, no, of course not!" He swallowed and continued. "Dennison did make a scene at school today, though."

Anna sighed and rubbed the heel of her hand across her forehead. She slowly got up and took her place back at the stove and resumed stirring.

"Well, tell us what happened, then."

"Must I, Mother? I really want to go help Papa!"

Bjorn directed his plea toward Christina who had stood and began cutting kernels of corn off an ear and into a pot on the table.

"Just tell us quickly what happened, Bjorn, and then you can tell us all the details tonight."

"Well, all right," the ten-year-old sighed. "Dennison came in late today, really late."

Anna nodded. Jed Dennison was rarely on time to school, but usually Miss Stevens just tried to ignore it.

"It was so late that my class had already started oral reading."

Anna gasped. That meant Jed Dennison showed up nearly two hours after the start of school. She couldn't believe that even he would have the nerve to show up so late.

"Well, Miss Stevens tried to be calm about it, like she always is," Bjorn continued, eyeing his sister, "but when she asked him to sit down and take out his books, he refused."

"So what happened?"

"That's when he told Miss Stevens that he planned to marry her!"

Elsie broke in, her blue eyes wide.

"He just walked right up and told her."

"I was telling the story," Bjorn complained.

"Bjorn," Christina chided. "You will speak nicely to your sister. Elsie, please let Bjorn finish the story.

"Well, it was sort of like Elsie said. When Dennison did not sit down the first time, Miss Stevens asked him again. At that point, he just walked up to her and got real close to her face. This close."

Bjorn held the palm of his right hand only a few inches in front of his nose, and then looked at his mother and Anna, visibly enjoying their reactions.

"The whole school was quiet now. Nobody knew what to do. Miss Stevens asked him to sit down again, and that's when it happened," Bjorn paused, taking another bite of his cookie and chewing thoughtfully. "Dennison grabbed Miss Stevens by both shoulders and said, 'Tina Stevens, I am a'going to marry you and take you to my farm. You kin live there with me and Pa and be my wife.' And then he kissed her, right on the mouth."

Anna dropped the wooden spoon on the floor and put her hand over her mouth in horror. To think that all of this had happened to poor Miss Stevens and Anna hadn't even been there to offer support. She heard Christina mutter something quickly under her breath.

"What happened then?" Anna tried to keep her voice steady.

"She pushed him," Elsie threw in, glancing at her brother.

Bjorn glared at Elsie and said, "Yes, then she pointed to the door and told him to leave. She seemed to be really mad."

"Did he go?" Anna asked, fearing the answer.

"Oh, yes," Bjorn replied. "But right before he left he turned around and winked at Miss Stevens and said he'd be seeing her very soon."

Anna's stomach clutched in fear for her friend.

"It was funny though," Bjorn added, setting his black felt hat on his head in preparation for joining his father and brothers in the field. "Jed Dennison smelled strange today. It was an odor I did not recognize . . . very strong."

The boy shrugged his shoulders and went out the door.

Anna turned back to the tomatoes, but not without catching a glimpse of her mother's head bowed quietly by the sink. She wondered if Christina was praying about the incident, and Anna felt a surge of anger. A lot of good prayer had done so far for Miss Stevens! Someone should have taken care of Jed Dennison after the first day of school instead of just sitting around and waiting for God to handle it. Anna furiously stirred the contents of the pot, her brow wrinkled.

Chapter Five

The day of the Allens' barn-raising dawned clear and warm, a pleasant surprise after the unusually cool week. Anna had stayed up late the night before helping Christina prepare a large pot of beans and several pans of Swedish pastries to take to the day's event. In the midst of baking, Christina had muttered several times about her lack of proper ingredients, but Anna knew the sweets would taste delicious.

Anna had returned to school on Wednesday, the day after Jed Dennison's unexpected proposal to Miss Stevens. She had worried about finding the teacher flustered and scared, but instead, the petite brunette had remained calm and professional the rest of the week, although, perhaps, a bit paler than usual. Miss Stevens had given a warm smile to Anna on the student's first day back. The teacher reassured her that the younger pupils had gotten along fine in her absence, even though she had been dearly missed.

The rest of the school week had passed without incident, although Anna noticed that Miss Stevens' eyes flew to the door every time it opened. Jed Dennison did not return to school that week, and Anna hoped that he had decided not to return at all.

When her father had heard Bjorn tell the story about Jed's untimely proposal, Oscar's face had grown stern in a way that Anna had rarely seen before. She caught the long glance her parents shared across the supper table, and she was not at all surprised when Oscar hitched up the wagon that evening and he and Aaron went for a visit to the Allens' farm. Anna also noticed the pain on her eldest brother's face as Bjorn and Elsie described the way Jed had grabbed Miss Stevens' shoulders and planted a kiss on her lips. For the most part, Aaron Svensen was a good-natured man, but Anna feared what he might do if he came across Jed Dennison alone.

Christina and Anna prepared a simple breakfast of cornmeal mush and fresh milk the morning of the barn-raising. Everyone ate quickly, anxious to get to the festivities. Oscar had laid out the few tools the family owned the night before, and he moved deftly, packing them and the food in the wagon. It wasn't long before the family set out, spirits high, for the half-hour wagon ride to the Allen farm.

"How about a song with your mother, Anna?" Oscar asked soon after the wagon pulled out of the shanty's yard.

Anna agreed readily, and soon the harmony of two female voices, long accustomed to each other, rang out across the calm air. As she sang, Anna looked around her and noticed the way the prairie had taken on a rich array of colors with the approaching autumn. The tall grass had mellowed into many deep shades of gold and brown, and the trees the wagon passed as it neared the river showed off bright leaves of red, orange, and yellow. Anna thought back to the heat of the previous summer and the greenness of the spring, and found herself amazed at the prairie's diversity. She smiled quietly to herself, wondering if she had begun to appreciate the hard life her family had chosen on this yet untamed land.

When Oscar finally guided the wagon into the Allen's yard, Anna felt a flutter of anticipation as she noticed the number of wagons and people already assembled. Aaron quickly swung down and unhitched the horses, letting them drink from the trough and then tethering them with all the other families' horses in a nearby pasture.

In the crisp morning air, the Allens' yard already rang with the sound of women chattering and children laughing. Oscar kissed Christina quickly on the cheek and grabbed his tool box, leading his three sons over to a small congregation of men. Anna felt proud as she watched her father stride confidently to the group. Oscar had worked with lumber most of his life, and she knew he would be an asset to the men assembled to build the barn.

Carrying the large bundle of sweet rolls wrapped tightly in two cotton towels, Anna followed Christina to the wooden benches where a large variety of food was already laid out. Elsie had spotted a friend from school, and had run ahead to join in a game of tag with several other children. Anna felt a pang of homesickness as she laid her bundle on one end of a long wooden table next to several pies and a pan of gingerbread. The abundance of food reminded her so much of the family dinners the Svensens used to attend almost monthly in Sweden, when all of Anna's aunts, uncles, and cousins would crowd around a common table, spending the day eating, singing, and visiting together. Many of the Svensens' extended family lived close to their home in the old country, and anyone's birthday or anniversary had proved cause for celebration. Tears threatened to fall as Anna remembered the dreary atmosphere of the going away party her Aunt Elena, Christina's sister, had thrown two days before they were to leave.

Wiping the back of her hand across her eyes, Anna shook her head slightly, determined not to let memories ruin the excitement of the day's events.

"Well there you are. I was hoping you'd make it."

Anna turned to see a welcoming smile from Tina Stevens, who carried a large blue bowl across the Allens' front yard.

"Good morning, Miss Stevens," Anna said, smiling back, and grateful to have a diversion from her thoughts. "Can I help you with that bowl?"

"Oh, thank you, but I think I'll just set it here."

The petite brunette set down a bowl filled with cornmeal muffins.

"Isn't this exciting? I've never been to a barn-raising before. In St. Louis, we just hire someone to do our building, or we build what we need by ourselves."

Anna nodded. "I have not been to a barn-raising either. We do it the same way at home. I mean, in Sweden."

The teacher turned a thoughtful gaze on Anna. "I would very much like to talk to you about Sweden some day, Anna, that is, if you want to. I'm so interested in travel and in seeing other parts of the world."

The teacher sighed and leaned closer, lowering her voice. "Can I tell you something?"

Anna nodded again, and felt a small thrill travel down her spine at the thought of Miss Stevens speaking to her confidentially.

"I'm to be married in two years. My fiancé, Samuel, is studying to be a minister. When he graduates from seminary, we plan on entering mission work."

Anna's mouth gaped in surprise. She had no idea that Miss Stevens was promised to be married, and from the admiring glances the teacher always attracted from the young men at church, Anna didn't think anyone else in West Bend knew about the engagement, either.

Tina Stevens gazed across the yard filled with children playing, and Anna could tell her thoughts roamed far from the homestead on which they stood.

"I don't know where we will be sent to do mission work, but I feel ready to go wherever the Lord wills."

Her gaze turned wistful. "I do miss Samuel, though. Two years can seem like such a long time."

Anna tried to mask her reaction to her teacher's surprising news. She felt a wave of remorse when she realized how sad Aaron would be when he found out about Miss Stevens' engagement. Although Aaron, with his blonde good looks and polite manner, often received attention from many young women, he had never really seemed interested in anyone until he met Miss Stevens.

Anna took a deep breath and garnered a smile for her teacher. "I am happy for you, Miss Stevens. I did not know you were promised to someone."

Tina blushed slightly and looked at her feet. "I haven't been trying to hide my engagement, but I haven't been sharing it too much either. With Samuel in seminary, he hasn't been able to afford an engagement ring. He worries about that, but I told him not to. I know I have his love, and that is better than any engagement ring."

Raising her head to meet Anna's gaze, she said, "And I did not want people to have the idea that I had just come to teach to pass the time until Samuel and I could marry. That is not what I intended at all. Teaching school has always been a dream for me. I truly feel called by God to teach, and I believe that, for whatever reason, God wants me to teach here."

"But," Anna began and then hesitated. After all this was her teacher's personal business. Maybe Miss Stevens did not really want to discuss it further with a mere pupil.

"Yes?"

Anna's curiosity overcame her hesitancy. "Do you not miss Samuel? Is this not hard, being apart? Why don't you find a teaching position closer to his seminary? At least then you could visit each other, even if you cannot marry yet."

Anna took a breath, wondering if she had said too much, had been too forward. But Tina Stevens just reached out her hand and touched Anna softly on the sleeve.

"I believe God has a plan for all of us, Anna. Following His will for my life brings the sweetest peace and joy that I have ever known. This was the only teaching position I was offered, although I did apply for many more. This is where God wants me. I firmly believe that."

Anna turned away from her teacher, feeling doubt well up in her heart. She had seen the same peace on Miss Stevens' face that she witnessed often on the faces of her parents. She felt Tina's hand on her sleeve again, and turned back.

"Well, anyway," Miss Stevens' serious look had been replaced by a wide smile, "I do miss Samuel dreadfully, but I love my work, and I have been looking forward to today all week. Shall we go join the other ladies?"

Anna nodded, and followed Miss Stevens across the yard to where a group of women had gathered and were busily looking through a basket of quilt patterns Mrs. Allen had brought out from the house.

The rest of the day passed quickly, the hours being filled with hard work, good food, and lots of laughter. Anna could not remember the last time she had laughed so much in one day.

However, in between serving food and watching the youngsters play, her thoughts had frequently turned to Miss Stevens' words. Anna found herself wondering if the peace that Tina Stevens and her own parents claimed could belong to her also.

At the end of the day, while wiping down a series of tables to clear them of crumbs, Anna watched as one last wagon pulled into the Allens' yard. Her heart nearly stopped as Jed Dennison dismounted from the driver's seat, his gait a little unsteady. A second man stayed in the wagon, his brown battered hat pulled low over his eyes and a tarnished rifle draped across his lap.

"We come to help ya with the barn-raising," Jed announced, speaking loudly to the group of men and women who had gathered in the yard.

There was a moment of silence, and then Tom Allen strode forward and stepped in front of Jed.

"That's right kindly of you, Jed, but I believe the work is all done for today."

Tom spoke deliberately, looking Jed in the eyes.

"You can see that everyone is packing up to leave now. Why don't you and your pa just run along home and get some rest?"

Despite his unsteady stance, Jed gazed levelly at Tom, and then turned to one side and directed a stream of spittle into the dirt.

"Me and Pa weren't invited to this here event. Why was that?"

Tom drew up to his full height.

"Why, I'm right sorry about that, Jed. I thought everyone here abouts knew they were welcome to come and help. I guess folks might not have known you were interested."

Jed shuffled one boot in the dirt, and looked down at his feet.

"We'd like an invitation next time."

"Well, sure, Jed. We'll make sure you get one. We can always use the help of two more able-bodied men."

The silence grew long again as Jed kept kicking at the dirt.

In the wagon, Jed's father shifted, almost imperceptibly.

"Oh, all right. I guess we'll be gittin' along, then," Jed finally said. He turned around and walked back to his wagon, stumbling only once.

"Goodbye, and thanks for the offer to help. We'll sure take you up on it next time."

Tom Allen waved and turned back to the group of men.

"All right, let's finish packing up the tools. Some of you have quite a ways to go to get home."

Everyone gathered seem to breathe a collective sigh of relief as they once more began making preparations to leave. Anna did not realize how tense she had been until she noticed her knuckles were white from gripping the dish cloth so tightly. She did not know what she had expected Jed Dennison to do, but after Miss Stevens' confrontation with him earlier in the week, she knew that he seemed to bring trouble with him wherever he went.

Anna quickly finished the wiping and then took the cloth over to a bucket of sudsy water the women were using for the clean up. Tina Stevens was already there, wringing out another cloth. As usual, she greeted Anna with a smile.

"Oh, it has been such a wonderful day," the young teacher said.

"I do not know why that . . . that Jed Dennison had to ruin it," Anna replied crossly. She quickly covered her mouth with her hand. "I am sorry Miss Stevens, it is just that, well, Jed Dennison always seems to ruin everything."

Miss Stevens looked at Anna thoughtfully and then replied, "Yes, he does cause quite a stir, but I think he might be getting better."

"Getting better! Why look what he did to you earlier this week at school. Thinking that you could . . . you would . . . ," Anna broke off, lifting her hands helplessly in the air.

"Oh, yes," Miss Steven chuckled. "Thinking that I would marry him? Well, Jed didn't really have his wits about him that day. But really, I took his proposal as a compliment, inappropriate though it was. And I think he was pretty embarrassed about it later, because he didn't come back to school."

Anna shook her head and a frown crossed her face.

"I'll continue to pray for him, of course," Miss Stevens continued, wiping her hands on a towel. "I'll turn Jed Dennison over to the Lord, just as I have turned over my engagement to Samuel, and our separation."

The teacher flashed one more smile at Anna, and then made her way inside the Allens' house.

All the way home, Anna sat quietly with Elsie dozing beside her and her two youngest brothers stretched out in the back of the wagon, but she kept thinking about Tina Stevens and the sense of peace and joy that radiated from the young woman. Anna couldn't help wondering if it might be time for her to discover some of that same peace and joy for herself.

The days grew shorter, yet Anna and her siblings daily trekked back and forth to the country school. Anna continued tutoring the youngest pupils in math and spelling, and she often listened to their reading lessons as well. Even though she stayed busy with the youngsters, she still kept up with her own studies, and she became more and more comfortable with speaking English every day.

As to be expected, Aaron reacted poorly to the news of Tina Stevens' engagement, at least, at first. He spent several nights eating supper with the family in silence, a grave look on his face. He would then take long walks late into the evening, and Anna would hear him return after the other children were already asleep.

Gradually, though, Aaron started to smile more, and Anna noticed that he began to wait after church so that he might speak to Minnie Johannsen. Minnie was a friendly girl with sparkling blue eyes and plump cheeks that would flush pink ever time Aaron looked her way. Anna felt relief when Aaron finally appeared to have given up his feelings for Tina Stevens.

Anna, however, began to spend even more time with the young teacher as the autumn lengthened into winter. What started out as conferring about lessons for Anna's young pupils soon developed into a friendship that went beyond the typical teacher-student relationship. Now that Elsie and the boys had close friends of their own, Anna would often stay in the school building during the noon recess, speaking with Tina about upcoming lessons, and talking with her about Sweden.

"You lived close to the hills, then?" Miss Stevens asked one day, a far away look in her deep brown eyes.

"Oh, yes," Anna exclaimed, clapping her hands together. "We did not live in the hills. We were in a valley, of sorts, but the hills were always in view. I miss them so much. All the colors – purple, and blue, and white. There is nothing like that here."

"I miss the trees, too," Miss Stevens said, wistfully. "It's so flat here."

Anna nodded silently.

"The prairie seems to stretch forever and the sky is so large," the teacher continued, "Sometimes I get overwhelmed with all of this space."

"Oh, so do I," Anna exclaimed. "And this weather! Who knows what it will do next?"

Tina Stevens chuckled.

"You know what Mrs. Allen says? She says that if you don't like the weather in Kansas, don't worry. All you have to do is wait five minutes, and it will change."

Anna joined in the laughter, reveling in the fact that she had finally found a friend. She had so long wanted to find a friend to make up for the pain she felt from missing all her school friends in Sweden. Now the closeness she shared with Miss Stevens lessened some of that hurt.

"Still," Miss Stevens continued, "I am growing to love it here. When I go outside on clear nights, I feel like the stars are surrounding me. I truly feel the peace of God then."

Anna sobered quickly, considering her teacher's words. Confusion filled her heart as Miss Stevens rose to call the rest of the students back in for afternoon classes.

Chapter Six

A few weeks later, during one of her frequent noon talks with her teacher, Anna finally worked up the courage to ask her teacher about her faith. Miss Stevens had just finished reading out loud a section of a recent letter she had received from Samuel. The letter went into great detail about the young man's studies.

". . . and, my dearest Tina, I miss you more than words can say, but I truly know I am following the Lord's will for my life. Every day I spend here I feel myself growing spiritually in so many ways. As the apostle Paul says in Philippians, 'For it is God who is at work in you, both to will and to work for His good pleasure.' I look forward to each of your letters. I'll continue to pray for you daily until we can be together again. All my love, Samuel."

Miss Stevens let the letter fall to her lap, and then she sat back at her desk and sighed.

"Oh, Anna, I miss him so much," she said, smiling slightly. "Even though I know he's where he needs to be right now."

The young teacher turned suddenly in her chair, looking at her pupil. "I do pray that some day, Anna, God will find someone for you to love as I love my Samuel."

Anna smiled, and then asked softly, "It means so much to you, doesn't it? This faith . . . this belief in God?"

Tina Stevens looked long into Anna's eyes before replying.

"It means everything. Have you given your heart to God, yet, Anna?"

Nearing tears, Anna shook her head, slightly.

"Would you like to hear how I came to know God?"

Anna nodded.

"It was when I was 12," Tina Stevens began. "My mother had just died from pneumonia. My father began working all of the time in his office – he is a lawyer – and he hired a woman to come in and stay with my three brothers and me during the days while he was away."

Anna leaned forward in her chair, hungering to hear what Tina had to say next.

"Her name was Mrs. Blackwood, and she came from the south. She had been a slave, before the Civil War. She was a large woman, but she always spoke quietly, and she was one of the gentlest people I've ever met."

Tina leaned back in her chair, closing her eyes, as if to see into her memory.

"I was not an easy child to be around at age 12. Being the only girl in the family, I had been spoiled dreadfully, by both my mother and my father. The pain from missing my mother was so strong, and I dealt with it in the only way I knew how – by being totally rotten to everyone around me."

Anna watched her teacher in disbelief. She found it hard to believe that Miss Stevens had ever been anything but the giving, loving, calm person who sat before her now.

"I was horrid to Mrs. Blackwood," Tina continued. "I was probably mad at her for trying to take my mother's place, although I really knew that she wasn't trying to do any such thing. But I refused to do anything she asked of me, I talked back to her, and I often would leave messes in the house, just so I could see her clean them up.

"I kept expecting her to get angry with me, to send me to my room or tell my father how horrible I was being. But she never did."

Tina paused for a moment, the remorse for her behavior as a child showing by the pained expression on her face.

"Finally, one day, after I had said something particularly dreadful to Mrs. Blackwood, I don't even remember what it was, she looked at me in such an odd, sad, way and said, 'Poor child, you got so much pain inside you, you just feel you got to be mean all the time.' Well, I don't know why that affected me so much, but for some reason it did. I found myself bursting into tears, and shaking uncontrollably. Mrs. Blackwood just sat down in a kitchen chair and pulled me onto her wide lap, rocking me until I could stop crying.

"After that, I was no longer mean to her. In fact, she became my best friend. I'd follow her around the house, helping with the chores and the cooking, and listening to her while she told Bible stories or sang hymns. She was the first one to tell me about God's love, and how he wants us to seek his forgiveness so that he can come into our lives and make us whole. My family had belonged to a church for a very long time, and we even went occasionally. But mainly, it was just for show, to support my father's social standing in St. Louis. It was through Mrs. Blackwood, however, that I learned how inviting God into my life could change me forever."

The teacher paused again, and with tears threatening to spill from her eyes, she looked deeply into Anna's own.

A sense of hope filled Anna's heart. Although she had heard the story of God's love offered through his son, Jesus, many times from her parents as well as in church, never had she felt so drawn to the promise it offered.

"God can change your life too, Anna. All you have to do is ask him."

Anna nodded. After several quiet moments, she asked, "Will you show me how?"

"Oh, yes," Tina said, drawing Anna's hand into her own.

The pair spent the next 20 minutes in prayer and reading Scriptures. Anna poured her heart out, and when they finally opened their eyes, she felt as though a tremendous burden had been lifted from her heart. She floated through the rest of the afternoon, her mind barely able to concentrate on her studies. She couldn't wait until school had ended so that she might share her news with her parents.

It didn't take long for Christina to sense a change in Anna. Rolling dough for biscuits, Christina looked up when she heard the door open. Immediately, Anna rushed over to her mother and encircled Christina's neck with her arms.

"Oh, Mama," Anna whispered in a quavering voice. "I wish I had known earlier how wonderful this could feel."

Christina hugged her daughter back and then held her at arm's length, examining her closely.

"Today I've prayed for God's forgiveness," Anna whispered, tears forming in her eyes.

"I've been praying for this for such a long time," Christina breathed, pulling Anna close again. "Was Miss Stevens there?"

"Oh, yes. She told me about how she had come to Christ. I've realized for quite a while now that something has been not quite right with my life, and I had wanted to ask Miss Stevens about her faith, but only today did it seem right."

Christina smiled at her daughter. "God sees to everything in his own perfect time. Today was soon enough."

The pair lingered over another hug, and then Anna pulled her apron off of a peg behind the door and began to help her mother with dinner preparations.

When he came in from tending the animals, Oscar felt as much happiness as Christina had about Anna's news, and he showed it by embracing his daughter warmly. During the simple meal of vegetable stew and biscuits, Anna related Miss Stevens' story of her childhood, especially the part about the teacher's loving caregiver, Mrs. Blackwood. Anna had asked Miss Stevens, of course, if she could share the story, and Miss Stevens had urged her pupil to do so. The young teacher thought that Anna's parents might enjoy hearing the story that had helped Anna decide to accept God's love.

Anna's siblings listened attentively to the story, although Anna did notice a frown cross young Elsie's face when Anna mentioned Miss Stevens' poor behavior as a child.

"I cannot think that Miss Stevens would ever be mean," Elsie said, shaking her head.

"Miss Stevens felt much pain because her mother had died," Oscar told his youngest child. "Sometimes people do not always behave the way they should when they are sad."

Elsie nodded solemnly, but Anna wondered if the child really understood.

Having come to Christ himself the year before the family left Sweden, Aaron rejoiced at his sister's decision. Anna noticed that

Bjorn seemed nonchalant about the news, but Joseph listened carefully to his sister, hanging on every word and almost forgetting to eat. Silently, Anna breathed a prayer that Joseph might soon make the decision to know the Lord like she had.

As autumn turned into winter, the cold, harsh winds began to blow across the prairie, but Anna's spirits remained high, even though it was often too cold for the children to safely make the trek to school. When the Svensens did make it to school, there were often many pupils absent. Many parents kept their children home during the gray months in fear of a quick snowstorm. All of the families near West Bend had heard stories of people getting lost during prairie snowstorms, and no one wanted to take that chance with their children.

The two weeks before Christmas, however, were unusually warm and temperate. Anna rejoiced at the weather because Miss Stevens had planned a Christmas program, and nearly all the students were making it to school during the warmer-than-usual days. The program was scheduled for the evening of December 23, the last day of school before Christmas break.

Miss Stevens had placed Anna and Mary Richards in charge of organizing the program, and the pair had great fun deciding what each student should perform. Mary had become a Christian two years earlier, and she and Anna often discussed Bible verses as they worked together.

"I've been talking with Pastor Heggarty about starting a youth group for the church," Mary's eyes shone as she talked. "Maybe you would like to help us plan?"

Anna agreed quickly, saying she would love to if she could spare some time away from helping with the farm chores.

The girls decided to put the youth group plans on hold, however, until after the Christmas program. Anna marveled at how organized Mary could be. After only one planning session, Mary had already drawn up a list of students and sketched in a possible piece for each of them to perform. Upon checking with Miss Stevens, the girls made a few changes in the original list, and then began working with the children on memorization and practice.

There were to be six songs, three Bible readings, and five poems. Elsie was going to sing a Christmas carol with two other children, and recite one small poem. Joseph and Bjorn, with their strong, clear voices inherited from their mother, had practiced adding harmonization to a favorite hymn. With her own love of music, Mary planned to lead the audience in several carols at the close of the program, as well as direct every student in an all-school choir. Anna had chosen to read the Christmas story from the book of Luke. She practiced the passage carefully, sounding out the words until she felt confident that she would not make a mistake.

As the night for the program drew near, Anna often felt flutters of anticipation and found it difficult to eat. There had not been such a large social event in the West Bend community since the Allens' barn-raising, and she knew that every family from miles around would make it out for the program, if possible. Never would Anna have dreamed just a year ago, while living in the cramped New York apartment with her uncle's family, that she would be able to help organize such an occasion.

Three days before the program, Anna and Christina were beginning dinner preparations after school. Anna had been busily chattering about the day's practice and how well it had gone.

"And Elsie, she said her poem perfectly, and even Jonathan Wilkes, who at first refused to do anything for the program, has finally chosen to sing with the two other boys in his grade."

Christina smiled as she heard the enthusiasm in Anna's voice. She breathed a quite prayer of thankfulness that Tina Stevens had thought to involve Anna in the responsibility of planning the program.

"How are the decorations coming, then?" Christina asked, knowing that Anna and Mary would surely have that part of the program in hand.

Anna beamed.

"Oh, Mama, it will be so beautiful! Mr. Allen has agreed to cut down a tree on his place, near the stream, and he is going to bring it to school tomorrow afternoon. When we can spare time from our studies, we have been making decorations for the tree. Mary's family sent some popcorn, which we strung on thread today into long rows."

Anna crinkled her nose.

"This popcorn is surely strange to see. Some of the boys kept taking little tastes of it, but I could not bring myself to."

Christina chuckled.

"Many of the children have collected items from their homes that we will use to decorate with, also. Remember the nest that Bjorn found on the ground near the well last week? Miss Stevens said he should bring it and he could place it on one of the branches. That made him so happy!"

Christina smiled again, marveling at how quickly her daughter's command of the English language had grown.

"Mama," Anna said, dusting flour on the table in preparation for rolling out biscuits. "Do you think there might be some lace or ribbon in your sewing box that I could add to my blue dress? I would like to look special the night of the program," she continued, a touch of shyness in her voice.

Christina's breath caught in her throat as she set down her spoon and looked carefully at her daughter. The excitement in Anna's voice reflected in her eyes making them seem even brighter than usual. Her fair complexion was accented by the pink in her flushed cheeks, and her blonde braids wrapped around her head shone like a golden halo. Oh, how she wished the family could afford to buy material for a new dress for the teenager! Anna had made do for more than a year with only two everyday dresses, now almost threadbare, and one Sunday dress, which was also beginning to look quite worn.

Quickly Christina remembered the two lace handkerchiefs she had brought from Sweden, those her own mother had given her one the day of her wedding, so long ago. She could remove the lace from one of those handkerchiefs and sew it on the collar and cuffs of Anna's good dress. It wouldn't be much, but at least it would be something special for her daughter to wear. After all, Anna had gotten by with so little, and since accepting Christ, she rarely complained any more.

"Yes, Anna, I think I can find something to add to your dress. I will work on it after dinner, while you are helping the boys and Elsie with their studies," Christina said, in careful English, being cautious not to let Anna hear the slight quivering in her voice.

"Oh, thank you, Mama," Anna said, smiling her gratitude. The teenager began to hum as she rolled out the dough.

Christina smiled back, but then turned aside to stir the stew. She was thankful for all the goodness God had bestowed on the family since they arrived in Kansas, but finding a way to keep her family fed and clothed was difficult. With the lack of rain during the summer and her husband's inexperience at farming, the family had not done well at harvest time. Christina had been supplementing the meager earnings of her husband by selling eggs at the general store whenever Oscar could venture into town. Her flock of chickens was young, however, and there often were few eggs left over after the family had been fed. She and her husband would just have to find another way to supplement their income, Christina decided with new resolve, silently asking the Lord for strength.

Chapter Seven

Gray clouds blanketed the sky the morning of Dec. 23. Anna felt the cold, sharp sting in the air when she walked to school with her siblings, and she worried that a storm might arise before the evening's scheduled performance. She soon forgot her fears, however, while busily seeing to the last minute details of the program.

Miss Stevens tried to keep the children occupied with their regular studies the first two hours of the day, but after several futile attempts, she gave up and let all the students spend the rest of the day rehearsing and decorating for the program. During a quiet lull in the afternoon, when most of the students were finishing the remains of their lunches, Anna approached the young teacher and shyly handed her a small package wrapped in a scrap of muslin.

Tina Stevens smiled in delight and unwrapped the gift, a small cross delicately embroidered on a rectangular piece of cloth.

"Oh, Anna, it's so beautiful!"

Anna beamed in response. "It is supposed to be a bookmark. I had hoped you would like it."

"I love it," the teacher said. "I have something for you, also. It isn't much, but I did want to thank you for all of your help with the younger students, and for your friendship."

The teacher pulled out a flat package wrapped with brown paper and tied with a white ribbon. Anna's heart fluttered with excitement as she took the package and unwrapped it, being careful not to tear the ribbon. She folded the paper and looked down at the thin book of Shakespearean sonnets in her hands.

"Oh, Miss Stevens! This is for me?"

"I wanted you to have it," the teacher smiled. "I know you love his plays so much. I have had this book for awhile, and I have just been waiting for the right person to give it to."

Anna's eyes glistened as she smiled at her friend. More words of thanks, however, were interrupted by Elise pulling on her sister's skirt.

"May I say my poem again? Please, Anna, may I?"

"Of course, Elsie. Right after lunch we will run through the entire program again, all right?"

Satisfied, the youngster ran off to join her friends. Clutching the book to her chest, Anna turned to make sure the final touches had been added to the evening's decorations.

Despite the ominous clouds, the snow held off through the evening's program. As Anna had expected, the school building was overflowing, with some visitors even having to standing in the aisle and behind the rows of desks. The warmth and light emanating from the building cut through the evening's chill, and the children performed their pieces without a hitch. Anna watched with pride as Elsie stood before a roomful of friends and strangers and spoke her poem confidently in English.

The boys sang heartily, and soon it was time for Anna to read her Bible passage. Her heart thumped as she approached the front of the room, but her voice rang clear as she carefully pronounced the words she had practiced so often that she knew them by heart. When she looked up from her Bible after finishing the story, she saw Tina Stevens and her parents beaming at her.

All too soon, the program ended and the guests and students dug into cookies and apple cider brought by the several families Anna and Mary had asked to help. Anna had just accepted a cup of cider from Michael Richards, Mary's eldest brother, when Pastor Heggarty came stomping into the coat room of the school, brushing off his shoulders and shivering.

"We best be loading up, folks," the preacher said. "It's just starting to snow, and it looks as if it might keep up for awhile."

Everyone in the room sprung to action. Even though parents and children alike hated to leave the party, they knew they couldn't tarry with the snowstorm approaching.

"Thank you for sharing your company with me," Michael said, taking the cup from Anna's hand. "It's too bad the snow couldn't hold off a while longer."

Anna returned his warm smile, thinking how much the smile and his red hair reminded her of Mary. She turned to find her family so they could load the wagon, when Michael stopped her by gently touching her elbow.

"May I call on you, Anna?"

Anna looked up to see if he was joking. All of the Richards were known for their sense of humor. But she could see no trace of smile remaining on his face.

"Why . . . why . . . of course. My parents would be happy to entertain your company," Anna faltered, finding it difficult to come up with accurate words in her nervousness.

Michael smiled widely.

"I'll take that as a yes, then," he replied.

Anna felt her cheeks grow warm as she smiled back, and then made her way across the room to her family. In her haste, Anna missed seeing her parents, who had witnessed the encounter between Anna and Michael Richards, exchange a knowing glance.

By the time the Svensens reached the homestead the snow was falling heavily. Anna could tell by the silence between her parents, huddled together on the wagon's seat, that they had been worried they might miss their home in the darkness. The heavy clouds blanketed any chance of light from the moon or stars, and muffled sound so completely that the horse's hoofs made a dull thud when hitting the ground. Finally, when he could see the shanty, Oscar breathed a loud sigh of relief and the horses seemed to pick up speed, hurrying to reach the warmth of the barn.

Aaron and Oscar quickly helped the rest of the family out of the wagon and went to take care of the horses. Anna helped Elsie unwrap her layers of clothing, while Christina started a fire in the stove.

"I can't get warm," Elsie said, her teeth chattering loudly.

Anna hung up her own coat, and then pressed her lips against Elsie's forehead. The heat coming from her sister's skin surprised Anna, and she tilted Elsie's face upward, peering into her eyes. As she had feared, Elsie's eyes looked abnormally glassy and bright. Quickly, Anna wrapped a quilt around her sister and helped her onto the mattress she normally slept on, tucked in one corner of the shanty's largest room.

"Joseph and Bjorn, please drag this mattress closer to the stove," Anna directed in a firm voice.

"But . . .," Joseph began.

"Just do it quickly, please," Anna interrupted, stepping to Christina who was feeding small sticks into the oven, trying to restart the fire.

"I hope the firewood outside has not gotten too wet," Christina murmured, trying to coax the small blaze higher.

"Mama," Anna said, placing a hand on her mother's arm. "It's Elsie. I think she is sick. Her skin is so warm, and her eyes . . . they do not look right."

Christina raised an alarmed face to her daughter's.

"Please finish feeding the fire. We must make some warm broth for her. Bjorn, Joseph," Christina turned to the boys. "Find the firewood stack outside and bring in several logs. Mind that you brush them off first, so as not to bring snow into the house."

Christina paused a moment, and then continued, "Do not let the house get out of your sight."

"Yes, Mama," Bjorn replied, and the pair began to put on their coats again.

Christina knelt beside Elsie, brushing the youngster's hair from her feverish forehead. She felt the child's burning skin against the palm of her hand.

"Do you not feel well, my love?" Christina murmured in soft Swedish.

"I am so cold, Mama," Elsie whispered back, "And my chest hurts, right here."

The child placed her shaking hand on her chest, and then let it fall back to her side.

"Shh, darling, you try to sleep. We will have some broth for you soon, and the fire will warm you."

Christina raised her head when her husband and Aaron stomped in the door.

"Brrr, 'tis cold," Oscar said, a smile widening across his face. The smile faded quickly as he met his wife's worried eyes, and he assessed the situation. He took his coat off, unwinding the woolen muffler from his neck and neatly hanging both on a peg by the door. Then he strode over to the stove and bent down beside his wife.

"And what is the matter with my little dove?" Oscar asked, peering into Elsie's face.

"I don't feel well, Papa," the small girl whispered. "It is my chest, and I'm so cold."

Oscar traced a finger down Elsie's cheek, trying not to flinch at its warmth.

"Just be patient, my love, and try to rest. Mama and I will make the room warm as soon as we can."

Gravely, Oscar stood up and motioned for Anna to follow him.

"'Tis the start of the pneumonia, I fear," Oscar said. "We must keep her warm and get some liquid down her. Your mother and I will stay up with her tonight, but you must take care of the boys and the chores. Can you do that, my Anna?"

Anna quickly nodded, frightened at the seriousness in her father's voice. She wondered how Elsie could have gotten so sick so fast. Elsie had performed so well at the program. Anna should have noticed that Elsie's flushed cheeks and rapid breath had been more than mere nervousness. Tears began to roll silently from Anna's eyes.

As is he could read her mind, Oscar put one finger under Anna's chin and tilted her face up to his.

"'Tis nobody's fault that Elsie got sick, Anna. We need all of us now to help, to work and to pray that she will soon be better."

Oscar pulled his daughter into a tight embrace.

"We must trust in God, Anna to see us through this. We cannot know God's will, but we must believe that he will take care of Elsie however he sees fit."

Anna nodded and wiped her eyes. Her father was right. God loved Elsie like he loved all of his children, and he would watch over her. All the rest of the family could do was to wait and pray. With resolve, Anna went to the stove and began heating water to make coffee. The entire family had been chilled through, and everyone needed warmth for the long night ahead.

The snow continued to fall steadily throughout the night and most of the next day. When morning finally came, the family discovered that the snow had drifted heavily against the shanty's wooden door, making it impossible to leave the house. Oscar tried pushing the door open and managed just a crack, enough to determine that there would be no going to the barn to check the livestock. In addition to the steady snowfall, the north wind had picked up during the night, and tall drifts lay tight against the house. Between the swirling thick snow and the heavy wind, Oscar could not even make out the shape of the barn.

All day the family stayed crowded around the stove in their small kitchen, listening to the wind howl. Anna knew that her father worried about the livestock surviving the storm without fresh food or water, but she also knew that his concern for his animals was overshadowed by his intense prayers for his youngest child.

In the middle of the night, Elsie had begun coughing – a dry, hacking cough that racked her delicate frame. Her fever continued to climb, and she had grown weaker as the night progressed.

Oscar and Christina had stayed awake nearly all night. They had decided to sit with Elsie in shifts, one watching over Elsie while the other one rested, but neither got much rest, concern for their child pushing aside their need for sleep.

It was near dawn, during one of Christina's watches, when Oscar placed his large, calloused hand gently on her shoulder.

After sleeping fitfully much of the night, Elsie had finally fallen into a deep, peaceful slumber. Christina turned to meet her husband's gaze, tears forming in her eyes.

"I think we should pray together," Oscar murmured, softly.

Christina raised his hand to her cheek, and nodded her head. Oscar helped his wife to rise and the pair made their way to the kitchen table. Sitting close together, husband and wife closed their eyes and asked their God to watch over Elsie and give them the strength to continue to minister to her needs. The pair continued in prayer for close to an hour. Finally, after several moments of silence, Oscar said, "Amen," and he and Christina raised their heads. Although they both still felt concern for Elsie, a new sense of peace filled their hearts, and they determined to face the day with courage. They had placed their daughter in God's hands.

Just then Elsie awoke and began to cough, and Christina hurried to her bedside.

"Mama, can I have some water, please? My throat hurts."

Christina quickly complied with her request. As she did so, Anna walked into the room, looking at Elsie with concern. The night had been long for Anna, also. She had spent much of it lying awake in her parent's room, listening to Elsie's coughs and restless movements. While awake, Anna had prayed fervently for her sister.

After receiving a tired smile from her parents, Anna began making breakfast. Fortunately, the boys had brought in enough wood the night before to last the family for a few days. Anna stirred the embers in the stove and added a few more pieces of kindling. She worked deftly, preparing hot mush and a fresh pot of coffee. Breakfast was ready by the time the boys entered the room.

By mid-morning, the snow continued to fall, but it became obvious that Elsie's condition grew worse. The racking coughs came more frequently, and she had begun to cough up a little blood. Oscar and Christina had discussed going for Dr. Markey, West Bend's only physician, but both knew that any rider would soon get lost in the blizzard.

As the long day wore on, Anna grew desperate. She continued to pray, but she found herself growing angry with God. How could he let someone as innocent as Elsie suffer without any hope?

To give her idle hands something to do, Anna began lunch preparations early. It was while she was in the lean-to, filling her apron with onions to make soup, that she came up with an idea.

"Mama, Papa," Anna cried, rushing in with her apron full. "These onions! They smell so strong. Can we make a poultice from them and put them on Elsie's chest? It may make her coughing easier."

Christina and Oscar looked at each other, and hope replaced the fear on their faces. There was an ample supply of onions from last summer's garden, and at least they could do something to try to help their daughter.

"Let us try it," Oscar said, his voice filled with quiet resolve.

Soon the whole family was involved with preparing the onions. Anna put a kettle filled with water on to boil, while Joseph and Aaron sliced the onions into thin rings. Oscar went to his bedroom and brought back his two extra work shirts. He held them up to Christina, who nodded her head, and then he began tearing the shirts into long, wide pieces.

Anna felt a knot in her stomach as she realized that the shirts were the only extras her father had. He would no longer have a clean shirt to change into on Sunday mornings. Instead, he would be forced to wear the work shirt he currently had on, with the elbows so worn they were almost threadbare. Pity for her father welled up inside Anna, but the feeling soon gave way to concern at the sound of Elsie fighting yet another coughing spell. Anna turned back to the onions. There would be time to figure out how to replace Oscar's shirts later; now they must concentrate on helping Elsie.

As the onions cooked, their pungent odor filled the shanty and brought tears to everyone's eyes. When the first batch began to soften, Anna and Oscar dipped a strip of his shirt into the mixture, and placed it in a cool frying pan to carry it over to the bed. They stood silent for a moment, letting the strip cool slightly so as not to scorch the child's tender skin. Then, they placed the fragrant strip on Elsie's bare chest, and watched.

In a few moments, Elsie opened her eyes and wrinkled her nose.

"What is that smell, Mama?" she asked, and then she began to cough violently.

Quickly, Anna rushed to the shelf beside the stove and brought back a mixing bowl. Christina and Oscar gently lifted Elsie so that she was sitting upright. A few minutes later, Elsie began expelling long strings of phlegm into the bowl. Anna felt her stomach lurch, so she stepped back and closed her eyes.

As horrible as it was to see Elsie racked with coughs, Anna knew that it meant the poultice was working to remove the infection from her sister's chest. She breathed a quiet prayer of thankfulness, and rushed back to the stove to prepare another strip of cloth.

Throughout the day, the routine continued of replacing the poultice on Elsie's chest as soon as it cooled. Without complaint, the boys continued to slice onions, and Anna's feet grew weary as she stood and stirred the pot. She did not notice her fatigue however, nor did she remember to prepare lunch for the rest of the family. Finally, the early evening began to near and Oscar lighted the two oil lamps. Elsie's coughing abated, and she fell into a peaceful slumber. Although pale, Elsie's breathing was no longer labored, and her skin felt much cooler than it had that morning.

"I think we may be over the worst," Christina murmured as Anna and Oscar brought yet one more poultice. "We should let her rest for a while."

Anna sighed, and for the first time all day, felt tired and hungry.

"I'll make something for us to eat now," she said, turning once again towards the lean-to.

"Please, Anna, nothing with onions," Aaron said, wrinkling his nose.

The room broke into quiet laughter, and relief was evident on everyone's face.

"Anna," Oscar said, placing one hand on his daughter's arm. "We are so thankful. The onions may have . . . they may have saved Elsie's life."

Tears fell from Anna's eyes, and she melted into her father's arms.

"Oh, Papa, I love her so much! I have been so scared!"

"Yes, my darling. We all have been," Oscar murmured, stroking Anna's hair gently. "We must continue to trust that our God is good, and whatever he wills for Elsie will be the best."

Anna nodded into her father's shirt, breathing a prayer of thanksgiving for the large crop of onions the family had harvested from their garden.

Chapter Eight

Elsie slept much more peacefully the second night of her illness, and Christina and Oscar even caught a few hours of rest. Christmas Day dawned bright and clear, and Anna woke to patches of sunlight filtering into the small window in her parent's bedroom. The sun's rays intensified as they bounced off the deep snowdrifts surrounding the house.

Anna, too, had found rest during the night. Before arising, she closed her eyes again, thanking God for the gift of his son so many years ago in Bethlehem, and asking for strength to face the challenges of the day. Elsie still could take a turn for the worse, Anna knew, plus the family had to find a way to dig out from the drifts around their home and reach the barn to check on the livestock. Determinedly Anna arose and went into the kitchen to prepare breakfast.

Both Christina and Oscar greeted their eldest daughter with smiles as she walked into the room. Elsie sat up, propped by pillows, and was drinking water thirstily.

"Good morning, Anna," the child said, a welcome smile crossing her face. "Merry Christmas."

"Oh, Merry Christmas to you, Elsie."

Anna hurried over to her sister's bedside, and after glancing at Christina, gave Elsie a tender hug.

"And how do you feel this morning?" Anna asked, gazing into her sister's eyes.

"I'm still tired, and my chest hurts a little from the cough, but I am also hungry. What's for breakfast?"

Elsie turned her now-clear eyes to her mother's face, amid the laughter of her sister and her parents.

It wasn't long before Anna had prepared a holiday breakfast of sugar-sprinkled muffins and thick slices of salt pork. She would have liked to prepare eggs to accompany the meal, but that would have to wait until someone could check the chicken coop. Her brothers awoke with the smell of freshly brewed coffee, and the family sat down hungrily to breakfast.

Just as Anna was starting to rise to begin the dishes, Oscar asked her to sit back down because he had something to say. He pushed his chair back from the table so that he might include Elsie, who still lay on the bed, in his conversation.

"You all deserve so much this Christmas," Oscar said in a clear voice. "Your mother and I have noticed all of the sacrifices you have had to make since we came to this new country."

A slight frown crossed Oscar's face, making him suddenly appear tired.

"We wish that we could give you all the presents you deserve, but times have been hard this first year on the farm," Oscar continued, and then brightened. "So what we have is not much, but we give it with love."

Oscar and Christina exchanged a loving glance across the table, and then Christina pushed her chair back and hurried into their bedroom. When she came back, she carried and armful of gray wool.

"These I've made for you. They will help to keep you warm during your walks to school, and doing the chores here."

Christina handed woolen caps to her three sons and long woolen scarves to her daughters. In her bed, Elsie rubbed her cheek against the scarf's softness.

"Oh, Mama, it is so beautiful," Elsie exclaimed.

Anna felt tears once again rush to her eyes.

"This was too much work for you, Mama," she began, but her mother silenced her by holding up one hand.

"It was not work, it was pleasure. With every stitch, I thought about all of the blessings God has given me."

Anna hugged the scarf close, and then thought of something she had almost forgotten during the past few days.

"We have something for you, too. Joseph, did you remember to bring it home?"

Joseph looked confused, and then brightened. "It's in my coat."

The boy grabbed his coat off of the hook by the door where he had put it two nights earlier after bringing in firewood. Carefully, he extracted a small object wrapped in brown paper.

"This is from all of us," Joseph said, presenting the package to his mother and father. "We made it at school."

Christina gently unwrapped the brown paper to reveal a small star made of twigs and entwined with dried flowers. The delicate object was not much worse for the wear it had received in Joseph's pocket.

"Oh," Christina said, her breath catching in her throat. "This is so lovely. How did you . . .?"

"Miss Stevens knew how to dry flowers," Elsie jumped in, proud of her knowledge. "We all looked for the flowers on the way to school every morning, but Aaron found some of the prettiest ones here in the pasture."

Aaron nodded, a smile on his face.

"This is a beautiful present," Oscar said. "Let us all thank God for our many blessing."

All the family members obediently bowed their heads together for the second time that day, joy and gratitude filling their hearts over Elsie's recovery and the end of the worst winter storm they had experienced since coming to Kansas.

It wasn't too long after the breakfast dishes had been washed, dried and stacked that the Svensens heard muffled voices outside their door. Oscar had just been discussing with his sons how they might dig out from the heavy drifts pressed against their door so that they could reach the barn. They all knew that the livestock must be desperately hungry and thirsty by now.

At the sound of the voices, Oscar pushed back from the table, a slight frown on his face. He reached the door and opened it as far as possible. Squinting his eyes against the whiteness, a wide smile soon replaced his frown.

"Welcome, neighbors!" Oscar's voice boomed through the crisp air. "I wondered how anyone could travel in this snow, but I see that you are not having any trouble."

"Hello, Mr. Svensen, and Merry Christmas! We thought maybe you would have a little trouble digging out from under all the drifts. This homestead has always taken quite a beating when the north wind blows."

Anna's face flushed as she recognized the voice. Peeking out behind her father she saw the bundled up figures of Michael Richards, his brother, Robert, and his father, George.

"An answer to prayer," Christina said softly, under her breath.

The Richards had driven over to the Svensens' farm in a sled pulled by their matching bays. The snow had frozen so solid that even the horses' weight did not penetrate the hard top crust. Although the hoses looked cold as they stamped their feet in the snow, they did not appear to be suffering.

"We would like to come help you to dig, but we cannot seem to get the door open very far," Oscar told the three men.

"Don't worry about that none, Mr. Svensen," Michael said, stepping as close to the door as possible. "We aim to dig out your front door first, and then maybe see if we can help you dig out your barn."

Catching a glimpse of Anna peeking behind her father's shoulder, Michael tipped his woolen cap and nodded.

Anna smiled, and then turned back to the sink, missing her mother's thoughtful gaze.

Soon the sound of shovels lifting the heavy, wet snow away from the door could be heard, along with some good-natured whistling and laughter. Oscar directed his sons to don their warmest clothing so that they might join the Richards as soon as the front door was free.

Wanting to join with the men in helping to shovel snow, but realizing that it probably wouldn't be proper, Anna decided to make a cup of warm tea for Elsie. Just as she finished the tea, Anna realized that Elsie had drifted off for a nap. Anna then decided to put on a fresh pot of coffee to warm their guests when they needed a break. After checking the lean-to for supplies, she decided she could make a quick batch of sugar cookies, also. After all, the family had not had many treats during the lean autumn, and it was Christmas Day.

It wasn't long before the door was free and the male Svensens joined their rescuers in surveying the damage to the small farm. The view just outside the door to the shanty was breathtaking. Bright winter sun glinted off drifts of snow, untouched except for the trails made by the Richards in their rescue work.

"It is so beautiful," Aaron murmured, glancing around the farm.

"Oh, come on now," George Richards said, a teasing twinkle in his eyes. "Don't tell me you boys ain't ever seen snow before. Why, you being from Sweden and all, I would have thought you'd be used to snow like this."

Oscar shook his head slightly, and replied, "We had snow, yes, but not drifts like this, so short in some places and so deep in others."

Oscar's hand swept across the expanse of land. "And see! White wherever you look. It is as if the blue of the sky just reaches down and touches the white of the earth with nothing in between. I am amazed."

The Svensens stood looking at the landscape a few minutes more while the Richards stood close by, respecting their friends' silence.

Finally, Oscar sighed and said, "It is time to check the animals."

The group of men and boys trudged toward the barn, just a lump in the snow. Oscar quietly braced himself for what he might find. He knew that he had made the right decision by not checking on the animals during the storm; he most certainly would have gotten lost in the heavy snow. But he also knew that for the animals, two and a half days was a long time to go without fresh food or water, especially while braving the cold in the barn. Would they have been able to survive?

When the group finally reached the barn and dug out the heavy snow from its doors, the scene was about what Oscar had feared. The horses had made it through the storm, although the men could tell by the pairs' drooping heads and clouded eyes that it would take some time for them to recover. Four of the chickens hadn't survived, and the rest appeared subdued. Oscar felt a pang as he thought of how hard Christina had worked to build up her flock. The worst loss, however, was the milk cow. The men found her lying in one corner of the barn.

"Was it the cold?" Oscar said, almost under his breath.

"Hard to tell." George Richards shook his head. "Cows can't tolerate not getting milked when they need it. This is a tough loss."

George put his hand on Oscar's shoulder and stood beside him, contemplating the situation for a moment.

"I know this probably won't help at a time like this, but a lot of folks hereabouts, well, they'll have losses, too."

George removed his hand and faced Oscar. "It will be a rough winter. Life on this prairie . . . well, it's just hard. It takes a tough breed to make it out here."

George paused and glanced in the direction of Oscar's sons tending to the horses. "From what I've seen, though, it seems like you all have what it takes."

Oscar nodded, and then his face broke into a large grin. "If, 'what it takes' is a lot of stubbornness and a dose of friendly neighbors, well yes, I guess we have it."

The men chuckled softly together, and then faced the difficult chore of tending to those animals that survived the storm, and the bodies of those that didn't.

It wasn't long before Oscar and his family discovered that George Richards' predictions had been true. Many families around West Bend had been hit hard by the storm. In addition to livestock dying at several farms, Jed Dennison's father, Jake, had also been lost.

Anna first heard about the missing man in church, two Sundays after the blizzard. The Svensens had not been able to attend church that first Sunday because both Elsie and the horses were still recovering. Oscar had led devotions at their kitchen table instead, praising God for Elsie's recovery and for seeing the family through the blizzard.

The second Sunday, however, all the Svensens were anxious to attend services. Due as much to the weather as anything else, school had not yet resumed for the spring term, and Anna had been missing her conversations with Miss Stevens and Mary

Richards. With great excitement, the Svensens bundled into their wagon and approached the small church. The excitement dimmed, however, as soon as they pulled into the yard.

As quickly as possible, Anna climbed out of the back of the wagon, helped Elsie down, and then hurried to meet Miss Stevens, who was standing with a group of women near the entrance to the clapboard building. But Anna slowed her pace when she noticed the young teacher dabbling at her eyes with a lace handkerchief.

"Oh, Anna," Tina Stevens cried. "Have you heard the news? Oh, it is just terrible!"

Anna looked at her friend in confusion and shook her head.

"It's Jed Dennison's father, Jake. They found him not fifty yards from his cabin. He was . . . oh it is terrible . . . he was . . . frozen, they say. And Jed found him. Oh, it must have been just awful for him!"

Anna lifted her hand to her mouth, and took a step backward. Her thoughts fled back to the Allen's barn-raising, the one time she had seen Jed's father. Picturing the man hunched down in the wagon, Anna tried to feel what it must have been like for Jed to find his father lying dead in the snow. She tried to conjure up a sense of sadness for Jake Dennison, unable to reach his door in the terrible storm, lost in the whirling snow and darkness. All she seemed to be able to feel, however, was a mix of anger and confusion. The unexpected anger welled up at Jed Dennison for once again ruining what Anna had anticipated being a wonderful day, the first day in two weeks that she had been able to leave their homestead. But the confusion Anna felt was overpowering. How could Miss Stevens show such compassion toward someone who had caused her such pain?

Anna regretted the thought as quickly as it had entered her head. She knew that, as a Christian, she should love Jed Dennison just as much as she loved her own family. But knowing that she should feel compassion towards Jed and actually being able to do it seemed impossible to Anna.

Quietly, she bit her lower lip and decided not to share her confusion with Miss Stevens. How the young teacher could feel such sympathy, Anna did not understand, yet she admired Miss Stevens for being able to do so.

"We must pray for Jed, Anna," Miss Stevens said, dabbing at the corners of her eyes with her handkerchief. "We must pray that God will use this terrible tragedy for some good."

"Yes, of course," Anna promised, taking her teacher's arm and accompanying her into the sanctuary for the beginning of services.

Anna resolved to keep her promise to Miss Stevens. Difficult though it may be, Anna would pray for Jed Dennison. She would also pray for her own heart to be softened.

Chapter Nine

A subdued congregation listened to the words Pastor Heggarty spoke that bright January morning. Many had lost livestock in the storm, and the horrifying picture of Jake Dennison freezing so close to his house had left its heavy mark on the parishioners. But however quiet the congregation seemed, Anna found the words of Scripture read by Pastor Heggarty inspiring, and she left church determined to strengthen her faith through prayer and Bible study.

Two more weeks passed before classes resumed, and by then, Elsie had recovered enough to make the daily trek with her siblings. Anna was all too happy to throw herself back into her studies and her lesson preparations for the younger children. Spending the long winter days stuck at home in the shanty had started to wear on all the Svensens. The resumption of school brought renewed energy to their days.

Still, despite the pleasure evident on the faces of the three youngest Svensens about the prospect of daily rejoining their school friends, Anna sensed a tension about the house. She knew something was bothering her parents, and she felt frustrated that she had not been included in the discussion of the problem, although Aaron evidently had.

It was while helping Aaron tend to the horses one windy Saturday morning that Anna confronted him about the somber mood she often found her parents in after she returned from school.

"What is it, Aaron?" she asked, watching her brother fork hay into the horses' stalls. "What is bothering Mama and Papa? They are so quiet lately. I do not know what to think."

Aaron set the pitchfork aside and looked at his sister.

"I do not suppose it would hurt to tell you. Everyone will find out soon enough, anyway."

Aaron sighed and rubbed his gloved hand across his forehead. "Papa is thinking about selling the farm."

Anna's breath caught in her throat.

"Oh, Aaron! This farm, it's not much, but it has been Papa's dream!"

Aaron's eyes began to get watery, and Anna watched as he wiped at them.

"I know. But the wheat . . . well, we did not get as much as we had hoped from it last year. You know, it was so dry. And now the cow is gone, and we must buy a new one. It's not good for the younger ones to go without milk."

Anna nodded her head, her thoughts solemn. She had been wondering when her father might buy another milk cow. Never before in her life had she gone so long without milk for drinking and cooking, not to mention butter and cream. Lately, there had not been much variation in the Svensens' meager diet. Although there was always just enough food, it all had begun to taste the same.

Aaron looked at his sister and said in a whisper, "Papa cannot afford to buy another cow. There is just no money for it. We all need new clothes, and Joseph and Bjorn, their shoes have holes in them. Papa is beginning to think that maybe God wants him to follow another path. Perhaps that is why there is not enough money right now."

Aaron, paused, bowing his head, slightly. "I am really frightened, Anna. I have not seen Papa like this before . . . so . . . so full of doubt."

The young man shook his head slightly. "I have decided to try to help, if I can. I am going in to West Bend on Monday, and I will look for a job."

"But what can you do? You have always wanted to work on the farm, too."

Aaron removed his right glove and ran one hand through his blonde hair.

"Once I thought my future was on the farm. But perhaps God has shown me another path."

Anna watched as her brother reddened slightly.

"I have been wanting to save some money. Minnie and I, we . . . well, we may want to get started on a home of our own, soon."

"Aaron . . . I did not know . . . this is a surprise to me," Anna stammered. She had known that Aaron had gone to visit the Johannsen house a few times before the holidays, but she hadn't anticipated Aaron and Minnie growing so serious so soon. As he finished pitching hay to the horses and then began to gather the buckets for their water, Anna examined Aaron with new eyes.

"We must pray for Mama and especially Papa," Aaron said, turning as he hung the pitchfork on a nail by the barn's door. "If they seek God's wisdom, I know the path will be made clear to them."

Anna nodded. She would seek God's wisdom, also. Surely there must be something she could do to help her parents stay on the farm and let Aaron and Minnie find the money to start their own home. As she stepped into the crisp bright January air, she determined to pray harder than ever before, seeking an answer to her family's dilemma.

Three weeks into the new spring term, a knock on the wooden school door surprised the students mid-morning while their heads were bent over their math and spelling lessons. Miss Stevens, who had been helping the intermediate students with long division, paused for just a moment, and then strode purposefully to the door.

There stood Jed Dennison, nervously rolling the brim of his black felt hat between his fingers. "I thought I might have a word with you, Ma'am," Jed said, his voice quavering.

"Why, of course, Jed. Step right here, into the cloakroom."

She quickly ushered the large boy in and shut out the howling February winds. A silence had fallen on the schoolroom. Noticing the lack of noise, Miss Stevens turned around.

"Boys and girls, please resume your studies. I will be with you in a moment."

Anna turned back to the addition problems she was working on with the children in Elsie's level, but she strained her ears, attempting to hear the conversation between Jed and Miss Stevens. Jed certainly did look like he had cleaned up his appearance; his worn boots had been recently polished, and his shirt was freshly pressed, but still Anna could not help but be suspicious.

"I am so sorry about the death of your father," Miss Stevens said. She patted his shoulder gently. "I know that it must be a terrible loss for you, and that you must miss him greatly."

Jed looked down at his hands still twisting his hat.

"Yes Ma'am, thank you," he said, "but me and Pa weren't that close."

He stopped and shuffled his feet a little.

"You see, Pa never took kindly to me wanting to come to school. He didn't see no need for an education. He said he could teach me anything I needed to know at home. He thought books and such was just a . . . well, just a waste of time."

Miss Stevens nodded, her sympathetic expression encourageing Jed to continue.

"Well, now I'm living with my Aunt Sylvie and Uncle Ray. Their place is down a piece from the school. It's a long walk, but if'n you'd have me back, I'd sure like to come back so's I could learn to read."

Jed looked earnestly into his teacher's eyes, which, by this point, were threatening to spill over with tears.

"Of course, you may come back, Jed," Miss Stevens said. "We'd be happy to welcome you."

Jed smiled a lopsided grin. Glancing up from her work, Anna noticed how much less sinister the young man looked when he was smiling.

"But you must remember," Miss Stevens continued, "that you have to take your schoolwork seriously from now on. No coming in late and unprepared, and no disturbing the other students while they are working."

"Yes, Ma'am . . . I mean, no Ma'am," Jed said.

"All right then," Miss Stevens smiled. "You may take your seat there, in the back row. I will finish the mathematics lesson I'm working on, and then I will be back directly to help you with your reading."

"Yes, Ma'am," Jed said.

The teacher turned around and walked back over to her pupils. Jed quickly shed his hat and coat and hung them on the empty wooden peg in the cloakroom. He hurried over to the last row, the one across from Anna and Mary's seat, and sat waiting.

The rest of the day passed without incident, and Anna reluctantly admitted to herself that Jed, indeed, did seem to have changed. Even Mary said as much as she and Anna prepared to leave at the end of the day.

"Jed Dennison seems to have cleaned himself up right nice," the bubbly redhead whispered. "I can't help but wonder how long it will be before he shows up and makes another scene, though."

"We should give him a chance. People can change," Anna replied.

"I suppose."

The pair exited the schoolhouse, and Anna began looking for the boys and Elsie.

"Have you talked to my brother lately?" Mary asked, her lips turning up in a playful smile.

"We spoke after church on Sunday."

Anna felt her face begin to redden.

Mary giggled, and then she grabbed Anna's arm and leaned forward.

"He's so sweet on you, Anna. He talks about you and your family all of the time. I really think he wants to court you, but he doesn't know whether or not you'd be accepting of him."

Anna could feel her entire face awash in a hot blush as a confusion of feelings swept through her. Michael always could make her laugh with his teasing bright eyes and good-natured smile, and she enjoyed his company. But did her feelings go any deeper than that? She thought of how kind Michael and his father were after the blizzard; of how her family may have been snowed in much longer if the Richards had not come to rescue them. Surely someone as kind as Michael deserved her attention, even if his name caused a flurry of confusion inside her.

"Tell your brother that he may come to call any time he wishes," Anna said. "I'm sure my parents would welcome his visits."

"Oh, Anna," Mary said, squeezing her friend's arm. "I am so excited! If you and Michael become . . . well . . . good friends, it would be so wonderful to have you as part of our family."

With that, Mary squeezed Anna's arm a final time, and turned to head home. Mixed feelings washed through Anna as she walked over to join her siblings. Michael Richards was sweet and kind, but was he the one God had planned for her life?

Anna did not have long to wait before exploring her feelings about Michael further. Two nights after her after-school conversation with Mary, the young man showed up at the Svensens' door, hat in hand, smiling broadly.

"Evenin' Mr. Svensen," Michael said as Oscar opened the door. "Right nice night out. I decided to go for a little ride, and I thought I might bring over some of my mother's famous sugar cookies."

After pausing for just a moment, Oscar smiled in return, and ushered the boy to the kitchen table.

"It is so thoughtful for you to visit," Christina said, choosing her words carefully. She rose from her chair by the stove, and set aside her mending. "Please thank your mother for these cookies."

"Elsie, find your sister and tell her we have company," Oscar said.

From where she was bent over her schoolwork in her parents' bedroom Anna listened closely. She suspected when she heard a rider trot into the yard that it might by Michael, but she had wanted to wait until the warmth left her cheeks before she joined the rest of the family.

"Anna," Elsie said, rushing into the room. "There is someone here to see you. It is a boy."

Elsie emphasized the final word with a giggle.

"Hush, Elsie, mind your manners," Anna reproached her sister. "Tell Mr. Richards that I will be there directly, as soon as I put away my books."

Elsie giggled again, raising one hand to her mouth, and then turn and fled the room.

"She's coming," the small blonde told the attentive group in the kitchen. "Her face is all pink, though."

To Anna's dismay, the room broke out into surprised laughter just as she walked through the doorway. Startled, she glanced around the room, and then, with her hands pressed to her cheeks, she laughed, also.

It wasn't long before Michael and all of the Svensens were gathered around the small table, eating sugar cookies and drinking strong, hot coffee. Michael was an avid storyteller, matching Oscar in his use of suspense and humor. All too soon, the evening came to a close. After tipping his hat to Anna with a wink, Michael stepped into the brisk evening for his ride home.

After the younger children had gone to bed, Christina and Anna washed the coffee cups and finally got a chance to speak.

"Michael Richards is a nice young man, I think," Christina said, handing Anna a cup to dry.

"Yes," Anna replied. "He always makes me laugh."

"It is good to laugh," Christina said, letting the silence linger for several more moments.

"I don't know if what I feel for him is love, Mama. He makes me laugh, and I like seeing him, but I keep wondering if that is enough to be called 'love.'"

Christina smiled gently and dried her hands.

"Bring your concerns to God, Anna. If Michael is the person He has chose for you, then He will put your heart at peace about it. If Michael is not the man God wants for your husband, then you will need to wait until God brings the right person into your life."

She sighed, carefully brushing the hair from her eldest daughter's forehead.

"God has such wonderful plans for all of us, Anna. I look forward to seeing how your life will unfold."

Anna smiled, and hugged her mother. She knew Christina was right. She would trust God to let her know if she should give her heart to Michael Richards, or if she should wait for another man to enter her life.

It wasn't long after Aaron's conversation with Anna in the barn that the young man came home announcing he had found a job in town. Proudly Aaron explained that he had checked first at the livery stable, because he felt comfortable around horses, but the owner hadn't needed any help. He went next to the blacksmith's shop, but he received the same reply. Finally, in desperation, he had gone to Jenkins Hardware. There he had found that Ralph Jenkins had just placed a "Help Wanted" sign in the front window of the store that very morning.

"I spoke with him for about thirty minutes before he offered me the job," Aaron reported that night over coffee following the evening meal. "Mr. Jenkins had some worries about my English; he thought the customers may not be able to understand me. After talking, however, he thought I'd make the perfect match for the job."

"Oh, that's wonderful," Christina said, a smile spreading across her face.

The family listened as Aaron described what his duties would be at the store, and how much money Mr. Jenkins planned to pay.

"As soon as I can, I will buy another cow, so that my brothers and sisters may have milk," Aaron finished, with resolve.

Elsie clapped her hands and giggled, but the rest of the family could not help but notice how Oscar sat silently, a slight frown upon his face. Aaron looked at his mother, but she shook her head slightly.

"Well, I think I will be going to bed, now," Aaron said, stretching his arms above his head. "Tomorrow I must pack my belongings to take to the store."

Earlier, Aaron had reported that Mr. Jenkins had offered, as part of his salary, to let him board in the small back room of the store from Monday through Saturday. He would take his meals with Mr. Jenkins and his wife. Aaron had readily accepted, knowing that the trek into West Bend was too long for him to make daily, especially during inclement weather.

The family picked up the remaining dishes and prepared for bed. While saying her prayers, Anna thanked God for providing Aaron with a job and the family with more income, but she also asked God to bring peace to her father's troubled heart. After what seemed like only minutes, Anna dropped off to a soundless sleep.

Chapter Ten

Rising earlier than usual, Anna's stomach fluttered with a mix of anticipation and dread. Aaron would be leaving this morning. She knew how desperately her parents needed the extra money that Aaron's employment would bring, but she also could not imagine the small house without her older brother's quiet, but strong presence. Ever since she could remember, Aaron had been there. Throughout the years, he had served as her protector and friend, despite the occasional bouts of rivalry the two shared. Since deepening her faith in God, Anna and Aaron had often read the Bible together, discussing the Word and their various understandings of it. Although Anna would miss this time, she knew the step that Aaron was about to take held great importance for his future, and the family's.

All these thoughts crossed Anna's mind as she mixed biscuit dough. She had only been up a few minutes when she heard Christina slowly walk across the room.

"Good morning, Mama," Anna said, scooting over to make room for her mother by the stove.

"Good morning."

Anna started when she heard quivering in Christina's voice. She turned to see tears rolling down Christina's cheeks. Christina brushed the tears away and smiled.

"I knew there would come a day when my children would grow and leave," she began. "I just did not know that it would be so soon."

Anna smiled. "Oh, Mama, he is nearly twenty. It is time."

"I know, I know, but it is hard to let go."

Christina put one had on her daughter's cheek.

"You will know, some day, what it is like, when you, too, have felt this . . . this mother love. It's so painful, and so wonderful, all at the same time."

"What is, Mama?" Aaron asked, coming up behind the two women.

"Never mind," Christina said, brushing her eyes. "Are you all packed? Did you remember to put in your extra shirt?"

Aaron smiled at his mother, noticing the wetness behind her eyes.

"Yes, Mama, I have packed everything. I am ready, but I would like to have a big bowl of your porridge. It will keep me warm on my long walk."

"Yes, yes, of course," Christina said, turning to the stove.

Anna winked at her brother.

Before long, the rest of the family was up and assembled at the table for breakfast. Anna was relieved to see that her father's face had lost its distressed look, and seemed once more to radiate a sense of peace and strength.

Following the blessing, Oscar spoke, directing his gaze towards his eldest son.

"Last night I was troubled," he began, everyone sitting around the table falling immediately silent. "I believed that Aaron should not have had to find a job. That it was my responsibility to support this family."

He paused, and Anna noticed that everyone had put down their spoons and forks.

"But then, after going to bed, I talked to God. I opened my heart to Him, and asked Him to guide my thoughts. I woke up this morning feeling refreshed. I had been praying for God to show me a way to let us stay on the farm. When God answered my prayer, I did not even realize it. All I could think about was my own fallen pride at having to let my son help support the family."

"Aaron," Oscar continued, reaching out his hand and placing it on the warm cotton of Aaron's blue shirt. "I am happy that you will bring support to this family. I am thankful that you will share the fruit of your labors with us."

Aaron nodded, unable to speak.

"And now," Oscar said, withdrawing his hand, "Let us eat this meal, before it grows cold."

Anna picked up her spoon again, taking a bite of the warm porridge but still noticing the glance shared between her mother and father.

Aaron planned to accompany his siblings on their way to school that morning, continuing after they reached the schoolhouse for the extra two miles it would take to reach West Bend. Just before leaving, Christina tucked a package into Aaron's bundle.

"Some ginger cookies," she whispered into his ear. "I hid them from your brothers last night. I wanted to make sure there would be some left for your first day. Who knows what kind of food you will be eating from now on."

Aaron hugged his mother.

"I am sure that Mr. Jenkins will take good care of him," Oscar said, walking up from behind his wife. "God be with you, my son."

Without embarrassment, he pulled Aaron into his arms and held him tightly.

"Now, you'd better be off, or all of you will be late," he said, releasing Aaron and pushing him gently toward the door.

Christina and Oscar stood side by side as they watched their offspring hurry out into the crisp, bright air.

"We are so blessed," Christina murmured.

"Yes, my love," her husband said, drawing her close.

As they trod across the prairie, Aaron and Anna noticed the first hints of tender green spears shooting their heads up between the brown grass. After the December blizzard, the Kansas weather had been unusually dry and cold. They lagged behind, letting the younger children run ahead in their haste to meet their friends.

"Are you scared?" Anna asked after several moments of silence.

"A little," Aaron admitted, raising his head and scanning the horizon. "But I am at peace, too. I have never really minded farm work, but now I do not believe it is where my heart is."

Anna nodded. She had seen Aaron working hard by their father's side ever since the family moved to Kansas, but Aaron's eyes never seemed to sparkle the way Oscar's did, or even Joseph's. Bjorn was more like Aaron, and Anna now wondered if he, too, would be lured away from farm life.

"You will be nearer to Minnie, living in town," Anna mentioned, glancing sideways at her brother.

Aaron reddened slightly, but his lips parted in a smile.

"Yes, that's true," he said. "I hope to be able to see Minnie, to visit more often at her home now that I will be so close."

They continued on in silence for several more moments, two blonde heads bowed in deep thought.

"Do you still wish to marry?"

"Oh, yes. Minnie and I have not known each other that long, but we both feel it is God's will. We are much at peace about it. But I believe I have a promise to keep to father and mother first. I must help father keep our land."

Aaron lifted his chin into the air.

"After I have bought a cow and paid for the spring seed, I will buy some lumber to add another room or two onto the house. Then I can begin to save for my own home."

Anna stopped and placed a hand on Aaron's worn jacket sleeve.

"But Aaron, all of that . . . why, it could take a long time. More than one year, maybe more than two. That is too long to wait . . ."

"Yes," Aaron said, a heavy sadness in his voice. "But I must help, Anna. I am the oldest son. It is my duty."

They continued on, both lost in their own thoughts. Confusion washed through Anna. On one hand, she admired Aaron for pledging to help their parents; yet, she could not help but pity her brother and his future wife. One or two years could be such a long time to wait to begin a new life with someone.

She wrinkled her nose and plodded through the grass. Several more minutes passed before she noticed Aaron smiling at her.

"What is so interesting that it is causing such a frown on my sister's face?"

"Oh, Aaron," Anna said, throwing her mittened hands up into the air. "I would so like to help, too. I wish there could be a way for me to make money. I want to help Mama and Papa, and I would like for you and Minnie to be able to get married."

Aaron stopped, touched by his sister's concern. Gently he took Anna's hand into his own, larger one.

"Your education has always been important to you. Me, I never cared too much about school. But you are different. You should finish. Let Papa and I worry about saving the farm. And, if God is willing, there will be a way for Minnie and I to marry soon enough. It is not to be your concern."

Gently Aaron squeezed Anna's hand before releasing it. The two walked forward, silent only a moment before Aaron spoke again.

"Besides, your time has been much spoken for lately. Perhaps you will not even be living on the farm much longer. On Papa's farm, that is."

"Oh, Aaron!" Anna's face flushed as she garnered her brother's meaning. "Michael Richards . . . he is . . . he is just a friend. He enjoys visiting with you and Papa as much as with me."

"Yes, he does like talking to Papa," Aaron replied smiling. Suddenly his tone took on a new urgency. "But Michael does not think of being just a 'friend' to you. This I know."

"You have talked to him, then?"

"No, not about this. But he cares about you deeply, sister. It is evident every time you enter the room. His eyes, they are full of you. I know what it means to look at someone like that. I have done it myself."

Anna nodded. She had noticed the change in Michael every time she was around him. He remained the friendly, funny friend he always had been, but a new tenderness had recently developed in the way he spoke to her.

"And you, my sister, do you feel the same way?"

"I don't know."

Anna shook her head, looking at the ground. "I am confused. Were you ever confused about Minnie?"

"Never. With Miss Stevens, yes. But what I felt for her was not love. It was more . . . admiration, I guess. With Minnie, I've always known."

Anna nodded and walked on, vowing to herself that she would not only seek a way to help Aaron and her parents support the farm, but she would also spend some time examining her feelings for Michael Richards. If she did not feel for him as he did for her, she owed it to him to tell him as soon as possible.

It was a troubled but determined sister that Aaron left near the school house. With a small wave of his hand, Aaron turned toward West Bend. Anna watched his back for a moment, then turned and went inside the school house door.

The Svensens adjusted to Aaron's absence quickly, although they continued to miss him when they gathered around the table every night for their evening meal. Joseph and Bjorn stepped up to the challenge of helping Oscar with the evening chores upon their return from school every afternoon, although both boys were drooping with fatigue by dinnertime. The weather continued to hold fair the rest of the winter as the calendar crept towards spring.

Daily Anna prayed for a way that she might be able to help her parents and her brother. She also dwelt on her confused feelings about Michael Richards. Although she grew restless for a solution to both of these issues, she tried to throw herself into her studies and her lessons for the younger pupils. Miss Stevens had given over nearly total control of the two primary grades to Anna and Mary Richards. Even though Anna seemed to do the bulk of both the preparations and the scoring, Mary could always be counted on to add creativity to the lessons.

It was during a planning session between Mary and Anna one lunch period that Mary brought up the subject of Anna finishing school the following year. The sun shone unusually bright and warm, and the two girls sat on a bench near the entrance to the school eating and watching the youngsters play.

"How important is it to you to graduate?" Mary asked as she nibbled on a gingersnap cookie.

Anna set aside the mathematics book she had been poring over. "It has always been a dream of mine. When we left Sweden, I didn't think it would be possible to finish. Then I lost a whole year our first year in the United States. When Papa told me last fall that I could return to school, well, it was almost like a miracle. I had just about given up hope."

Mary looked at Anna. "Would there be anything that could stop you from finishing. What I mean is, would you be willing to make . . . say . . . other plans?"

"Oh, yes! If there was a way I could help my Papa. With money I mean. Aaron . . . he works so hard, but everyone knows he wants to get married. If I could do something . . . if I could help, then maybe Papa could keep the farm and Aaron could get married."

"Oh," said Mary, "I see."

The redhead slowly took another bit of her cookie, then brightened.

"But couldn't there be another reason not to finish school? I mean, what if, say, someone ask you to . . . well to . . . ."

"Mary!" Anna exclaimed, finally grasping her friend's meaning. "Are you talking about . . . about your brother? He and I, well, we have never discussed such things!"

Mary giggled, and grasped Anna's arm.

"But, Anna! Surely you've thought about it! Michael is just crazy about you. I can tell. He gets flustered every time he is around you. And I know he is thinking about marriage, because he asked Pa about building a house on that piece of land we own down by the stream . . . ."

Mary cut her sentence short when Anna began violently shaking her head.

"We mustn't talk about this, you and I," Anna said firmly. "It is not fair to Michael."

"All right," Mary conceded. "But I tell you, you'd better be prepared to have an answer for him. I truly believe Michael will ask you to marry him soon."

With a slight nod, Mary flounced away, leaving Anna to ponder her friend's words.

Could it be true? Would Michael Richards ask her to marry him? And if he did, how would she respond? Marrying Michael certainly would help her family by providing one less mouth to feed every day. Besides, the Richards seemed quite prosperous and generous. Surely, Michael's family would help her parents keep the farm. Was this the answer to prayer that Anna had been waiting for?

It was a preoccupied girl that led the primary grades in spelling recitation that afternoon. Try as she might, Anna could not get Mary's words out of her head.

Miss Stevens couldn't help but notice Anna's lack of focus. After the second time that Anna asked Tommy Jensen to spell the word, "success," Miss Stevens approached and gently touched Anna on the shoulder.

"I'll finish with the lesson today. Why don't you go back to your seat and work on your composition?"

Anna smiled in gratitude at her teacher, and made her way back to the last row where she shared a seat with Mary. Thankfully, Mary was listening to a third level student read, so Anna was alone on the bench. She took out her composition, an essay on the definition of "love" as shown in William Shakespeare's sonnets. Wryly, she smiled at the irony of her topic. Why could she write about love in poems, but not even be able to identify her own feelings on the topic? This was the longest essay Anna had ever attempted to write in English, and it took only a few moments for her to become absorbed in the words.

Before she knew it, Mary had slipped back to her seat, and the entire school began closing exercises for the day. As the pupils filed out of the building, Miss Stevens quietly put her hand on Anna's arm and asked her to wait a moment. Anna waved to Elsie and her brothers to tell them to go on home without her.

"I think there is something bothering you," Miss Stevens said after the two had gone back inside the building. "Would you like to talk about it?"

Miss Stevens' sensitivity did not surprise Anna. The teacher had an uncanny way of knowing when one of her students was bothered, and because of the friendship the two shared, Miss Stevens was especially aware of Anna's feelings.

Anna sat on the step leading to Miss Stevens' desk. She looked out the window for a moment, noticing that robins had returned from their winter nesting grounds.

"It is about Michael Richards." Anna paused, searching for the right words. "Mary told me today that he . . . that he may ask me to marry him."

Miss Steven finished wiping the blackboard at the front of the room and then turned around, smiling broadly.

"And how do you feel about that? I have noticed that the two of you have been spending quite a bit of time together at church. And, a few people have mentioned that he has been calling at your farm."

Anna's cheeks flushed warmly at the idea of Michael and herself being the topic of West Bend gossip.

"I am so confused. Michael is warm and kind and he makes me laugh, but, well, I just do not know if I wish to marry him. I don't know if I wish to marry anyone right now."

Lifting her skirts, Tina Stevens sat down on the step next to Anna.

"I think you do know, Anna." She let her words sink in. "In my opinion, the only reason to marry someone is because you love him. All the other reasons, no matter how convincing they sound, cannot make up for love."

Wiping tears from her eyes, Anna nodded quickly.

"But what if it is God's will for me to marry Michael? What if Michael is an answer to my prayers about helping my family?"

"If it were God's will for you and Michael to marry, then you would be in love with him. I believe that is the way God works." The teacher threw her head back and chuckled. "That is certainly the way it worked with Samuel and me."

Anna took the lace-edged handkerchief Miss Stevens handed to her and gently wiped her eyes. As she contemplated her teacher's words, a sense of calmness descended upon her. Suddenly, she knew what her answer to Michael's proposal would be, if he should offer one.

"Thank you," Anna said, handing the handkerchief back.

"I hope that I've been able to help."

"Yes, and now I know what I must do."

With her chin set firmly, Anna rose, smiled at her teacher, and hurried out into the sunny afternoon. If she walked quickly, she might be able to catch up with her brothers and Elsie.

Chapter Eleven

Aaron continued to visit his family nearly every Sunday, although he had spent two Sundays in town, calling on Minnie's family during the afternoon and then walking back to his room at the store in the early evening. On one unusually warm Saturday in April, Aaron appeared in the evening guiding a black and white cow behind him.

"Papa! Mama! Look!"

Elsie had been playing in front of the shanty, and, without her parents' permission, had removed her shoes to walk in the new grass. Anna and Christina put aside their mending and rushed to the door.

"Oh, my," Christina exclaimed, raising one hand to her brow and squinting to get a better look at the two figures plodding along the wagon ruts that led to their homestead.

Oscar, stepping out from the barn, gazed into the distance.

"Thank you, Lord," he murmured.

As he grew closer, Aaron lifted one arm in greeting. A wide smile spread across his face.

The family hurried to meet him, with Elsie in the lead. When she reached her older brother, she stuck out her hand to touch the cow's soft nose.

"Her name is Sophie," Aaron said. "She is supposed to be a good milker. She gave birth to a calf about two months ago, so she should give milk for at least another two years."

There was an unmistakable ring of pride in Aaron's voice as he spoke.

"She looks fine, son," Oscar said, slowly walking around the cow. "A fine animal. Where did you get her?"

"Mr. Richards knew we were looking for a cow, and his neighbor had two for sale. His cows weathered the December storm well."

Oscar patted Sophie's head.

"Was she . . . did she cost much?" he asked, searching for the right words.

Aaron looked down and scuffed his foot in the dirt.

"She cost a little," he admitted.

Oscar nodded. "How much?"

Aaron shrugged his shoulders.

"Son," Oscar said, his voice deep and commanding. "How much did she cost?"

"All," Aaron said, tipping his chin defiantly in the air. "It took all that I have saved so far. But you have to have a cow. The children, they need milk."

Anna drew in her breath and bit her lower lip. What a sacrifice Aaron had made, spending all the money he had earned so far, saving none to set up his own household.

"Well, then," Oscar said, taking Sophie's lead rope and touching his son gently on the shoulder. "We must take very good care of her."

Aaron smiled and patted the cow's side.

As her father and brothers saw to settling Sophie in the barn with a bed of straw and some hay to chew on, Anna joined her mother in the house to begin preparing the evening meal. Aaron soon brought in two buckets of warm milk, and the family had milk with their supper for the first time since the Christmas snow storm.

Soon after the meal was finished and the last dish washed, Michael Richards appeared at the door. Anna felt no surprise as she heard his familiar knock and friendly voice.

"Evening folks," he said, striding into the room after Elsie opened the door. "Fine night, isn't it? Pretty warm for this early in the spring."

Oscar nodded his assent. "Can you sit down, Michael? It's a fine cow that Aaron brought home. You must thank your father for finding it for us."

"I'll be sure to do that Mr. Svensen."

Michael placed his lanky body on a bench near the table, the bench closest to Anna. He discussed the weather with Oscar and

Aaron for a few more minutes, only including Anna occasionally by smiling in her direction. At last, gripping his hat tightly, he turned to Anna.

"Would you like to go for a walk? The stars are mighty pretty tonight."

A cold knot formed in Anna's stomach. She breathed a silent prayer for strength, and then looked into Michael's eyes, nodding her assent. She dreaded having a confrontation with her friend about the prospect of marriage, but now was as good a time as any. Besides, Michael Richards was a friendly, honorable young man; it was not fair for her to give him any false expectations. She got her wraps, then stepped through the door as Michael held it open.

"We will not be gone long," he said, directing his comment toward Oscar.

"Oscar smiled and nodded.

"Well, my love, I think this may be an eventful walk for our Anna," he murmured, placing his arm around Christina as she came to join him on the bench.

"'Tis too soon, I think," Christina said, laying her head on her husband's broad shoulder. "I just pray that Anna follows her heart."

Michael led Anna past the barn toward the wagon tracks leading into the Svensens' yard. Almost tentatively, he reached for one of her red-mittened hands. She stiffened slightly at his touch, then let her hand rest in his.

They walked without speaking for several minutes, and then Michael said, "It is a fine night, isn't it? Even though it is still a little chilly, you can see now that spring is here to stay, and summer won't be far behind."

"Yes," Anna agreed, nodding. "After the first storm, the winter was not as bad as I had feared. We managed to make it to school nearly every day. I didn't think we would be able to do that."

Michael led Anna away from the wagon tracks towards the creek that wound close to the Svensens' wheat field. They approached an outcropping of limestone next to the creek, and Michael sat down, pulling Anna to sit beside him.

"Your schooling is important to you, isn't it?"

"Yes," Anna said. "Finishing school has been a goal of mine since even before we came to America. I love to learn, to read books and find out about the world."

Michael nodded, holding tightly to her hand.

"What are your plans next year, after you finish?"

Anna's heart beat faster. She felt tears threaten to fall from her eyes at the thought of hurting her friend, but she knew she must be brave.

"I do not know, yet. But I know what I would like to do."

"Yes?" Michael turned to face Anna, looking deeply into her eyes.

Anna glanced at the creek, listening to the sound of it gurgling softly.

"I would like to become a teacher. Like Miss Stevens. There is a new training school in Wichita . . . if I could speak English just a little better . . . maybe I could . . . ."

Anna's voice trailed off as she felt Michael's grip on her hand tighten even more.

"Would you even consider doing anything else? I mean . . . ."

He reached across and put the fingers of one hand gently under Anna's chin and tilted it upward so that their gazes met.

"Oh, gosh, Anna . . . I think you know what I mean. I'm just crazy about you. You are so kind and gentle and pretty. Would you ever consider marrying me and helping me make a home?"

Anna's blue eyes watered as she looked into those of her friend.

"Oh, Michael," she murmured, moving her head away from his grasp, and pulling her hand from his. "I am so . . . so . . . honored. It's a great compliment you give me."

Michael smiled.

"We could wait until a year from now, until next summer I mean. That way you could finish school. Of course, I don't want to wait. I want to get married right away, maybe June. I've talked to Pa, and there is a little stretch of land on the north side of his property that he would give us for a little cabin. I've got some money saved, so I could begin building as soon as the weather clears for good. There is plenty of work around Pa's place for me, too, and Pa and I have been thinking about buying the land to the east...."

"Michael, please stop," Anna said, turning to him and placing her hand in front of his mouth. At his surprised look, she dropped her hand and took a deep breath.

"Oh, Michael, you will make a wonderful husband for a lucky girl some day, but not for me. I have been praying and praying about this, and my heart, well, God is telling me that this is not the path he has chosen for me."

She glanced at the man beside her, saw his familiar smile turn troubled.

"But Anna," he said, so quietly that she could barely hear him. "Don't you think you could learn to love me? I love you so much. I've prayed about this, too."

"I am sorry, Michael. I do love you, but as a brother, or a good friend. My heart is not what it should be towards the man I should marry. I have felt much confusion for a long time, but I am not confused any more. I cannot marry you."

There was silence for several moments until he finally spoke again.

"Okay," he said, a touch of tension entering his voice. "Okay, but please, just think about it. Maybe you will change your mind. Maybe after one more year of school, marrying me and settling down in West Bend won't seem like such a bad idea."

Anna's mind raced. She knew that if she agreed to think about Michael's proposal, that he would return to his kind, cheerful self, and the anger and disappointment he felt towards her would be gone. But she also knew that agreeing to think about his words would give him false hope. Her mind and her heart had made their decision, and she owed total honesty to the red-haired young man sitting beside her.

"Michael," she said, softly touching his hand.

He raised his head and looked at Anna, hope filling his eyes.

"Michael there is no use in thinking about it. My mind is made up. This is not that path that I am to follow right now, or next year. I cannot . . . cannot lead you on to think . . . to think that there is hope where there is none. I am sorry, but this is the way it must be."

He sat perfectly still for what seemed to be a long time. Finally, he gave a small sigh.

"I see," he said, rising and pulling Anna up to meet him, then releasing her hand. "I must take you home, now."

He turned, and began quickly walking back toward the shanty, the oil lamp sitting on the kitchen table visible in the darkness. Anna yearned to comfort Michael, but instinctively she knew that silence to be alone in his thoughts was what Michael most needed.

When they reached the door, Michael stopped and looked at Anna again. It was as if a mask had fallen over his face.

"I'll say goodnight to your parents, then," he said.

Anna pushed the door open and Michael followed her into the small room. Oscar had been reading from the Bible out loud while Christina mended a sock. When the door opened, they looked up, questions filling their expressions.

"Goodnight Mr. Svensen, Mrs. Svensen."

Michael tipped his hat and nodded slightly. "Goodnight, Anna."

He paused, and Anna felt his eyes on her face, but she didn't meet them. He turned and closed the door softly behind him.

Anna took off her shawl and began to prepare for bed. Her siblings had already gone to sleep, so she moved quietly.

Finally realizing that his daughter was not going to speak unless prompted, Oscar said, "Well, daughter, have you some news for us?"

Anna sat down on the edge of her mattress in the far corner of the room. She sensed more than understood her parents' concern.

"Yes," she said, choosing her words carefully. "Michael will most likely not be coming to visit us anymore. He asked me to marry him, and I told him, 'no.'"

"Oh, my daughter," Christina said, rising and coming to sit beside Anna. She held the teenager in her arms, gently stroking her hair. "There, there, my love. It will be okay."

Anna sobbed softly, resting her head on her mother's shoulder. Oscar gazed at her with a concerned, yet peaceful, look.

"You have prayed about this, I suppose?"

"Yes, Papa. I have spent much time in prayer asking God if Michael was the one I should marry."

She wiped her eyes.

"I am at peace with my choice, but I do not like hurting someone who has been so kind to me and to our family."

Oscar nodded, reaching out to pat Anna's hands. Christina loosened her grip on Anna's shoulders and leaned back, brushing the hair out of her daughter's eyes.

"You should have seen his face," Anna continued. "His hurt was so much. I could not bear to see it."

Oscar pulled back his hand.

"We shall pray for Michael," he said, reaching out again this time to take both his daughter's and his wife's hands into his own.

The trio bent their heads and spent several long minutes in prayer, asking God to ease the pain of the one who had flattered Anna so by his attention. When they finished, they went to bed and slept peacefully, feeling confident that God's will had been done.

Spring melted into summer as the days grew longer and warmer. The school term ended the first week in May, allowing the children to return to their farms to help their parents in the fields.

After closing ceremonies on the final day of school, Anna bid a tearful goodbye to her beloved teacher, Tina Stevens, who was returning to St. Louis for the summer break. Although she would miss the friendship and the times of shared confidences, Anna's heart grew joyful at the thought of Miss Stevens finally getting to see her Samuel again.

"One year has passed," Miss Stevens said, her eyes shining. "Half of the time is over. Only one more year remaining until Samuel and I can be married. Oh, I can't wait!"

Anna smiled with Miss Stevens, rejoicing that her friend had found someone to share her life with, someone who had been chosen by God especially for her. Wistfully, Anna felt a pang of regret as she wondered if there would ever be such a person in her life.

Trying to push such thoughts aside, Anna threw herself into working around the farm. With Aaron continuing his job at the West Bend hardware store, there seemed to be no shortage of chores needing attention around the Svensen homestead. Thankfully, Joseph and Bjorn, each being a year older than the previous summer, were able to spend more time with their father in the fields, leaving Anna and Christina to manage the vegetable garden and the household chores. Even small Elsie helped more this summer than the last, pulling weeds out of the garden, and helping her mother to hang the wash.

With little time for reading or quiet study, Anna's arms grew strong and her face browned as she hoed the garden and brought buckets to water it from the well, trying to coax life from the stubborn soil. Anna knew how important the garden was; the vegetables she had helped Christina preserve the previous fall had fed the family all winter.

The summer months passed quickly, and several times Anna thought of the sullen girl she had been, standing under the hot July sun only a year ago, sulking and feeling sorry for herself. Anna's feelings ran along a much different vein now. As her hands worked the soil, breaking up the large clumps so that the tiny seeds would take root and grow, gently plucking string beans from the tender stalks, and later, digging in the earth for new potatoes, Anna began to love the ground like her father did. She began to see the complete miracle of new life springing from a tiny seed, and the beauty of a golden field of grain waving in the wind.

Although he did not come to the farm anymore, Anna ran into Michael Richards often that summer: every week at church, at the Jaspersons' mid-summer barn-raising, and at the Fourth of July picnic in West Bend. The young man always seemed polite and friendly while talking to Oscar about the weather or joking with Joseph and Bjorn. He'd tip his hat and smile at Anna, but it seemed to her that his face was closed and guarded. She still felt sadness over the pain she had caused him, but her heart remained at peace with her decision.

At the end of August, Tina Stevens returned to West Bend for her final year of teaching. Anna hummed the entire two miles as she walked over to the Allens to greet her friend. The crops were growing well, the summer had been one with plenty of rain, and Anna had noticed that her father had recently regained the twinkle in his eye, the one that had been missing most of last winter.

The two young women greeted each other with hugs. Then, over a plate of sugar cookies, Anna listened while Miss Stevens wistfully spoke of her weeks in St. Louis, of taking long walks with Samuel, and of the pain of leaving him once more.

"He is learning so much in seminary," Miss Stevens said, her face shining. "He will be ready to take on whatever mission work is assigned to him next summer, after we are married."

The pair exchanged another hug and a giggle of excitement.

"And you, Anna? How was your summer?"

The teacher listened as Anna talked about the hot days tending the garden and completing the house chores. Miss Stevens nodded as Anna expressed her desire to still find a way to help her family stay on the farm.

"I've been praying about this, Anna," Miss Stevens said, "as I am sure that you have been. When it is time, the answer will come."

Anna sighed and brushed a wisp of blonde hair from her face.

"Yes, I know. But I get so . . . so im-pu-dent."

Miss Stevens laughed good naturedly at her student's mistake.

"Impatient, you mean."

Anna chuckled; then the pair continued to visit for another hour.

Anna left in time to help her mother with the dinner chores, her heart warmed by spending time with her friend, and her mind full of lesson plans for tutoring the primary grades. What Anna did not know, however, was that she would never get the chance to help Miss Stevens that year. Her prayers were finally going to be answered.

Chapter Twelve

It happened in church, the Sunday before school was to resume the following Wednesday. The morning dawned hot, even though it was near the middle of September, and Anna wondered if fall would ever come. Bouncing in the back of the wagon with Elsie, Bjorn, and Joseph, however, she smiled, remembering how she feared in March that summer would forget to return.

Sweat poured down the backs of the parishioners as they gathered in the wooden clapboard church and sang their first hymn. The ladies in the congregation mopped their faces with handkerchiefs, while the children shifted uncomfortably in their seats.

After the hymn and before the sermon was to begin, Pastor Heggarty stood and introduced the tall stranger sitting in the first pew. Anna had noticed him, of course, when she and her family had first arrived at church. It had been impossible not to notice him; strangers were uncommon in West Bend, and if a new family attended church, Pastor Heggarty always made a point of introducing them.

But this was a man alone, not accompanied by his wife, children, or even his parents. Anna couldn't help but notice how his brown hair, slightly too long in the back, curled up at the edge of his collar, or how dark and solemn his eyes looked. She caught herself staring at him, before she saw him smile slightly and nod in her direction. Blushing, she averted her eyes and concentrated on Pastor Heggarty's words.

"This morning I would like to introduce a young man who I hold very near to my heart," Pastor Heggarty said, smiling in the stranger's direction. "My nephew, Wesley Smith."

The pastor reached out his arm to the young man who stood and turned to face the congregation.

"Wesley is an attorney in Kansas City. He has been in Denver, on business, and he will be staying with me for a few days before he returns home. Also, he is on a mission of sorts. Do you want to explain it your dilemma, Wesley?"

The young man nodded, and smiled at his uncle.

"Thank you, Uncle Bill," Wesley Smith said. "My uncle is right. As I have been traveling back to Kansas City, I have been thinking about a problem that has been weighing heavily on my heart."

He paused, and Anna noticed that, despite his calm appearance, his hands were twisting his hat nervously in front of his body.

"My mother, Patricia Smith, is not well," he began again. "She is bed-ridden. The doctors, well, they think that there is a good chance that she will live for quite some time longer, but she is not able to care for herself."

Wesley paused, and stared down at his hands. He took a deep breath, and then continued.

"Although my mother has plenty of household help, someone to cook and do the cleaning, she needs a . . . well, a companion ... someone to keep her company and attend to her personal needs."

Here Wesley paused again, looking towards his uncle with pleading eyes.

"My sister," Pastor Heggarty said, "has not been well since her husband unexpectedly passed away two years ago. What Wesley is trying to say, I believe, is that he is looking for a person who might wish to attend to his mother."

Wesley nodded relief evident on his face.

"I believe," the parson added, looking to his nephew for confirmation, "that Wesley is able to pay quite well for the right person."

Again the young man nodded.

"Yes," Wesley said. "My mother is not easy to care for. I have hired several women from Kansas City, but they never seem to stay more than a few weeks."

He looked down for a moment, and then raised his head. "I have been praying that God will help me find the right person to look after my mother. As I travel on business, I always keep my eyes and ears open. I believe that before long, my prayers will be answered."

With that statement, the corners of his mouth turned upwards slightly, and then he sat down.

"Thank you, Wesley," Pastor Heggarty said. "Now, the scripture reading this morning is from I Corinthians, chapter 13 . . . ."

Anna had sat silently throughout the appeal from Wesley Smith, and as the preacher began to read, she tried to concentrate on the words. But inside, her heart pounded wildly and her mind raced. This was it, she knew. This was God's answer to her prayers.

Anna quietly looked across the aisle to where Tina Stevens sat with the Allens. The teacher glanced back at Anna, and her eyes shone as she nodded her head. At that moment, an understanding passed between the two women, and a sense of peace descended upon Anna. Even though attending to Wesley Smith's mother would mean leaving her family and possibly delay finishing school, Anna knew that she would be following God's call.

By the end of the sermon, Anna's decision had been made, and she resolved to speak to Wesley Smith as soon as church had ended.

"But Anna," Christina said later that evening. She held her daughter's shoulders and looked into her eyes. "Do you realize what this will mean? Do you know that you will not finish school?"

"Yes, Mama," Anna nodded. "But I have prayed about this. I believe it is the right thing to do."

"I don't like this," Oscar said, rising from the table and pacing around the room. "It's not correct for a young girl to go so far from her family."

Anna bowed her head and said, quietly, "Please, Papa, you must trust me. I have been looking for a way to help the family.

When Mr. Smith spoke at church, I felt a great sense of peace. This is the right step for me to take."

She finished with a small lift to her chin, but her eyes were pleading. Wouldn't her father change his mind and accept her decision?

After a few moments of silence, Oscar stopped his pacing, sat down, and placed one arm around his wife's shoulder.

"I think, my wife, that our Anna may be right." He stopped and took a deep breath. "We must accept her decision," he said. "If it is God's will for her, who are we to stand in the way?"

Anna smiled in relief, and threw both of her arms around her father's neck.

"Oh, Papa! Thank you for understanding. I will try so hard to make you proud of me."

"I will miss you. I will miss you, my child," Oscar murmured huskily, and then planted a kiss on the top of Anna's head.

After her parents accepted her decision to move to Kansas City, Anna spent the next few days preparing her few belongings to take on the train ride east. She and Wesley Smith would be leaving only six short days from the Sunday when Anna first heard about the job opening. The days passed in a flurry of activity, including the sewing of a new dress for Anna.

"I had been saving this piece for your graduation from school," Christina had said, pulling out the blue cotton print. Tiny pink and white flowers dotted the material whose background perfectly matched Anna's eyes.

"Oh, Mama! It is so beautiful. Thank you so much. It must have cost..."

"Hush, child. It doesn't matter."

Anna threw her arms around her mother's neck quickly enough that she missed the pained look on Christina's face. Finishing school had been so important to her eldest daughter. Were she and her husband making the right decision to let Anna leave home just one short year away from graduation?

Christina pushed such thoughts aside as she helped Anna measure and cut the material. The mother and daughter team worked deftly to finish the dress in just a few short days. Christina's concerns, however, were put to rest on the first day of school when her children came home. Anna had accompanied Joseph, Bjorn, and Elsie to school to bade Miss Stevens and her other friends farewell. It was difficult to leave the primary children, those Anna had come to know so well through tutoring the previous year. But Anna knew that the most difficult goodbye would come at the end of the day, when she had to bid farewell to her teacher and friend.

"I have wonderful news for you," Miss Stevens said after the other students had gone home. Anna had sent her siblings home without her in anticipation of a long conversation with Miss Stevens.

"I have spoken to Mr. Webb, Mr. Allen, and Mr. Sorenson, from the school board," the teacher continued. "They have agreed to let you continue your lessons in Kansas City. I will send assignments and books with you, and then, when you complete them, you'll mail them back to me. I will then send you some more. Oh, Anna, isn't it exciting?"

Anna stood still for a moment, and then clapped her hands. It was too good to be true! A way to help her parents and finish her studies.

"Oh, Miss Stevens . . . it is too . . . too . . . ." Anna began, and then stopped abruptly, a sudden thought darkening her mood. "But what if this . . . arrangement is not acceptable with Mr. Smith?"

But the teacher just smiled back at her pupil.

"I had already thought of that," Miss Stevens said. "I spoke to Pastor Heggarty about it two days ago. He talked to his nephew, and then Wesley Smith came to see me. He did not have any objection to you finishing your studies, as long as his mother's needs for companionship were being met first."

The teacher finished with a nod of her head.

"So you see, there, it is decided."

Unable to restrain herself, Anna threw her arms around her teacher.

"Oh, Miss Stevens, how can I thank you?"

"No need to, Anna. Your friendship is thanks enough."

With many tears and more hugs, the pair finally said goodbye. Although her excitement was tempered by having to leave her dearest friend, Anna's spirits were light with the thought that she would receive her high school diploma and still be able to help her family. She said a heartfelt prayer of thanks as she made her way home through the warm autumn evening.

Two evenings before she was scheduled to leave, Anna was surprised to see Wesley Smith riding up to the small homestead on Pastor Heggarty's horse. Setting down the two buckets of water she carried from the well, Anna greeted the young lawyer.

"Good evening, Miss Svensen," he replied, tipping his black hat. "I wanted to come and discuss the final travel arrangements with you and your parents."

"Yes . . . yes, of course, Mr. Smith," Anna stammered, feeling a hot blush creep up her face. "Please come in."

She picked up the two buckets and headed toward the door. Oscar and the boys were still finishing up the evening chores, but Christina and Elsie were inside, putting away the last of the supper dishes.

Wesley rushed ahead of Anna to hold the door open for her.

"Here, those look heavy. Let me help you," he said, looking down at Anna. He stood almost a head taller than her.

"Oh, they're not too heavy," she said, wishing she wasn't so keenly aware of how close she stood to him as she passed through the door. "Mama, Mr. Smith is here to speak to us."

Christina had already turned when the door opened. She greeted Wesley with a warm smile. Although the young attorney soon would be taking away her eldest daughter, Christina had instantly liked the handsome young man with the soft brown eyes.

"Come in, Mr. Smith. Can you not please sit down?"

Anna flinched at her mother's grammatical mistake. She carried the buckets of water to the stove and set them down. Noticing how sweaty her hands felt, she wiped them on a dish towel.

"Mrs. Svensen, I wanted to come and make final travel arrangements for Saturday," Wesley began.

Leaning forward slightly, Anna sat close to her mother.

"Yes," Christina replied. "Anna is to leave on the train first thing in the morning. We shall have her there."

Christina looked mistily at her daughter and then continued.

"We are nearly packed, yes Anna?"

"Yes, Mama."

Anna nodded and then folded her hands in her lap. She hoped the nervousness she felt inside did not show to the dark stranger seated before her.

"Would you like for me to call for Anna early that morning?" Wesley asked. "It would save you a lot of time to not have to accompany her to the train station."

"We would want to bring Anna to town," a booming voice said from the door.

The trio turned to see Oscar enter the room. For the second time that evening, Anna felt embarrassed as she noticed her father's disheveled appearance next to Wesley Smith's cool elegance. Oscar tried to keep himself neat and clean, but working with animals under the hot sun did not lend itself to good hygiene.

Wesley Smith stood and nodded toward Anna's father. "Good evening, Mr. Svensen. I just stopped by to finalize our travel plans for Saturday."

"I am glad you did so, Mr. Smith," Oscar said, stepping into the room and shaking Wesley's hand. "Christina and I are happy to see that our daughter will be in the care of a man so concerned."

Anna's face flamed upon hearing her father's words. Why must they speak as if she wasn't even in the same room?

Wesley stayed for several more minutes, discussing final plans with Oscar and Christina, and writing down the address of his mother's home so that Anna might receive mail. Anna found herself growing more and more impatient with the way the three seemed to make decisions without even consulting her, as if she was a child, and they the only adults. Finally, as Wesley rose to leave, Anna stood up herself and spoke.

"Excuse me, Mr. Smith," she said, in a firm but slightly higher than normal voice. She felt the sudden gaze of all eyes in the room.

"Yes?" Wesley said, after a slight pause.

"I . . . I was wondering just what my . . . my responsibilities will be when I am with your . . . your mother."

"Yes. Well, that is a good question."

Wesley turned again and addressed Anna's parents. "Miss Svensen will be responsible for keeping my mother company. She needs someone to sit beside her during the day to see to her needs. Anna will serve my mother's tea, read to her, and possibly fluff her pillow, those sorts of things."

Oscar and Christina nodded their heads.

"I have discussed with Tina Stevens the opportunity for Anna to continue her schooling by correspondence this final year, and I do not see any reason why she cannot. My mother often naps in the afternoon, and this should provide ample time for Anna to work on her assignments."

"That will be good," Oscar said. "Finishing school is important to our Anna."

Nodding his assent, Wesley Smith took his leave, only glancing Anna's way once quickly as he exited.

With furious eyes, Anna followed Wesley Smith to the door and watched as he mounted the brown mare. He tipped his hat at Christina and Oscar as he left.

She may be young, Anna thought to herself, but she was not too young for Wesley Smith to acknowledge her presence. Anna vowed to herself that before long, Mr. Wesley Smith, attorney-at-law, would be speaking to her directly, and not just talking to her parents. With a flourish, Anna lifted her skirts and flounced back into the house.

Wesley Smith was lost in his own thoughts as he rode back to the parsonage. Young Anna Svensen seemed capable, but would she be strong enough to withstand his mother's personal attacks? Could she put up with being criticized, condemned, and yes, even screamed at day after day?

Wesley sighed and shook his head. What was he to do about his mother? Once a refined, gentle lady, she had quickly turned into a bitter, resentful old woman following the death of her husband, his father, Arthur Smith. Of course, his father's death had been sudden. Wesley vividly remembered the last time he had seen his father alive, waving broadly as the older man left for a three-day hunting trip with two of his law partners. His father had ridden the new bay, and his mother had worried that the horse was too spirited for such a long trip. But Arthur had been confident of the horse's strength, and he had looked forward to the trip with enthusiasm. That had been four years ago, when Wesley was in his last year of law school.

Word had reached Wesley and his mother late the following day that Arthur had been thrown from his horse that morning. Landing on his back on a fallen tree, his neck had snapped and he had died instantly. At least, he hadn't suffered, Wesley thought. It would have been terrible for his robust, hearty father to have been crippled, dependent upon others for his basic care. No, Wesley thought. It was better that his father had died doing something he loved.

Not so for his mother, Patricia Smith, however. Her suffering was deep and great, and her illness slow and painful for all those who knew her. Soon after being informed of Arthur's death, Patricia had taken to her bed. The doctors could find no medical reason for her illness, but she increasingly refused to eat or to see anyone. At first, visitors to the grand house remained plenty. Patricia Smith, being the wife of a prominent Kansas City attorney, had a wide circle of friends and acquaintances. As time wore on, however, visitors became more and more infrequent, until they dwindled to no one at all.

After several months of watching his mother refuse to leave her bedroom suite, Wesley finally hired a woman to keep Patricia company. Mrs. McAfee, the Irish grandmother Wesley hired first, was plump and jolly, and she reassured Wesley that she would put life back into his mother's faded cheeks. For a while, it seemed that Mrs. McAfee would succeed. She definitely brought color into the pale ivory room where Patricia spent her days and nights. Mrs. McAfee set large bouquets of cut flowers on every spare surface of the bedroom, so that when Wesley entered to visit with Patricia, he immediately noticed the sweet floral perfume filling the air.

It only took a few months, however, before Mrs. McAfee had given up and taken her bright cheerfulness away. Patricia had begun yelling at the good-natured woman, and once had even thrown a vase full of roses at her when Mrs. McAfee had refused to shut the curtains.

"She's a sad woman, your mother," Mrs. McAfee told Wesley on the day that she left, shaking her gray head as she swished out of the room.

After Mrs. McAfee, a succession of hired help followed, some staying a few weeks, and others only a few days. Just before Wesley left for his trip to Denver, the latest girl, a small, terrified, dark-haired thing, had left the house in the middle of the night, never to be heard from again. It was then that Wesley had vowed to find the perfect replacement – someone who could withstand his mother's verbal attacks, maybe even see beyond them to the caring woman underneath the pain, the one Wesley knew still existed. Diligently, Wesley prayed for the perfect person. Would Anna Svensen be the one?

Chapter Thirteen

On Saturday, the Svensens rose early. Unable to sleep well, Anna had been up before sunrise. Before her parents entered the kitchen, she had already prepared a hearty breakfast of biscuits and sausage gravy, a dish Tina Stevens had taught her how to make. She felt a stab of sadness as she thought of her friend and all of the time and confidences they had shared.

"My daughter, that smells so wonderful!" Oscar said, coming into the room and walking up behind Anna, placing a kiss on the top of her head. "We will miss your cooking skills."

"Oh, Papa!" Anna said, turning suddenly and throwing her arms around her father's waist. Sobbing, she buried her head into Oscar's chest, just as she remembered doing when she was a small child.

"There, there, my daughter," Oscar murmured. "Have you changed your decision? Do you not wish to leave with Mr. Smith?"

"Oh, no Papa," Anna said, pulling back and shaking her head. "I know this is the right decision for me. But I will miss you so much, and Mama, and the boys, and Elsie . . . oh, I do not know how I am to stand it!"

She embraced him again with fresh tears flowing.

"What is going on here?" Christina demanded, walking into the room. "All of this work to do, getting Anna ready, and you two standing there wasting time!"

Anna turned in surprise at the sharp sting in Christina's voice, only to see her mother smiling with wet eyes.

"Oh my daughter," Christina said, reaching her arms out to Anna. After holding her daughter for several moments, Christina pulled back and chuckled, "A fine sight we are! We really will get nothing done this way. Come, let us wake the others and prepare to leave."

Feeling secure in her parents' love, Anna set about the morning tasks of waking her younger siblings, helping Elsie dress, and getting everyone settled at the table for breakfast.

The faces were somber at the table, and Anna could not help but be reminded of the morning that Aaron had left to work at the hardware store in West Bend. The difference was, this time, Kansas City was a full day's train ride away, and she did not know when she would see her family again. Anna blinked as tears once more threatened to spill from her eyes.

Oscar and his sons fed the livestock quickly that morning, and soon after breakfast the entire family piled into the wagon for the ride to the train station. Sitting in the back of the wagon and holding Elsie tightly on her lap, Anna looked back at the small homestead as it faded into the distance. Anna had agreed to work for Wesley Smith and his mother for one year. What would happen to the homestead and her family during those months? Would the struggling farm make it? Anna smiled to herself. Only a year ago, she would have been almost happy with the idea of the farm failing. She had wanted so desperately to leave the hot prairie. But not now. Now she knew that the tall grass, the blue sky, and even the gusting winds had invaded her soul, becoming a part of her that would be carried into the bustling streets of Kansas City.

Aaron met the family at the train station. Anna knew he would, yet the sight of her handsome older brother brought a new lump to her throat. Aaron was standing by Wesley Smith, and Anna noticed how the two were almost the same height. In fact, from a distance, Anna could only distinguish between the two by the fact that one had dark hair, and the other was blonde.

When the wagon pulled up, Aaron rushed over, helping down first his mother, and then Anna.

"Are you ready sister?" he asked, holding Anna's gaze in his own.

"Yes," she replied, tilting her chin confidently.

Despite his sister's self-assurance, Aaron thought he could see the nervousness in her eyes. "Remember to place your trust in

God, Anna," he said, drawing his sister into an embrace. "If you are sure that you are following his will, then all will be well."

Anna returned Aaron's hug, knowing already how much she would miss him.

Suddenly, a long, low whistle broke the silence. Wesley Smith, who out of consideration for the family had been waiting several feet away, stepped forward and bent down to pick up Anna's bag.

"The train will be stopping soon folks," he said, his voice gentle, yet matter-of-fact.

"Yes," Anna said, breaking free from Aaron's grasp and turning to look at her new employer. Wesley, however, had already taken Anna's bag and moved nearer to the tracks. With another low whistle, the train came into view, beginning to slow as it snaked its way toward the West Bend station.

"Oh, Mama," Anna said, turning back to her family and hugging her mother. Tears flowed freely now, out of everyone's eyes.

"God be with you, Anna," Oscar said, joining his wife and daughter's embrace.

The next moments seemed to blur as Anna gave one last round of hugs and then allowed herself to be ushered onto the train by Wesley Smith. It wasn't until she was seated in a private compartment next to the window, and waving one last time, that she saw Michael Richards ride up a short distance away from her family. He dismounted and stood beside his horse, staring intently at the train.

Anna hesitated, then smiled and waved her hand in his direction. Just as the train began to pull out, Michael tipped his hat, smiled tentatively, and then swung back onto his mare.

"A friend of yours?" Wesley Smith asked, settling himself in the seat across from Anna.

Surprised that he had noticed, Anna felt herself blush.

"A friend of my family. His sister and I . . . we went to school together."

"I see."

Seeming not to notice Anna's discomfort, Wesley lifted a black briefcase onto the seat.

"There will be several hours of traveling before we stop for lunch," he said, opening the case and lifting out a stack of papers. "If you don't mind, I believe I will do some work."

Anna nodded stiffly, but Wesley Smith, already engrossed in reading the top paper on his stack, did not seem to notice.

Relieved that she would not be expected to make conversation, Anna took the opportunity to examine her surroundings. Glancing out the window, she noticed that West Bend was already just a dark spot in the distance. The rolling prairie stretched in all directions, and all that could be seen was the tall grass bending in the wind, and the blue sky dotted with a few wispy clouds.

Turning her attention to the inside of the compartment, Anna rubbed her hands across the soft, red velvet on the upholstered seats. She had dreaded the train trip, remembering the crowded seats her family had occupied in the coach section of the trains they took from New York to Kansas. Other families, many of them also immigrants, had shared their crowded conditions. The lack of privacy had been the worst. They had to sleep sitting on the hard wooden seats, and there always seemed to be a child crying nearby.

Of course, Anna had soon realized when Wesley led her onto the train that a young man of his standing would only travel in the first class compartments. She blushed anew at her assumptions.

At that moment the conductor, dressed in a blue wool uniform, opened the heavy red curtains that separated the compartment from the narrow hallway.

"Tickets?" he questioned, holding out his hand.

Wesley pulled two tickets from the breast pocket of his coat and handed them to the conductor. The man tore them in half and passed the bottom sections back. Without saying a word, Wesley went back to his reading.

Watching the exchange, Anna wondered if Wesley Smith's mother was as quiet as he was. If so, Anna would have to find a way to make her open up. Coming from a large family that lived in small quarters, Anna was used to noise and activity. Wesley Smith, she decided, was altogether too quiet. Sighing, Anna reached into the bag she carried at her side and withdrew a book Tina Stevens had given her before she left.

The train made only one stop before lunch, and that was at a small station that looked very much like the one in West Bend. As the train approached the station and slowed, Wesley Smith looked up from his work.

"We'll only be here for a few minutes, maybe fifteen," he said. "I believe that I will stay here and continue working."

Anna nodded.

Turning his gaze back to his papers, Wesley added, "Of course, if you would like to get up and stretch your legs a little, I would be glad to accompany you. However, we will be stopping for lunch in a few more hours."

"I am fine."

Although her legs did ache a little from sitting for so long, Anna did not want to inconvenience Wesley Smith. The thought of having to make conversation with the quiet man while they walked around the small train station made sitting for a few more hours without stretching her legs seem far less daunting.

Anna was curious, however, about the town. Only three people were waiting on the platform: a thin woman dressed in gray and holding the hand of a boy maybe three or four years old, and an older man, standing to one side, obviously unrelated to the woman. As Anna watched, the woman cautiously stepped up to the platform and entered the train. Noticing how poorly they were dressed, Anna knew that they would not be riding in the first class section.

As Wesley Smith had predicted, the train pulled away from the station within fifteen minutes. Looking back, Anna noticed the town had a general store and a livery stable, much the same as West Bend's. Idly, Anna wondered how many other small towns in Kansas would remind her of her family's home. How many other farmers were struggling to make ends meet on rough plots of land? Sighing, Anna turned back to her book and soon became engrossed in its contents.

At the sound of her sigh, Wesley Smith raised his eyes without moving his head and peered at Anna over his stack of papers. Of course, when Anna had first introduced herself to him at his uncle's church, he had noticed the brightness of her eyes and the firm way she tilted her chin. Still, ever since they had left her family back at the West Bend train station, Wesley could not help but sense a vulnerability about the young Swedish girl. Obviously intelligent, as evidenced by her reading and her resolve to finish her schooling, Wesley still felt that Anna Svensen was, in some ways, like a young child first venturing out into the world.

Wesley became aware of conflicting emotion inside himself. He had a strange urge to protect Anna, yet he wanted to avoid her at the same time. Her presence disturbed him in ways he could not identify. Shaking his head slightly, he returned his gaze to his work. As his father before him had discovered, work often allowed one to bury feelings and avoid dealing with difficult situations. Perhaps such dedication was why, at age 26, Wesley Smith was already considered to be one of the most competent attorneys in Kansas City.

Two hours later, the train slowed as it approached the station in Salina.

"We'll be stopping for lunch here," Wesley said, returning his stack of papers to his briefcase.

Anna raised her head and looked out the window. Although still a small town when compared to cities such as New York or Stockholm, Salina was the biggest town she had been in since settling in Kansas. Anna's eyes widened as she watched the train platform, crowded with people, grow larger in the distance as they approached.

"Might I get out and stretch my legs?"

"Yes, of course," Wesley said, standing as the train came to a halt. "There is a hotel just a short way from the station. I had planned on eating there. The atmosphere isn't much, but the food is quite good."

Anna nodded. Her mother had wrapped some buttered bread into a dishtowel and pressed it into Anna's hands as she was leaving. She hadn't thought to pack enough for Wesley.

Wesley cleared his throat and startled Anna from her thoughts. She looked up at him, realizing that he was waiting on her to leave the compartment first. She stood, then reached for the wall as she wobbled slightly on her legs. Sitting for hours in the same position had taken more of a toll than she had realized. Carefully she walked out of the compartment and into the hot sun of the Kansas midday.

Upon reaching the platform, Anna stopped and blinked. The sights, sounds and smells of the busy train station assaulted her senses. Looking to the left, she saw cattle milling about a large pen, and she surmised that they would soon be taken to slaughter. To the right, she observed the crowd of people, pressing closer to find their relatives and friends who had just disembarked from the train.

"Let's go this way."

Anna felt a soft pressure on her elbow and found herself being guided through the crowd by Wesley Smith. Within a few moments, they had cleared the crowd, and Wesley released her arm.

"See the sign?" Wesley pointed to a white clapboard building a short distance ahead. "That's the hotel."

Continuing to walk beside her employer on the wooden sidewalk, Anna asked, "Shall I meet you there after you have finished your lunch?"

Stopping, Wesley turned to peer into Anna's clear eyes to determine if she was joking.

"No, of course not," he said, and then, noticing how quickly Anna's head dropped and her chin quivered, swiftly added, "We shall dine there together."

Embarrassed by her mistake, Anna fell into step beside Wesley as he strode towards the hotel's door. Upon entering the building, Anna was immediately reminded of the few times she had eaten at a restaurant before. The room was cool and pleasant with three mechanical ceiling fans purring overhead. Anna and Wesley were ushered to a small table covered with a white cloth in one corner of the room. A waitress clad in a simple gray dress with a white ruffled apron rattled off the day's specials.

"We'll take the fried chicken, two orders please," Wesley said, and then added, almost as an afterthought, "will that be all right with you, Miss Svensen?"

Anna nodded. She was relieved that Wesley had ordered for her, yet she could not help noticing how he always seemed to take charge without consulting the feelings of others.

When the waitress left, Anna sipped her water, grateful for something to keep her hands busy. Wesley seemed intent on studying two men loading feed sacks into a wagon across the street from the hotel. Finally, he spoke in a halting voice.

"I wrote in my telegram to my mother that she should expect us this evening, but it may be too late when we arrive for you to meet her tonight. I won't expect you to begin your duties until tomorrow afternoon. That will give you the morning to rest and to acquaint yourself with some of the other employees in the household."

Anna nodded, and then hesitatingly asked, 'Will I be sharing a room with another . . . employee?"

"No," Wesley shook his head. "You will have a room adjacent to Mother's. There are times, at night, when she is restless and cannot sleep . . . ."

He looked down and rearranged the napkin on his lap.

"She likes to have someone to sit with her then, until she falls back to sleep."

Anna looked at Wesley and noticed a grimace cross his face. Without thinking, she reached across and touched his arm.

"It will be all right," she said. "I am used to being awakened by my sister and my brothers. They have often woken me when they have trouble sleeping."

A smile crept across Wesley's face, and Anna could not help noticing how handsome he looked when he smiled. She wondered why he didn't smile more often. Wesley then glanced down at her hand on his arm, and Anna quickly drew it back. With her face flaming, Anna put her hand in her lap.

"I'm sorry," she stammered. "I . . . ."

"Don't apologize," Wesley said, his eyes dancing with a touch of humor. He considered making a joke about how he enjoyed having a pretty girl touch his arm, but Anna's obvious embarrassment stopped him.

Luckily, the waiter arrived bringing two steaming plates of food. Anna's eyes widened as she observed the crispy fried chicken, the soft mound of mashed potatoes smothered with gravy, the browned biscuits and the dark green beans.

She hadn't realized she was hungry until she smelled the food. Waiting while Wesley said a quick word of thanks, Anna soon dug into her food, enjoying it with relish.

Out of the corner of his eye, Wesley observed the young Swedish girl. Anna Svensen was a mystery to him. Bold, yet shy at the same time, Anna's actions and words had taken him by surprise more than once already.

"Well, Lord," Wesley prayed silently, "I hope she can handle my mother. But as with all things, I place the situation in Your hands."

Chapter Fourteen

Wesley had accurately predicted their late arrival. Darkness had fallen by the time the train pulled into the station in Kansas City, and Anna woke with a start when Wesley Smith gently touched her shoulder.

"We're here, Miss Svensen," he said, smiling at her slightly as she sat upright and blinked her eyes.

"Oh, yes . . . yes," Anna said, rising and running her hands down her skirt in a futile attempt to wipe away any wrinkles. "I am sorry. I must have fallen asleep."

"No matter," Wesley said. "I'm sure you arose early this morning. Traveling has a way of making people tired. This way please."

He led Anna out into the narrow passage between the first class compartments and down the stairs at the end of the car. Anna blinked again as they stepped into the night air. The station was large, with many tracks stretching into the distance. Wesley once again took Anna's elbow and guided her through the crowd assembled on the platform.

"Mr. Smith! Over here, sir!"

Wesley turned to the left and broadly smiled at the young man striding towards them.

"Anna Svensen, meet Simon McNeil, our gardener, handy-man, occasional groomsman, and great friend."

The young man, who appeared to be about 19 or 20, took off his gray wool cap and made a slight bow. Raising his head, he smiled at Anna.

"Pleased to make your acquaintance, Miss," he said, with a slight Irish accent. "Shall I be getting the bags, sir?"

"Would you please, Simon? I shall escort Miss Svensen to the carriage."

"Right. It is just over there, on the left."

Simon bounded off and Wesley led Anna toward a row of black carriages lined up along the street. Anna remembered a similar scene near the train station in New York City. Stepping toward the third one in line, Wesley released Anna's elbow and went to speak softly to the matching bays attached to the carriage.

After gently stroking their noses he returned and helped Anna into the carriage. Still sleepy, Anna gratefully sank into the soft velvet seat. Wesley waited outside the carriage until Simon returned, and then he stuck his head in the door.

"Would you mind, Miss Svensen, if I rode up front with Simon? I would like to catch up on the news from home."

Anna shook her head and smiled, secretly relieved that she would not once again have to find a way to make conversation with Wesley Smith. The day had taken its toll on her, and she ached to go to bed.

The carriage soon started and Anna pulled the curtains aside to look out the window. The scenery quickly changed from the bustling train station to quiet, residential streets. At first the houses appeared small and neat, much like the home she and her family shared in Sweden. Soon, however, the houses became larger with wide lawns and high fences separating the homeowner's property from the street. Anna gasped as the carriage pulled up to the gate of the largest house yet. Simon got down and opened the gate, and then returned to guide the carriage up the winding path.

Instead of stopping by the front entrance, Simon guided the carriage to the back of the house. Anna peered out. She wasn't sure, but it appeared that there was a large English garden, complete with a fountain, stretching out behind the house.

"This way, please."

She started to the sound of Wesley's voice. Gathering her skirts, she allowed him to help her out of the carriage.

"We'll enter in the back today so as not to disturb Mother," Wesley explained, dropping Anna's arm as she reached the ground. "Of course, you can use the front door whenever you like if . . . ."

The young man halted, startled by the sight of Anna's eyes, wide in the darkness.

"Yes?"

" . . . if you have the opportunity. I mean the inclination . . . I mean . . . well . . . ."

"Would you like me to get Miss Svensen's bags?" Simon interrupted.

Anna turned toward the sound of the groomsman's friendly brogue.

"Yes, please, Simon. Bring them to her room if you don't mind."

"I'll be up directly, sir."

Wesley paused for a moment, and then led the way up the back porch to an oak door. Anna caught her breath as they entered a large, cool room. As her eyes adjusted to the further darkness, she looked around at what appeared to be the kitchen. She smiled to herself as she thought that her family's entire shanty would easily fit into this one room.

"This way," Wesley said, walking through the room into a wide hallway.

They passed several doors, all of them closed but one. Anna peeked into the room and noticed that it appeared to be a library. Tall shelves reached from the ceiling to the floor, holding row upon row of books. What a treasure!

She turned back toward Wesley and noticed he was watching her.

"That was my father's study," he said, in a matter-of-fact tone. "It is not much used now, although I do use some of his law books from time to time. You are welcome to borrow any books you want."

He turned and began ascending a winding staircase. The stairs were wide, and the banister carved intricately. Anna followed silently, awed by the splendor of the smooth, polished wood under her hand and the carpeted stairs.

After passing two closed doors, Wesley stopped by a room whose door was opened. He entered and lit a gas lamp resting on a table near one of two large windows.

"This will be your room. You may put your things in the bureau, or the closet over there. This door leads to Mother's room. I'll leave it closed tonight, so that you may catch up on your rest, but most nights you will need to leave it open so that you may hear her if she needs you during the night."

Anna nodded.

Wesley edged toward the door. "Feel free to sleep in tomorrow as late as you'd like. I'll arrange with Jenny to show you around in the morning. The staff and I eat breakfast at seven. However, you will take most of your meals with Mother. If you need anything, don't hesitate to ask."

Anna again nodded, feeling apprehensive. She suddenly felt the miles stretching between her and her parents' farm, and tears pressed at her eyelids.

There was a soft knock at the door, and Simon appeared, carrying Anna's bag.

"Thank you," she said, giving him a tired smile.

"My pleasure, Miss Svensen," he said, tipping his cap and backing out of the room.

"Well, I guess I will leave then. I will probably be at work in the morning when you wake up, but Jenny and the others will see that you find your way around. I will check in with you tomorrow evening to see how Mother is doing and to see if you have any questions. Good night."

Without waiting for a response, Wesley left the room. Anna sat down on the lace-covered bed, her heart pounding. What had she gotten herself into? Closing her eyes, she said a quick prayer, asking for strength.

A little calmer, she opened her eyes again and examined her room. Cream-colored wallpaper dotted with tiny pink rosebuds covered the walls. The four-poster bed she was to sleep in sat in the center of the room, pushed against the far wall. Two windows framed the bed, and their lace curtains matched the lace covering on the bed. A tall oak bureau was pushed against a wall next to a door that Anna assumed opened to the closet. The door to Mrs. Smith's room loomed to the right, and Anna looked at it with apprehension. What would happen behind that door tomorrow?

A full length mirror was attached to the wall next to the bureau. Walking over, Anna examined her reflection. Tired blue eyes with dark circles underneath stared back at her. Never before had she felt so alone and so vulnerable. Had she made a mistake?

Anna awoke with a start. What had she heard? There it was again. A long, low moan. Someone's in pain!

Sitting up in bed, Anna focused her eyes and remembered. She was at the Smith's in Kansas City. She was here to care for Mrs. Smith. The moan had obviously come from the adjacent room.

Anna swung her legs over the side of the bed and reached for her robe. Padding on bare feet to the door joining the two rooms, she carefully cracked it open and peered in.

She was not prepared for what she saw. The room was grand, decorated with the same cream and rose wallpaper and lace lines as hers, but the space was at least three times as much. A high bed rose up from the center of the room like a pedestal, and on it, a frail-looking, gray-haired woman lay, tears streaming down her cheeks. From the vague description Wesley had given of his mother, Anna had maintained the impression that Mrs. Smith would be a large, imposing figure. Why, the tiny person on the bed couldn't possibly cause anyone any trouble, Anna thought.

Mrs. Smith moaned again. Just as Anna was about to enter the room, the door leading to the hallway opened, and Wesley Smith came in, carrying a lit candle. He set the candle by his mother's bed, and grasped one of her hands.

"Shh, Mother, it will be all right," Wesley whispered.

"Arthur, Arthur, the pains are coming now. Get the doctor, get the doctor! Something will go wrong again. You must hurry!"

The tiny woman suddenly sat up and stared at Wesley.

"Mother, it's me, Wesley. You are having a dream. Please lay down." Gently, Wesley tried to help his mother lie down, but the woman didn't budge. She blinked rapidly, staring at her son. Finally, when he released her, she lay down of her own accord.

"I'm tired, Wesley," she said, her voice so soft now that Anna could barely make it out. "You must leave me so that I can sleep. I will hear about your trip tomorrow. You have been gone so long."

"Yes, Mother, but I am home now," Wesley said, pulling the blankets close around his mother's shoulders. "We will talk more in the morning."

Mrs. Smith's eyes quickly closed, and she seemed to instantly fall into a deep sleep. Anna watched as Wesley stayed a few moments longer, bowing his head, his lips barely moving.

Tears welled up in Anna's eyes as she softly closed the door and got back into her own bed. Mrs. Smith was obviously an ill woman, but the gentle concern her son showed toward her had caught Anna off guard. All of the time she had known him, Wesley Smith had been nothing but business-like and impersonal. Anna found herself suddenly drawn to the caring side of Wesley Smith. Although she was still fatigued from the journey, she lay awake for a long time. She used the sleepless hours to pray, asking God to give her direction on how to best help Mrs. Smith and her son. When she finally was able to doze off, the sun had just begun to rise and shine through the lace curtains.

Anna awoke when she heard a soft rapping at her door.

"Excuse me, Miss Svensen, but I thought you'd best be liking to wake now."

Anna propped herself on one elbow and squinted at the doorway. A girl of not more than fourteen or fifteen stood holding a silver tray with coffee and muffins. The girl, with her friendly smile, reminded Anna instantly of the groomsman from the previous night.

"Oh, I am so sorry . . . I did not mean to sleep so late."

"That's no matter, Miss," the girl said again, her head bouncing with brown curls. "I reckoned that the Missus had awoken you in the night with her carryin' on, and you needed to get your sleep out."

The girl brought the tray to the small table near Anna's bed and set it down.

"I'm Jenny McNeil. Pleased to meet you, Miss."

Anna took the girl's outstretched hand and smiled at her.

"You are related to Simon McNeil?" Anna asked, warming to Jenny's friendliness.

"Yes, he'd be my brother, sorry to say." Jenny smiled to show that she was teasing. "Our mother and father work here, too. Ma does the cookin' and Pa, he helps Simon in the garden and watches over the animals. We have a house in the back, behind the stables, that the Smith's built for us when Simon and I were just wee ones."

Anna followed Jenny's gaze to the window and looked where the younger girl pointed. In the distance, beyond a large garden full of flowers and the fountain she had seen last night, eaves of a white clapboard house peeked through the trees.

"Oh, what a lovely place to live!"

"Yes," Jenny said, turning to the bed and beginning to fluff Anna's pillows. "The Smiths have been very good to our family. They have always been nice ones to work for."

Anna turned and saw that a dark cloud had crossed Jenny's face.

"The Missus, though, well . . . she ain't been the same since the Mister's passing. It'll be a big job for you, caring for her."

Anna gazed at the younger girl, and then smiled.

"Thank you for bringing my breakfast, Jenny," she said, trying to use proper English. "You don't need to wait on me, though. I was planning to come down to the kitchen."

"Oh, no bother, Miss," Jenny said, smiling again. "We have been done with breakfast for at least two hours now. It'd be almost nine o'clock."

Anna felt her face flush with shame.

"I do not usually sleep so . . . so late," she stammered.

Jenny busily pulled up the coverlet on Anna's bed and fluffed her pillows.

"I am sure that is true," she said, laughing. "I am to take you on a tour of the house when you are ready. I'll be back in about half an hour."

"Make it twenty minutes, please," Anna said, hurrying over to the tray on the table and picking up the coffee cup. "I am not very hungry today, and I will dress in a hurry."

"All right, then," Jenny said, turning at the door to throw one more smile Anna's direction.

After Jenny left, Anna took a deep breath and another swallow of coffee. She turned to her bags, still unpacked from the evening before, and pulled out a fresh petticoat, blouse and skirt. Shaking the clothing first to try and remove some of the many wrinkles, Anna dressed quickly and downed the rest of the coffee. Her stomach churned, and she knew that she'd be unable to eat. After quickly combing her hair and putting it in place with a few pins, she paced the room until Jenny returned several minutes later.

"All ready, then?" Jenny bustled into the room.

Anna nodded and smiled.

Let's start with the kitchen so that I may take this tray back."

Jenny picked up the tray and led Anna out of the room.

The pair padded down the hallway that Anna and Wesley had navigated the night before. Admiring the wall covering, done in dark blues and mauves, Anna couldn't help but run her hand across it. Following Jenny down the grand staircase, Anna remembered the room with the books, and tried to peek in to get a second glimpse of the shelves. All of the downstairs doors, however, remained shut.

Using her back to push through a wide set of swinging doors, Jenny led Anna into the kitchen. Anna's senses were immediately assaulted by an array of tempting smells.

"Why, there ye be!"

A robust woman who shared the same warm smile and sparkling eyes and Simon and Jenny came toward Anna with her arms outstretched.

"We knew he'd found a young one this time, but I didn't know ye'd be just a mite older than my girl."

The woman embraced Anna and planted a kiss on her cheek. Anna found her eyes watering over with homesickness.

"Miss Svensen, this is my ma, Trudy McNeil."

"Pleased to meet you. And Jenny, please call me Anna."

"Well, Anna, how do you like our little house?" Trudy asked, returning to the stove where she began stirring something simmering in a pot.

"I have not seen much of it, yet. Jenny is going to give me a ... tour."

"Yes, and I believe we'll be starting with the pantry," Jenny said, opening a door off the kitchen.

Anna followed Jenny into another room, only slightly smaller than the kitchen and lined on all sides with shelves. Well-organized jars of every shape and size filled the shelves, and Anna opened her mouth in wonder.

"'Tis a lot of food, you think?" Jenny laughed at Anna's response.

Anna chuckled, too, and shook her head, then followed Jenny into another room. For the next hour, the two girls traversed around the mansion, opening and shutting door after door. Anna carefully listened to Jenny's explanation of how each room was used. They had just reached the library when Anna heard the frantic ringing of a bell coming from upstairs.

"Jenny!" a woman's voice demanded. "Jenny where are you? I want you here, now!"

Anna stopped looking at the books and turned in horror to her companion.

"That'd be Mrs. Smith," Jenny explained, all sunshine gone from her face. "The last companion she had left last Tuesday, a week earlier than she had planned. My ma and I've been trying to look after the Missus since then. 'Tisn't easy, though."

Jenny raised her eyes to the ceiling as the bell began to ring again.

"My ma will be having lunch ready in the kitchen in about 30 minutes. Whyn't you rest in your room a bit and then join us?"

"Would it be all right if I visited the garden instead?"

"Of course! Enjoy yourself!"

Anna watched her new friend disappear up the grand staircase, and then made her way back to the kitchen.

"Did ya get a good look-see around, then?" Trudy McNeil asked when Anna entered through the double doors.

"Yes, it was a wonderful tour," Anna said. "I was going to take a short walk in the garden, but I could help you if you need me to."

"Oh, thank you, my dear, but don't fret yourself. Go on out and enjoy the garden."

Trudy put down her wooden spoon and gazed thoughtfully at Anna.

"You will have plenty of work to do this afternoon."

Anna smiled at the older woman, again feeling the pang of missing her own mother. She stepped through the doorway she and Wesley Smith had entered the night before. Just as beautiful as Anna had seen from the window of her room, the garden proved a delight to explore. Anna followed the stone pathways, stopping to examine a variety of flowers and plants that were unfamiliar to her. She had just discovered the fountain, an elaborate stone sculpture of a child pouring water from a pitcher, when Simon McNeil approached.

"Are ye finding your way around then?" he asked, his brown eyes dancing.

"Yes, it is so beautiful here!"

"That it'd be. Me and Pa, we work hard to keep this place nice. Sometimes I wonder, though, if it is worth the trouble."

Anna looked up at the gardener.

"Why would that be?"

"When Mr. Smith was alive, why, there'd be parties here all the time. Everyone would comment about the garden. It was a thing to be proud of."

Simon stopped, and darkness clouded his face.

"Now, though, the only ones who enjoy the gardens are us. The young Mr. Smith, he works too hard to ever throw a party. And Mrs. Smith, well . . . she just never leaves her room."

Anna nodded, once again feeling the apprehension of wondering just what she had gotten herself into.

Simon lifted his head. "Are ye hungry? My ma is the best cook in Kansas City! Come, let's eat lunch."

Anna joined the young man as they retraced her steps and entered the kitchen.

Chapter Fifteen

Anna thoroughly enjoyed her lunch shared with the McNeils, although she did notice how often Mrs. Smith summoned Jenny upstairs. In fact, Anna thought that Jenny barely got a chance to eat at all.

The rest of the McNeil family made her feel much at home, however. Ian McNeil, Simon and Jenny's father, spent the time relating stories about the Smith family's activities, including many stories of Wesley Smith and his childhood that made Anna laugh. She sensed, however, that Ian McNeil was not just engageing in idle gossip about his employer. The entire McNeil family felt a fierce loyalty to the Smiths – that Anna could tell. As she rose from the kitchen table, Anna felt determined to help Mrs. Smith to the best of her ability.

"Are ye ready to meet the Missus then?" Jenny asked.

"Yes, but I thought I could help your mother with the dishes first," Anna replied, carrying her own plate toward the basin.

"No, no, darling, you go on ahead with Jenny. Mrs. Smith knows you are coming. She may have a whole list of items for you to care for this afternoon."

Trudy gazed at Anna with concern evident on her face.

"Try to remember, dear, that she will jest be testing ye, trying to see if she can make you angered. Mrs. Smith, she be a lady with much pain. Sometimes, the pain fills her so much that it just spills out all around, and it hurts the people nearby. Don't forget that inside, somewhere lost in her sad self, there is a lady who once knew how to laugh and love.

With her eyes damp, Trudy gave Anna an encouraging smile, and then continued clearing the table. Thinking about Trudy's words and the sincerity behind them, Anna once more followed Jenny through the long, quiet hall and up the wide staircase.

Pausing before Patricia Smith's room, Jenny hesitated and looked back at Anna. Trying to appear more confident than she felt, Anna smiled and nodded. Jenny lifted a hand and knocked softly. Without waiting for a reply, she turned the knob and stuck in her head.

"Mrs. Smith, Anna Svensen, your new companion, is here."

"Well, it's about time. Bring here in, bring her in. Maybe she'll be able to get some work done around here. I hope she isn't as lazy as you and your mother."

Anna flinched as she heard the harsh words. Although she had known the McNeils only a few hours, she certainly wouldn't characterize any of the family members as lazy.

Walking forward, Anna saw the same slight woman she had seen the previous night, only this time, the woman was propped up in a sitting position surrounded by large pillows.

"Well, come closer so that I might get a look at you."

Anna stepped near the bed.

"Well, you're pretty enough, but younger than I had thought. You'll probably get it in your head to find yourself a beau as soon as possible and run off to get married. I had wondered why your mother let you come all this way, at your tender age, too, but now I know. She thought you'd be able to better yourself here; maybe meet a nice city gentleman who takes a fancy to you. You with those blue eyes and shiny hair. Well, you better not waste any time courting while you are being paid to work. That's all I have to say about it."

Although she had thought she had been prepared to accept anything Patricia Smith might say, Anna felt her temper rise. How dare this woman criticize her mother's judgment? Taking a deep breath, Anna prayed for help in managing her reaction.

"Well now, Mrs. Smith," she said, looking Patricia Smith directly in the eyes. "Of course, my mother did have concerns about me traveling so far to find work, but my family and I prayed about it many times, and we felt a peace that comes from knowing this was the right path for me."

Patricia's eyes narrowed. "So. That's the way it is then. You are religious. I should have known, what with Wesley's tendencies and all. Well, I suppose you will want Sunday mornings off to go to church."

The woman sighed and rolled her eyes.

"At least, I can understand you, even with your accent. Almost all of the help Wesley finds for me can barely speak English. Isn't anyone born in America anymore?"

Anna felt her temper once again flare at the woman's words, which were delivered with heavy sarcasm. She quickly took another deep breath, and deliberately made herself smile, deciding to ignore Patricia's last comment.

"Mr. Smith and I have not yet made arrangements for what day will be my day off, but I do believe he did mention something about Sunday. He said that he is usually home to sit with you on Sundays."

Without waiting for a reply, Anna turned and nodded at Jenny, who was watching from the doorway. Jenny smiled and gently closed the door.

"Now then, Mrs. Smith, since I am to be your companion, is there anything I can do for you?"

Patricia Smith glared at the younger woman for several long moments. Finally, she spoke.

"After lunch, I usually rest. I like to keep the curtains shut while I sleep. You can do as you like, but don't make any noise. I can't sleep with noise or light."

The last words were said in a whisper, and Anna couldn't help but notice how frail and vulnerable the woman suddenly looked. She felt an unexpected surge of sympathy for Patricia Smith.

"Well, we can shut the light out easily enough," Anna said, stepping to the windows to draw the curtains shut. "As for noise, I will probably just do some reading while you rest. That should not keep you awake."

Anna turned back to the bed to find Patricia already laying on her side, her eyes closed and her mouth slightly open, her breathing regular. She quietly walked backed to the bed and drew a thin blanket around the woman's shoulders. Thoughtfully, she studied Patricia's face. Almost without wrinkles, Anna could see the same high brow and strong nose that Wesley had, although

Patricia's features were slightly thinner. Everything about the woman seemed delicate, and Anna relaxed, again feeling pity. How could anyone think this slight woman could be the cause of so much trouble? Yes, she had tried to make Anna angry with the comments about her mother and her accent, but Anna could handle comments like that easily enough.

Anna tiptoed across the room to the door that led to her own bedroom. Once there, she selected a book on world geography that Tina Stevens had sent with her. She opened the first page to find a carefully scripted list of instructions on how to complete assignments. Anna mentally made a note to write a long letter thanking her teacher when she sent her first lessons back.

Entering Patricia's room again, Anna chose to sit by a small table near one of the windows. Even without the curtains opened, the window let in enough light so that Anna could see what she was reading. After examining the assignment list again, Anna opened the book and turned to the first page.

After only a few moments, Anna found herself engrossed in the book. She spent the next hour studying intensely, only stopping when Patricia groaned softly in her sleep.

Putting the book aside, Anna rose and hurried to the older woman's bedside. Finding her still asleep, Anna rubbed her eyes and leaned back, stretching her shoulders. She could feel the beginnings of a dull headache, the result of reading too long with inadequate light. She thought of going downstairs to have a quick chat with Trudy and Jenny, and then decided not to. It was, after all, her first day of work, and she did want to make a good impression. But did she want to make as good of impression on Mrs. Smith as she did on her son?

Anna shook such thoughts from her head and glanced around the room. Although elaborate, the room seemed lifeless. The objects and furniture, while carefully coordinated, did not have the appearance of being loved. Anna felt a pang of homesickness for her parents' small shanty on the prairie. It had never been beautiful or large, but with her mother's brightly colored rugs on the floor and neatly patched quilts on the beds, the house had always felt like home.

Anna's eyes stopped when they reached a bureau stuck away in a far corner of the large room. The bureau probably wasn't used much, because a larger one sat closer to the bed. This one was small and the furniture pattern did not match the pattern of the rest of the furniture in the room.

Anna crossed the room to the bureau and opened her eyes wide with surprise. On top of the bureau lay several photographs, all neatly framed, but none of them sitting upright. One by one Anna examined them. There was one that included four people, two parents and a boy and girl. Anna recognized Wesley Smith as the boy because of the large dark eyes that smiled out of the photograph, and she assumed the handsome man next to him was his father. But could this dainty woman, dressed in lace and smiling widely, be Wesley's mother? And who was the small girl? Yes, there was a resemblance....

Anna chose another photograph to examine; this time, the wedding photograph of the two parents in the other picture.

"Patricia Smith, why she positively glowed!" Anna thought to herself.

The third photograph was of Wesley again, only this time more recent. He looked much like the man Anna knew, and she felt her palms dampen just upon holding his image in her hands. Quickly she put the photograph down, dropping it gently onto the wooden bureau.

"I do not remember giving you permission to sort through my things."

Anna turned abruptly at the sound of Patricia Smith's voice.

"I . . . I . . . ." Anna searched for the right words.

"No need to make excuses. I have been watching you look at those photographs. Trying to determine the value of the frames, aren't you? I know exactly what I have in this room. If anything is missing, I will promptly inform my son, and he will take the proper measures."

Anna's face flamed hotly. She fought desperately for control of her emotions, but she felt herself losing the battle.

"Mrs. Smith," she began, balling her hands into fists at her sides. "I may be curious, but I am not and never have been a . . . a

. . . thief. I am here to take care of you, and that I will do. But I will not have you threatening me all of the time. My parents raised me to be an honest person, and that I am."

Anna stopped and took a breath.

"Well," said Patricia, a smug look on her face. "Now that your little tirade is over, the least you can do is to bring me my afternoon tea."

Anna wished to respond, but realizing she had already spoken more sharply than she had meant to, she turned and walked out of the room.

Trudy turned when she heard the kitchen door open, and her face softened as she gazed at Anna.

"Already at it, eh?" Trudy asked, gently nodding her head. "I suppose the Missus'll be wanting her tea, then. I'll have it ready directly."

Knowing that she had never been able to conceal her feelings, Anna assumed her frustration with Mrs. Smith showed on her face.

"Will she keep this up, Trudy? This . . . this attack? She said such mean things about my mother, and she accused me of being a thief!"

"Come dear, and sit a moment."

Trudy pulled a chair out for Anna at the kitchen table.

"Remember what I said about the pain that Patricia feels?"

Anna nodded.

"Well, that pain is all mixed up inside her with anger. She is downright mad that the Mister died. He and she . . . well, they loved each other very much. They had been through so much together. People see this house and think that the people who live inside are all happy because they have money, but that ain't the truth, not always."

Concentrating on Trudy's words, Anna felt her frustration with Patricia Smith begin to subside just a little.

"Mr. Wesley, he's the only child the Missus has, but he's not the only one she carried. She lost three babies before Mr. Wesley was born, and a little girl after. The girl reached five years of age before she died. The pneumonia it was."

Trudy shook her head before continuing. "Losing children like that; it's hard on any woman."

Anna had had no idea. She remembered the photograph upstairs on the bureau. The tiny girl with the blonde curls and the big smile. Tears came quickly to her eyes as she imagined poor Patricia Smith losing her precious daughter. She thought of her own brothers and of Elsie. How would her mother have reacted at the loss of any of her children?

"But the Mister," Trudy reached out and clasped Anna's hands into her own. "He was strong throughout. He loved those children as much as she, but he loved her even more. He brought her comfort and gave her peace about the losses. So when he died, well, she just couldn't take any more."

Anna nodded, understanding washing through her.

Trudy rose and bustled about, putting the finishing touches on the silver tray containing the tea service.

"I hadn't told the other helpers about this, I'm not sure why. 'Course, they knew about the Mister's death an' all, but you're the only one who knows about the babies and the little one. Somehow it just seemed right."

"I thank you for telling me," Anna said. "Of course, I'll not say anything to Mrs. Smith, but it will help me, when I get frustrated with her, to remember the pain she is feeling."

Anna wrapped an arm around Trudy's shoulder and gave her a gentle squeeze. The older woman smiled in pleasure and handed Anna the tray.

Determinedly, Anna strode off to Mrs. Smith's room with a new purpose in mind. Not only would she meet Mrs. Smith's physical needs, she decided, she would try and help the woman find a way to mend her broken heart. Never had a person more need of knowing God, Anna thought as she climbed the stairs. Maybe, with patience, she would find an opportunity to talk with Patricia Smith about God and the peace and healing a relationship with him could bring.

But despite her changed attitude, Anna found tending to Patricia throughout the rest of the afternoon frustrating. She did not seem able to please the woman. The tea, when Anna first brought it up, was too hot, so Anna returned with a small pitcher of tepid water to cool it down. She added too much, of course, so she had to pour out that cup and brew a second cup, making sure to add just the right amount of cream and sugar.

After the tea had finally been consumed and Anna had returned the tray, Patricia then wanted her pillows fluffed. This Anna could not seem to complete to her employer's liking. The afternoon wound on in a similar vein. Finally, when Anna felt that her patience had been pushed beyond the breaking point, Jenny knocked on the door and popped in her head.

"Excuse me, Mrs. Smith, but my ma is wonderin' if you and Anna will be taking dinner in your room?"

Patricia Smith eyed Jenny coldly.

"Well, child, where else do you think I would eat? I haven't been able to rise from this bed for over a year. Of course we'll eat here."

"Yes, Ma'am."

Before shutting the door, Jenny winked at Anna.

Anna knew, without being told, that Jenny had really been asking if Patricia Smith wanted Anna to eat dinner with her. She couldn't help but feel that being asked to eat with the older woman was a breakthrough, however small it may be.

She followed Patricia's orders for another hour or so until Jenny finally brought up a tray full of dishes. Upon strict instructtions from her charge, Anna spent several long minutes adjusting the tray and the dishes until Patricia was satisfied and began to eat. Anna picked up her own plate and sat at the nearby table. She folded her napkin on her lap, and then bowed her head to say a silent grace.

"Dear Lord, please bless this food that we are about to eat. Please be with the one that I am helping, Lord, and let her find the peace that she is seeking. Amen."

Anna opened her eyes to find Patricia Smith staring at her.

"Well, aren't you going to eat?"

"Yes," Anna replied, "but I was saying a blessing for the food."

"Humph!" Patricia wrinkled her nose and turned back to her food. "A lot of good that will do you, I'm sure. God doesn't listen to prayers, don't you know that?"

For a brief moment, Anna tried to decide whether to respond to the older woman's words, muttered almost under her breath. Finally, she decided that this may be the opening she was looking for, the chance to try and introduce Patricia Smith to her God.

Just as she was about to speak, there was yet another knock on the door. This time Wesley Smith appeared. Anna immediately noticed that he was accompanied by an attractive, dark-haired, young woman.

"Hello, Mother," Wesley said, his presence seeming to fill the room as he entered. "We didn't mean to interrupt your dinner, but Jessica and I are going to the theater tonight, and we wanted to see you before we left. I thought you might be asleep when we returned."

Wesley stepped over and kissed his mother lightly on the cheek.

"Oh, Wesley," Patricia said, losing her stern voice and suddenly becoming more childlike. "I've had such a trying afternoon with this new girl. Her accent is so difficult, I can barely understand what she is saying, and she refuses to do the things I have asked. I'm afraid you are just going to have to send her home."

Wesley glanced over to where Anna sat.

"Why, Mother, affairs seem to be very much in order here. You are eating your dinner, and your tray is just as you like it. It seems to me that Miss Svensen is working out very well."

He threw an encouraging smile in Anna's direction.

The svelte woman at Wesley's side chose that moment to step forward. Gently she touched Patricia's hand.

"So good to see you again, Mrs. Smith. I've been thinking of you often. Did you get the floral arrangement I sent over?"

The woman's voice was lower than Anna had expected, but quite smooth, like a cat purring.

"Yes, I did, my dear. They were beautiful flowers. It was very thoughtful of you."

Anna looked at Patricia Smith. Her response to this Jessica had been the only civil words she had spoken all day.

"Well, Wesley, we must be going if we wish to arrive in time."

Jessica placed one hand on Wesley's arm.

"Yes, but in a minute. I would like to speak to Miss Svensen alone."

Anna rose, noticing that Jessica looked at her coldly as she followed Wesley into the hall.

Once in the hall, Wesley leaned toward Anna. She felt disturbed, yet strangely pleased by his closeness.

"How are things really going with Mother?" He spoke in a low voice, which further unnerved Anna. She collected her thoughts and spoke honestly.

"It has been trying at times. Your mother, she seems so angry. I have tried to do exactly as she has asked, but she never appears to be satisfied."

Wesley nodded his head.

"That is the usual pattern. I had so hoped it would be different this time."

"I will not give up, though," Anna responded. "Your mother ... she is in much need of love comfort. I thought . . . ."

Her voice trailed off.

"Yes?"

"Well, I thought, if you would not mind, I could speak to her about God. His peace, I mean. The peace that I have felt since I have accepted His will."

Anna felt her face grow warm, yet she stood resolved. Wesley looked at her for several moments before he answered, his dark eyes piercing into her.

"Miss Svensen, I would like that very much. I have tried to talk to Mother repeatedly about God's love, but she never wants to hear it. I have prayed for her acceptance of His peace. Maybe she will listen to you."

Anna lowered her head under his strong gaze.

"I will look for an opportunity to speak to her then."

At that moment, Patricia's bedroom door opened and Jessica stepped out, again reaching for Wesley's arm.

"Darling, we really must be going. Perhaps you and Miss . . . Stephensen is it? Perhaps you two can speak tomorrow."

She flashed a brilliant smile in his direction, once again not addressing Anna directly. Anna felt a sudden flash of anger, and tried to swallow it.

"Yes, well, you're right. Thank you, Miss Svensen," Wesley said, stepping aside so that Anna could reenter his mother's bedroom. "I do appreciate your help and your concern."

Anna gave a quick nod and then stepped into the room, feeling her heart flutter as she accidentally brushed his arm. Throughout the rest of the pleasant evening, a beautiful, attentive woman accompanied Wesley Smith to the theater and then to a late dinner, but his mind never wandered far from the farm girl sitting patiently with his mother at home.

Chapter Sixteen

For Anna, the days began to fall into a predictable routine. Upon rising, she would have a quick breakfast with the McNeils, and then enter Patricia's bedroom to begin a long day of trying to meeting the older woman's demands. She would first help Patricia with a sponge bath, and then she would place fresh sheets on her bed. Patricia Smith took tea mid-morning and mid-afternoon. Despite having refreshment almost constantly available, however, Anna noticed that the woman never seemed to eat very much.

Anna studied her lessons whenever she got the chance, usually after Patricia finished her lunch and took a short nap, and again in the evening. Boredom soon fell upon Anna, and she found herself staying up late at night reading, trying to shake the monotony of her days by burying herself in her books. Although she had not yet found the opportunity to speak to Patricia about her beliefs, Anna faithfully prayed for the chance to come along.

Each week, Anna wrote a long letter to her family and includeed most of her weekly salary. Although she filled her letters with descriptions of the elaborate house and her new friends, the McNeils, she kept her discussions about Patricia Smith short and positive. She knew her parents worried about her enough.

One sunny afternoon while her charge dozed, Anna decided to go for a walk in the garden. She had barely set foot outside the house since her arrival. As a person used to spending long hours outside walking to school and doing chores, Anna desperately missed the fresh air and sunshine. Trudy McNeil had volunteered to sit with Patricia for a short time in the afternoons if Anna needed a break, but so far Anna had not taken her up on the proposal. Anna knew that Trudy had many responsibilities also, and she hated to impose on her friend. But as she felt the frustration building, she asked Jenny, when the younger girl brought the noon tray, if Trudy could spell her for a short while that afternoon. Jenny had nodded eagerly. She and her mother had, just that morning, discussed that fact that in the few weeks Anna had been there, she had not even taken one day off.

After lunch, as soon as she had gotten Patricia settled for her nap, Anna opened the door and saw Trudy striding down the hall.

"Now you just take your time, dear, and enjoy this fine day." Trudy pushed her toward the stairs. "Don't hurry back. I've sat with the Missus before, and I'm a guessing she can stand my company. I think she'll miss you, though."

Anna expressed her thanks and hurried down the stairs, thinking about Trudy's words. It was true that Mrs. Smith had been softening a little. She still issued orders and made occasional sarcastic comments, but she didn't raise her voice as frequently. Anna had, however, interpreted the woman's softening not as her acceptance of her new helper, but as a sign that she was sinking even further into her sadness and despair.

Walking through the kitchen and out into the garden, Anna took a deep breath. Never had she smelled the air so fresh, and it made her realize she had been cooped up in a sick room far too long. Gingerly she stepped out and gazed around the garden. Autumn had arrived while Anna sat with Patricia; the air contained a touch of coolness, and the leaves had just started changing into their colorful fall foliage.

Slowly, she strolled around the cobblestone paths, stopping occasionally to smell a mum, to touch a leaf, or to marvel at a bird. The sunshine felt wonderful on her skin, and she felt the tension begin to ebb out of her shoulders and neck. She must work up the nerve to ask Wesley Smith about a day off, she decided. She would ask for Sundays, so that she might attend church. A picture of her church in West Bend popped into her mind.

Anna wiped away a tear that unexpectedly rolled down her cheek. Home. Finally alone, she allowed herself to think about home and all the people she missed. Elsie and the boys would be in school, now, she thought, and Aaron would be measuring lumber and selling nails at the hardware store. Her father would be bringing in the last of the fall crops and preparing for spring planting, and her mother might be canning, or baking bread. When she closed her eyes, Anna could almost see them, hear their voices, smell the bread baking. She sank down on a stone bench near the fountain and let her tears flow.

From his bedroom window, Wesley Smith watched Anna Svensen stroll around the garden. Earlier in the day, he had left the office to work on a case at home. He often did that when he had a lot of paperwork to complete. The distractions of his office could keep him from focusing. However, after arriving at home on this particular day, he found it unusually difficult to concentrate, so he had left his study to spend a few minutes in prayer in his bedroom.

Wesley did not feel angry that Anna had taken a break from her duties; in fact, he was happy to see her do so. He knew that caring for his mother could be daunting, and frequent breaks were necessary to regain perspective.

He had purposefully been avoiding conversation with Anna. Ever since the night he and Jessica had gone to the theater, his thoughts had often turned to Anna. Her blue eyes and open smile were inviting, but what really intrigued him was her honesty and devotion to her duties.

"Oh, Lord," Wesley breathed as he watched Anna sit on the bench. "Please give me direction as to your will. I can't stop thinking of her, Father, yet she is so young. And there is Jessica to think of. Please guide my thoughts in the proper direction."

Feeling better, Wesley decided it had been unfair of him to avoid Anna. He must speak to her and ask if she needed anything and see if she had made any progress with his mother.

By the time Wesley arrived in the garden, most of Anna's tears had stopped. However, when she raised her head at the sound of his footsteps, he could see that her eyes were red-rimmed and puffy.

"Excuse me," Wesley said as he approached. "May I sit down for a moment?"

"Of course," Anna replied, desperately wishing she had a handkerchief.

Lowering his body next to Anna's on the stone bench, Wesley became suddenly aware of how closely he sat to her. He tried to clear his head of such thoughts and focus on the purpose of the conversation.

"I was wondering, Miss Svensen, how you feel about your position here. I mean . . . is there anything you need . . . anything that I could do to . . . well to help you adjust?"

The young man who had nerves of steel while facing juries and judges found himself turning nearly incoherent around Anna. She, however, lost in her own thoughts, did not seem to notice.

"Yes, Mr. Smith, there is something I was wondering about." Anna hesitated, and then gathered her courage. "I was wondering if I might have a day off during the week. I find that it is difficult to sit with Mrs. Smith week after week without a day of rest."

Horrified at his faulty memory, Wesley immediately grew apologetic. In his delight that his mother had seemed to somewhat accept Anna, as well as to avoid the nervousness he felt in Anna's presence, he had completely forgotten to discuss setting up a day off with his new employee.

"Of course, of course. I didn't mean to forget that," Wesley stammered. "I just, well, I just was so happy with the way that Mother has seemed to adjust to your being here that I forgot. I apologize sincerely. Which day of the week would you like?"

"If it wouldn't be too much trouble, I would like to have Sundays. If you could direct me to the nearest church, one that I could walk to, I would like to attend services."

"Yes, yes," Wesley frowned. On Sundays, he usually attended church with Jessica and then accompanied her to dinner at her parents' house. Jessica would not be pleased with the sudden change in plans. With Anna taking Sunday as her day off, he would need to be available to meet his mother's needs in the afternoon. He glanced over at Anna and caught her wiping her eyes. How could he be so selfish?

"Of course you may have Sundays off, Miss Svensen. I would be glad to take you to the church that I attend, and if you find it not to your liking, then I will direct Simon to drive you to whichever church you'd like."

A smile broke across Anna's face and Wesley felt like he was melting.

"Oh, thank you, Mr. Smith! I have been missing the fellowship I found in your uncle's church in West Bend."

"You're quite welcome, Miss Svensen. Anything I can do to make your job easier."

"Well, I must get back inside," Anna said, rising and smoothing her skirt. "I'm sure Trudy will need to get back to her own chores."

Wesley felt panic at the thought of losing Anna's company, and he quickly thought of an excuse to keep her longer.

"Miss Svensen, if you could sit a moment longer, I would like to ask you a few questions about my mother's condition."

"Yes," Anna said, sitting again.

Wesley noticed a shadow cross Anna's face.

"What is it?" he asked, leaning closer.

"Well, it is true that Mrs. Smith has seemed to be more accepting of me lately," Anna said, pausing to put her thoughts together.

"Yes?"

"But I fear that she is growing worse – sicker I mean. She does not seem to have as much spirit as she did even when I arrived. She grows thinner and thinner and refuses to eat, although Trudy makes the most delicious dishes. I fear, well...."

"Yes?"

"Well it almost seems to me that she is giving up. That she is, well, willing herself to . . . to stop living. She is so unhappy all of the time, I do not think she sees anything worth living for."

Wesley nodded and sighed.

"I hadn't noticed her thinness, but I must look the next time I visit with her."

"You have been working too much," Anna said. "I do think your mother would enjoy visiting with you more."

Without meaning to, Wesley laughed out loud at the reprimand he heard in Anna's voice.

"Well, Miss Svensen, I do feel much like a schoolboy who has been caught sleeping during recitation."

Horrified, Anna glanced at her employer. Once again she saw the twinkle in his eyes that indicated he was teasing her.

"Excuse me, please, Mr. Smith. I did not mean to be so forward. But your mother, she always becomes much livelier when you visit her."

"Miss Svensen, you're right," he said, taking one of her hands into his own. "I very much appreciate your concern for Mother. I must confess that with the heavy caseload I have been carrying lately, I haven't had as much time to spend with her as I would want. I will begin to rectify that tonight."

Anna felt herself tremble involuntarily at the touch of his hand. She quickly withdrew it, and stood again.

"Thank you, Mr. Smith. I shall then return to my duties."

Wesley noticed the slight shakiness in her voice and mentally chastised himself for throwing her off guard. He usually wasn't so animated.

"Miss Svensen," he said as she began to walk towards the house. "Services begin at 10 a.m. on Sunday morning. The carriage will be waiting outside the front door at 9:30."

"Yes, thank you Mr. Smith," Anna replied as she hurried into the house.

Stepping into the kitchen, Anna stopped and caught her breath. Why did she always feel so nervous in his presence? Why did the touch of his hand or the sound of his voice send shivers up her back?

She must stop this foolishness, she decided. She set her chin firmly and headed toward the hallway stairs. She did not come to Kansas City to develop a crush on her employer, who, after all, appeared to already be spending time with another young lady, one who shared his own social class and background. No, she would push all thought of Wesley Smith out of her mind. She would spend her time finishing her course work and looking for opportunities to make Mrs. Smith comfortable, and perhaps, happier.

When the mail arrived the following day, Anna was thrilled to find not one, but two letters addressed to her. It was the first time she had received mail since arriving in Kansas City, and she immediately felt her spirits lift upon holding the heavy envelopes.

Tina Stevens had written one of the letters, and Anna expected to find grades for the first assignments she had sent to her teacher. Anna recognized her father's careful handwriting on the other envelope, and tears involuntarily came to her eyes. She could picture him bending painstakingly over the paper and writing the letter.

Anna quickly decided to open the letter from Miss Stevens first, savoring the thought of reading the one from home at night, just before she went to bed. As she was about to tear into the first letter, Patricia Smith awoke and demanded her afternoon tea tray.

Anna obliged, but felt disappointment as she set the unopened letter aside. A half an hour later, after serving Mrs. Smith's tea and taking a cup for herself, the older woman spoke.

"Well, aren't you even going to open your letters?"

Anna looked at her in surprise.

"Yes, . . . of course, I am planning too, but I thought I would wait until I had some quiet time to read."

Patricia Smith looked at Anna over her cup of tea.

"I am a grown woman, you know. I would think you'd realize that I can care for myself for a few minutes while you read your letter."

Anna paused for a moment. She really wanted to save both letters for a time when she could read them slowly, enjoying every word. But Mrs. Smith was sitting so quietly, and this was the first time that the older woman had ever seemed concerned about any of Anna's affairs. Anna realized that, in her own strange manner, Patricia Smith was trying to be kind.

"Why, thank you, Mrs. Smith. I am interested in reading this letter from my teacher, Tina Stevens. I believe that she may have included a response to some of the lessons that I have been sending her."

"Go ahead then. I'll just drink my tea and wait."

Anna set her cup down carefully and went to the small table near the bed. Sinking into a chair, she opened the letter, seeing her teacher's face in her mind as she did so.

"Dearest Anna," the letter began . . .

"I am so pleased with the work you have been sending back. It is, of course, the same high quality as the work you completed last year in the classroom. I have enclosed responses to your first two geography lessons, and a response to the mathematics lesson on fractions . . . ."

Forgetting her charge entirely, Anna engrossed herself in the letter. She could almost hear her friend's voice as the teacher described, in great detail, the new students at the school and some of the antics they had been performing. There was also a description of the news Miss Stevens had received from her fiancé, and a long discussion about the hayride and bonfire the church was planning for its young members.

"Finally, dear Anna, I have some wonderful news for you. Do you remember Jed Dennison? Well, it appears that our prayers have been answered! Jed has been attending church quite regularly now for the past month, and last week at the end of services, he approached Pastor Heggarty and asked to pray with him. Jed will not be back in school, but he has been hired on at the livery stable. I truly believe he is a changed person."

Setting the letter aside, Anna brushed tears from her eyes. Who would have thought after the first day of school last year that Jed Dennison could be so changed? Anna said a silent prayer of thanksgiving for Miss Stevens' news, even as she suffered from the loneliness of missing her friend.

"Has something happened?"

Patricia Smith's voice interrupted Anna's thoughts. She realized that she had been so engrossed in reading the letter that she had quite forgotten that Mrs. Smith was even in the room.

"Oh, no, no," Anna responded, forcing a smile to her face. "In fact, I have received some good news."

"Well," said Mrs. Smith, "you wouldn't have known it, not with all your carrying on."

Anna thought she detected a small note of concern in the older woman's voice. She thought for a moment, and then decided that this may be the opportunity she had been praying for. She brought her chair closer to the bedside.

"I would like to share with you the reason for my tears, Mrs. Smith," Anna began.

The older woman glared at her, but Anna saw a hint of curiosity behind the impatient expression.

"At home, there is this boy – a man really – who has always brought a lot of trouble with him. Last year, in school, he often scared or insulted our teacher. Some people even thought he stole things, he and his father."

Anna paused, seeing Jed's leering face in her memory.

"But all of that has changed now," she continued. "You see, Jed Dennison has accepted Christ into his life. Pastor Heggarty, your brother, helped Jed through his sermons, and many, many people have been praying for him."

Anna looked deep into Patricia Smith's troubled eyes, trying to read the expression she found there. She felt a glimmer of hope as she let her words sink in.

After a long silence, Mrs. Smith spoke.

"That's ridiculous. The young man has everyone fooled; it's easy to see that. If everyone is thinking he has changed, they'll let their guard down. Then he'll take advantage of them again."

Mrs. Smith pushed the tea tray away and sunk down into her pillows.

"My brother has always had such silly ideas. Please take this tray away. I'm feeling tired again. I'd like to be alone for a while."

"Yes, Mrs. Smith."

Anna's hopes faded as quickly as they'd come. She picked up the tray and started toward the door. Before opening it, however, she turned, feeling suddenly brave.

"Mrs. Smith, God's love is available to all of us, especially when we are hurting." Without waiting for a reply, Anna opened the door and started down the hall.

In the bedroom, Patricia Smith turned her face into her pillow and began to cry softly.

"Not for me, Anna," she murmured. "Never for me."

Chapter Seventeen

On Sunday morning, Anna donned her best dress, the deep blue cotton with her mother's lace at the throat and sleeves. She took extra time pinning her hair, and she pinched her cheeks to bring a little color into them. She looked in the mirror and found herself pleased with what she saw. Gently she chided herself.

"Oh, stop being so silly. You are just going to church."

But Anna knew, without admitting it, that she was looking forward to church not just because she wanted the fellowship and to hear the sermon, but also because she would be accompanied by Wesley Smith. She shook such thoughts from her mind and went downstairs to wait for the carriage.

Simon pulled up to the front of the house exactly at nine-thirty. However, the carriage door opened before Simon had dismounted, and Wesley Smith stepped out. Bravely Anna strode forward and accepted his help into the carriage. Upon entering, she saw that she and Wesley wouldn't be alone.

"Miss Svensen, I believe you have met Jessica Thompson?"

Wesley sat down next to the dark-haired Jessica.

"Yes, yes, a few weeks ago," Anna forced a smile to hide her disappointment. "So nice to see you again, Miss Thompson."

"Thank you, Anna. It's lovely to see you again, also."

Anna bristled at the way Jessica felt free to use her first name, but she quickly tried to swallow her pride.

"Wesley has been so pleased with the way you are caring for Mother. It has been a great burden off his mind – off both of our minds."

Jessica glanced at Wesley, and then placed her arm through his.

"He works so hard, my Wesley. He doesn't need to spend so much time worrying, too."

Anna managed another weak smile, noticing the fond way Wesley looked at Jessica.

The couple made small talk the rest of the ride, occasionally including Anna in their conversation. She did her best to look interested, but inside she felt like hiding. She had never harbored any real hope that there could be a relationship between Wesley Smith and herself, yet her heart had yearned for him without her even willing it to.

In a short while, the carriage pulled up in front of an impressively large church. Stained glass windows shone from the building, and a long row of carriages lined up to let finely dressed men and women get out.

Anna glanced down at her own cotton dress, the one she had donned with such pride just an hour earlier, and she suddenly felt insecure and out of place. Her cotton looked so dowdy next to the fine silks and taffetas descending from the carriages. She desperately wished she were back at the Smith mansion, reading the Bible alone in her room, or better yet, with her own family attending church in West Bend.

"Well, ladies, here we are," Wesley announced.

Simon opened the carriage door and helped Jessica out, and then extended his hand to Anna. He winked and smiled as Anna dismounted, and she managed a small smile in return. Wesley followed the women, nodding to Simon, who drove off with the carriage.

Anna couldn't help but feel awe as the trio entered the building. The sunlight filtering through the stained glass cast a soft, colorful light on the church's furnishings, and it took a minute for her eyes to adjust. A large pipe organ filled the area behind the pulpit, and there was a choir loft to one side, Wesley seated the two young women in a pew about half of the way to the front, then slid in himself beside Jessica.

The service proved to be just as impressive as the building, although Anna could not seem to get much meaning from the sermon. Many of the words the pastor used Anna had not heard before. She tried to focus on the words, but she found her thoughts drifting to the man sitting beside Jessica.

At the end of the service, following the last impressive performance by the choir, the pastor stepped down from the pulpit and spoke again.

"I have the pleasure of making a wonderful announcement this morning," the gray-haired gentleman said. "I would like to announce the engagement and approaching marriage of Miss Jessica Thompson and Mr. Wesley Smith."

Surprised smiles followed by gentle applause rippled through the congregation. Anna joined in, and desperately wished to be alone in her room. Jessica and Wesley stood and faced the crowd.

Soon the service was over, but Anna thought they'd never make it out of the building. Many well-wishers stopped to congratulate the couple, and even though Wesley always remembered to introduce Anna, it was Jessica and Wesley who garnered the attention.

When they finally did get to the carriage and were safely seated, Jessica chatted most of the way home. The conversation centered around who was wearing what and did Wesley see that so and so had returned from Chicago?

"On and on. Doesn't she ever quit?" Anna thought, and then chided herself for thinking so. Jealousy was an emotion Anna seldom experienced, and she struggled with it all the way to the mansion.

Once home, Wesley left the carriage and walked Anna to the door. He was planning on sharing dinner with Jessica and her parents, and then returning in mid-afternoon to spend the rest of the day with his mother. Patricia Smith did not yet know of his engagement.

"Did you enjoy the service, Miss Svensen?" Wesley asked politely.

Anna lifted her eyes to his.

"Oh, your church is very grand," she said. "But everything is too . . . too formal for me. Thank you so much for taking me, but I believe I will attend church with the McNeils next week."

With that, afraid that the tears she had been holding back all morning might burst, Anna turned and entered the house.

Wesley stood a moment, still staring at the place her face had been. Her eyes were so blue and her face so open. He felt his stomach churn as Anna ran lightly up the steps.

He had asked Jessica to marry him the night before in a somewhat desperate attempt to forget Anna. He had known Jessica all of his life, and she came from a quite respectable family. It had seemed to him that Jessica was the one the Lord had planned for him to marry. Love could come later.

"I should feel pleased and excited today," Wesley thought. "Instead, I feel like my heart is breaking."

"Wesley?"

Jessica had opened the door of the carriage and leaned out.

"Shouldn't we be going? Mother and Father are expecting us."

Wesley turned and walked back to the carriage, his steps heavy.

"Oh, Lord," his heart cried. "Show me the way. If I have made a mistake, help me to undo it, Father. Help me to follow your will."

Anna struggled with her emotions throughout the next few weeks. She did everything possible keep her thoughts from returning to Wesley Smith.

It seemed to her that his mother, Patricia, who had become almost docile during the past few weeks, had suddenly returned to her demanding ways. Anna tried to meet her needs and pacify the woman, but she found herself frustrated by the constant demands. There was little time for studying, for Mrs. Smith only slept in short spurts now, and Anna began to worry that she wouldn't complete her lessons on schedule. She tried to stay up late during the evenings, poring over her books, but Mrs. Smith often woke at night, causing Anna to rush in and try to soothe her. The lack of sleep and the fatigue brought on by racing up and down the stairs to the kitchen, caved in on Anna at night and she always sank quickly into a dreamless sleep.

Even so, when there were a few spare moments, Anna found her thoughts turning to Wesley and his bride-to-be, Jessica

Thompson. Without willing them, tears would often threaten to spill, and she would have to turn her head lest Mrs. Smith should notice her crying while fluffing pillows or arranging the tea set. One Thursday night, it was a physically and mentally exhausted Anna who, after tucking Mrs. Smith in, threw herself across her bed and wept.

"I am in love with Wesley Smith," Anna thought as her tears finally subsided. "As much as I don't want to be, I am."

A sudden feeling of peace descended on her after she finally realized her love for her employer. It was as if, after admitting it to herself, Anna could finally face the pain of dealing with her feelings. She went to bed and slept soundly, determined to start the next day by pushing thoughts of Wesley Smith from her mind while caring for his mother as best as she could.

In the morning, Anna decided to try a new tactic with her unsettled charge. After Patricia Smith had been fed, bathed, and tucked back into bed, Anna pulled out a large, leather-covered book, and arranged herself at the woman's bedside.

"What are you doing?" Mrs. Smith asked, using her bitterest tone of voice.

"I am going to read to you, Mrs. Smith."

After glaring at Anna for a few moments, the older woman turned away and announced, "No, you most certainly are not."

Anna slowly counted to ten, a technique she had learned from her mother.

"Yes, I am."

She opened the book and began the first chapter. It was one she had chosen early that morning from the Smith's extensive library. Although it was a thick book, the vocabulary looked fairly simple, and Anna felt confident that she could manage the reading.

For the first several pages, Patricia Smith seemed disinterested, yawning occasionally, but mostly just keeping a dissatisfied look on her face. After reading for about twenty minutes, Anna paused to take a breath, and Patricia interrupted.

"I will tell my son about this, you know. You have no right to keep me hostage while you read such . . . such drivel."

Anna calmly looked at her, and then returned to reading, making no comment. When she had finished the first chapter, she gently closed the book and asked, "Would you like your morning tea now, Mrs. Smith?"

The woman glared at her and then turned away.

"I'm not feeling well. Don't bring me any tea this morning."

"Fine. Then I am going to get some of my schoolwork to complete while you rest."

Anna brought her mathematics book in from her bedroom and sat at the table by the window, quietly working, until Jenny tapped on the bedroom door thirty minutes later.

"We were wondering if the Missus was wanting her morning tea," the girl said, dropping her voice to a whisper as she noticed Mrs. Smith's slumped form on the bed.

"Mrs. Smith has decided not to have her tea this morning. Thank you anyway, Jenny. I will come down for the lunch tray in about an hour."

Anna gave the girl a bright smile, and firmly closed the door. She looked at her charge for a moment, and noticing no response, she went back to the table to work on more of her mathematics.

An hour later, Anna closed the book and announced loudly, "Mrs. Smith, I am going downstairs now to get the lunch tray. After lunch, we will sit in the garden for a short time, and then we will come upstairs and read another chapter."

Without waiting for a reply, Anna left the room. She did not turn around to see Patricia Smith's eyes open wide with fright.

"Please Lord, help me to know if I am doing the right thing," Anna breathed silently as Simon and Ian McNeil carefully carried Patricia Smith on a cot down the stairs, through the kitchen, and out into the back yard. Anna had already fixed a makeshift bed laden with blankets and cushions by using a wooden bench with a sturdy back she had found in one corner of the garden. So far, Patricia Smith had remained silent ever since Anna had announced that they were going outside. She had refused to touch her lunch, and she did not look at either Ian or Simon as they lifted her.

"Well, something must be done, dear," Trudy McNeil had replied after Anna had confessed her plan to take Patricia outside. "That poor woman is just wasting away up there. I don't see any harm in her getting a little fresh air if the day be warm enough."

Indeed the day was warm enough, gloriously warm. Anna thought the garden had never looked more beautiful with the fall foliage in full bloom and the trees sporting their brilliant colors. Ian and Simon carefully placed Mrs. Smith into the makeshift bed, and tucked the blankets around her thin shoulders.

"There you be, Missus Smith," Ian said, smiling as his employer. "We'll be back in a half an hour or so to return you to your room."

"Thank you so much," Anna told the two men, pulling them aside.

"It'd be much courage you have," Ian said, nodding in Mrs. Smith's direction. "This is the first time she has left her room since Mr. Smith died. I don't rightly know what the shock of fresh air will do to her."

"Well," Anna replied, setting her chin firmly. "Staying shut up in her room does not seem to be doing her any good."

Simon smiled and tipped his hat, and the two were off. Anna pulled a white wicker chair close to Patricia and breathed deeply.

"Isn't it lovely, Mrs. Smith? Look how colorful the trees are. You surely have a beautiful garden."

Anna noticed that not only did the woman not respond, she didn't even raise her head. She just stared silently at the blanket covering her legs. Quietly the pair sat for about thirty minutes, and when Anna had just about decided she couldn't take the silence anymore, Ian and Simon returned to carry the invalid back to her room.

Once back in bed, Mrs. Smith uttered only one sentence. "Shut the blinds now."

Feeling like she had pushed the woman enough for one day, Anna decided to forgo the reading of a second chapter in the novel, and acquiesced to Mrs. Smith's request. She quietly drew the blinds, and then retired to her own room, keeping the door open so that she might check on her charge frequently.

Mrs. Smith stayed quiet the rest of the afternoon. When Anna went to check on her to see if she was ready for afternoon tea, she found the woman lying with her eyes shut. For a moment, Anna panicked, wondering if the woman was even breathing. She relaxed after she saw the light rise and fall of Mrs. Smith's check under the blanket. Anna spent the rest of the afternoon poring over her school books, getting caught up on some late assignments.

When it became time for dinner, Anna entered the room with resolve, opening the blinds and announcing firmly, "It is time to wake now, Mrs. Smith. You must sit up so that you may have some supper."

The older woman's eyes opened slowly.

"I'm not hungry. I want to speak to my son."

"I will tell the McNeils to send Mr. Smith up as soon as he arrives home. But you will eat something, Mrs. Smith. You didn't touch your lunch at all."

With that, Anna left the room, shutting the door firmly behind her. She made her way to the kitchen for the evening tray, meeting Trudy's questioning gaze.

Anna shook her head.

"She is a stubborn one, that Mrs. Smith. She is determined to show her anger at me by not eating and barely talking."

Trudy clucked her tongue.

"Hold on to your courage, Anna. You'll wear her down soon enough, I'm thinking"

Anna pondered over her friend's words.

"But is it the right thing to do, Trudy? I mean, is it my place to force her outside if she does not want to go?"

Trudy placed dishes on the sliver tray she was preparing for Anna and Patricia. When she finished, she turned and spoke.

"Who knows what is the right thing to do? All I know is that the day the Mister died it seemed like the whole house died, and everyone in it, too. You are the first breath of fresh air that we have had around here in a long time. If you believe, in your heart, that what you are doing will help Mrs. Smith, then I say keep to it."

Trudy smiled at Anna and handed her the try. Thankful for her friend's trust, Anna strode back up the stairs.

Just about when she was ready to push her way into the room, Anna heard Wesley's voice. She was thankful to hear it, because in her concern about her actions, she had forgotten to ask Trudy to send Wesley upstairs when he arrived home.

"I don't think a few minutes of fresh air will do you any harm, Mother," Wesley said. "In fact, remember what Dr. Bronson said? He said there was no reason why you shouldn't get up and take short walks through the garden as long as the weather held."

"But Wesley, I am feeling so much worse now that I was the last time Dr. Bronson was here. I want you to fire that girl. She is bossy and unfriendly, and she is often lazy, too."

Wesley looked at her mother, thoughtfully. He found it difficult to believe that Anna could ever be bossy or unfriendly, much less lazy. But still, he had not seen his mother in such an upset state since the day his father . . . .

Wesley sighed.

"I will speak to her, Mother. But I think you should consider getting some fresh air every day. It cannot help but make you feel better."

Anna chose that point to knock softly on the door and bring in the tray. She nodded in Wesley's direction and said brightly, "Here is our dinner, Mrs. Smith. It seems that Trudy has made many of your favorites tonight."

It was true. Concerned about her employer's lack of appetite, Trudy had spent hours that afternoon baking and cooking. Fragrant plates of roast chicken, potatoes with cream sauce, and warm biscuits smothered in melting butter rested on the tray next to a plate full of frosted fruit tarts.

Ignoring her remark, Patricia Smith glared at Anna. "I believe my son would like to have a word with you."

"Of course, Anna replied. "But let me get you settled with your dinner first."

Anna deftly placed the tray on a small bedside table and then transferred plates and dishes to the tray that she had set on Mrs. Smith's lap. She helped her employer to sit up, and then placed two large pillows behind her so that she could lean back without slumping down. The whole procedure took less than a minute. Wesley watched, admiring Anna's efficient yet gentle manner she exhibited with his mother.

When Patricia was duly settled, Anna stepped into the hall, followed by Wesley. Sensing that this conversation might take more than just a few minutes, he suggested that they talk in the drawing room adjacent to his bedroom.

Anna agreed and followed him down the hall to a room she had not entered before. She caught her breath as she entered the room. Unlike her own and Mrs. Smith's room, Wesley's drawing room exuded masculinity. Decorated in dark blues and greens, the room seemed less formal and more comfortable than many of the other rooms in the house. Two overstuffed chairs sat next to a small sofa near the fireplace. Three framed photographs rested on the fireplace mantle, and Anna held back her urge to walk over and examine them. A desk, covered with papers and books, faced a large window. Bookshelves filled with leather-covered volumes lined two walls of the room. Just by entering, Anna felt like she was getting a glimpse into Wesley Smith's usually reserved life.

"Please sit down," Wesley said, gesturing toward the chairs near the fireplace.

Anna chose one of the overstuffed chairs and Wesley took the other. She looked at him, expectantly, hoping to be able to conceal her newly-discovered affection for this man sitting so near.

Wesley sighed.

"Mother seems to be highly upset today," he began. "It appears that you took her outside this afternoon?"

"Yes," Anna admitted, nodding her head.

"And you read to her this morning?"

"Yes."

"May I ask why you suddenly have decided to become so assertive with her?"

"Assertive?"

"Sorry. It means forceful, stern...."

Anna continued to look confused.

Wesley sighed and then smiled.

"Mother says you are making her do things she doesn't want to do."

Anna nodded, catching the understanding.

'That is true. I am."

Wesley pondered this for a moment. "Why?"

Anna took a deep breath, willing her voice to be steady.

"Mrs. Smith has gotten so much worse since I first came here. She barely eats at all, and she seems to sink further and further into her bed every day. I have been praying about what to do. Yesterday, I came to the feeling that she could still be saved from her illness if only those of us around her could try a little harder."

Anna paused, finding it unexpectedly difficult to make such a long speech in front of Wesley. He waited, patiently.

"You see," Anna leaned forward, "I have learned so much about your mother, from Trudy and Ian, and from her photographs. I know that she was once a wonderful woman, full of life and love. I just had to try to help her find life again, and I thought that being outside, in all the beauty of your garden ... well, I...."

Anna lifted her hands, and then leaned back in the chair, exhausted from trying to make her point and from the stress of the long day. Wesley stood up and strode to the fireplace. He reached to the mantle and selected a photograph from those on display. He held it for several moments, examining it carefully. Then, thoughtfully, he put it down and returned to stand in front of Anna. Dropping to his knees, he took both of her hands in his own. She caught her breath, unable to still the beating of her heart. Finally, she raised her eyes until they met his.

"Anna, please continue to try with Mother. Nothing I have done seems to be working. I, too, feel like I am losing her more every day."

He looked deep into Anna's eyes, and then, as if suddenly conscious of his position, he dropped her hands and stood up, backing away.

"She will continue to resist, but I will tell her that you and I have talked, and we both agree that daily time in the garden is necessary."

Anna placed one hand to her chest where her heart still beat wildly.

"And the reading? Should I continue with that?"

"Yes," Wesley replied firmly. "Mother used to be an avid reader. Most of the books in the library belonged to her. Only the law and history books were my father's. Please, continue to read to her."

Wesley walked over to the door and held it open. Anna felt a sudden sadness that their conversation was coming to a close.

"And Anna, please continue to pray for Mother," he added, his voice small.

She nodded, fighting off the urge to gather him into her arms and comfort him. She chided herself. He was a man, not a boy like her younger brothers. She rose and nodded curtly and then walked down the hall, not conscious that Wesley Smith's eyes followed her until she disappeared into his mother's room.

Wesley shut the door and leaned against it, willing his own heart to still its heavy beating. There was one thing he knew after speaking to Anna, after holding her hand in his; he could not marry Jessica Thompson.

Chapter Eighteen

Shortly after his discussion with Anna, Wesley saddled his favorite horse and rode to Jessica's house, determined to inform her of his decision to break their engagement. It wouldn't be an easy task, and it was made even more difficult by the warm reception he received from the Thompsons. They invited him into their parlor and fussed over him, making him accept a cup of coffee and a slice of yellow cake still warm from the oven.

Finally, however, Jessica's parents left him alone with his fiancée. He paced around the room, trying to find the right words, until Jessica asked, in a tight voice, "Wesley, whatever is the matter?"

He stopped pacing and came to sit beside Jessica. He looked at her intently, and memories flooded back to him. He had known her since he was a child. They had attended each other's birthday parties as their parents had always been good friends. It had been assumed by both families that the two would marry ever since Wesley could remember.

Gently, he took her hand and tried to look into her eyes. He found coldness and resistance there.

"Jessica," he began, his voice cracking with emotion. "I cannot marry you."

She drew away and stood, turning her back to him.

"It's that Swedish girl, isn't it?" she demanded. "You have not been yourself ever since she has been living at your home. I see the way you look at her, the way you watch her when you think no one else is noticing."

She turned to him, her face red.

"You silly, silly man! You could never marry her, you know! She isn't like us. She is a mere . . . mere . . . peasant!"

Wesley first felt astonished at Jessica's ability to perceive his feelings for Anna, and then he felt anger. Any doubt he had about his decision to break their engagement faded under Jessica's strong criticism of Anna. He should have seen through Jessica long ago.

"No, Jessica," Wesley said, calmly. "It isn't Anna Svensen. It is me. I value your friendship. You are a beautiful, intelligent woman. But I don't feel for you the way I should. I believe God has other plans for me."

At this, Jessica's anger abated and she crumpled into a heap on the sofa.

"Oh, Wesley! I have loved you forever. If you would just give me a chance, I know I could make you love me, too. Please, please, darling!"

Gently, Wesley sat beside her and said, "Jessica, there will be another man for you. One who will cherish you and love you in the way I never could. I'm sure that God has someone already chosen for you. It has to be this way."

Jessica continued to sob noisily into her lace handkerchief while Wesley sat beside her.

"Would you like for me to tell your parents?" he asked after several moments.

"No, they will accept it better coming from me."

She gave him a wry smile.

"They won't want to see you for awhile, though."

Wesley nodded, glad to see a smile, however small, cross Jessica's face. Quietly, he rose and let himself out the front door. As he rode home, he felt pain for Jessica's distress, but a great sense of peace descended upon him as well. Even if he never would be able to express his true feelings to Anna, he knew in his heart that marrying Jessica would not have been following God's plan for his life. He breathed a quick prayer that God would comfort Jessica and show him the right time to approach Anna with his feelings. He breathed in the cool autumn air, his soul at peace for the first time in several weeks.

News of Wesley's broken engagement reached his home quickly the following day. Even though Wesley himself had not yet spoken of it, Simon had heard about it at the hardware store while speaking with one of the Thompsons' gardeners. He came home and quickly informed his parents in hushed, solemn tones, and they, in turn, told Jenny and Anna.

"We're not ones to gossip," Trudy said, her head bowed close to Anna's ear, "but I thought you'd be wanting to know in case the Missus seems unusually upset."

Anna's heart leapt with hope when she heard the news, but soon after she chided herself. She had no right to feel joy when presented with the news of others' pain. The McNeils did not seem to know why Wesley broke his engagement, and Wesley did not approach the subject with his employees.

Anna soon knew that he had told his mother, however. Inadvertently, she had overheard him speaking to Patricia one night as he visited with her before dinner.

"I didn't like her anyway," Patricia had unexpectedly announced in her bitterest voice. "She was always pawing and fawning all over a body. It made me sick."

Wesley had gently rebuked his mother for such harsh words about a family friend, but Anna noticed a trace of humor in his expression as she brought in the dinner tray. In fact, Wesley seemed to be in a better mood almost all of the time now. Without Jessica's company to keep his social calendar full, he spent more and more time at home, visiting with his mother. Anna knew Patricia appreciated her son's company, and she had to admit that she enjoyed having him around as well.

As the fall turned into early winter, Anna continued to take Patricia outside for her daily visit to the garden. All of the leaves had turned by now, and most had fallen off the trees. Simon and Ian attempted to keep up with clearing the garden paths, but Anna knew it was too large a job for them alone. Still, she noticed that the small space where she and Patricia Smith rested was always carefully tended.

Slowly, slowly, Patricia Smith had begun to give up a bit of her stubbornness about being outside. Small spots of color were coming back into her cheeks, and after the first few days outside, Anna noticed that Patricia's appetite had grown dramatically.

Anna praised God daily for the improvements she saw, although the older woman was still barely communicative.

One day in early November, Anna awoke feeling quite chilly in her room. She jumped out of bed, not bothering to put on her robe, and padded to the window. She caught her breath as she observed the splendor in the garden. A thin blanket of snow carpeted the landscape, and large, wet flakes were still coming down. Anna remembered the horrible snowstorm on the prairie the previous winter and felt thankful to be in a warm, safe, house. She dressed quickly and went to check on her charge.

She found Patricia huddled in her bed, frowning.

"Why Mrs. Smith, whatever is the matter?"

"This snow! It will make it impossible for me to go outside."

Anna bit back the words that threatened to spill from her lips. It was the first time that Patricia Smith had ever admitted liking her daily treks to the garden. She thoughtfully looked at the woman a few minutes.

"Well, if we bundle you up properly, I do not see why we couldn't go out for just a few minutes."

Patricia looked up, and her tight frown loosened.

"Do you really think so?"

"I don't see why not," Anna paused. "I probably should check with Mr. Smith first, however."

"Yes," Patricia said, brightness entering her eyes, "but please go now. He leaves so early for his office."

Anna nodded and slipped back to her room. Hurriedly she checked her hair, replacing a loose pin, and then she walked down the hall toward Wesley's suite where she knocked on the door. Garnering no response, she fairly flew downstairs to the dining room where she assumed Wesley took his meals. Finding it empty also, she rushed into the kitchen only to find Wesley sitting at the table eating bacon and biscuits with the McNeils.

"Oh," Anna said, placing one had to her chest. "I was looking for you, and I did not think you were still here."

Wesley looked up and felt his heart leap, as it always had done for the past several weeks each time he saw Anna. His gaze softened as he saw her flushed cheeks gotten from hurrying through the house.

He tried to steady his voice. "Good morning, Miss Svensen. Is something the matter?"

Anna remembered her purpose and set her chin firmly.

"Yes. I would like your permission to take your mother outside for just a few minutes today. I know that it is snowing, but she is so afraid that she might miss her daily time in the garden...."

Anna lifted, then dropped her hands.

Wesley didn't respond immediately, concern crossing his face.

"I don't know . . . I mean, she is starting to look a little well ... I'd hate it if she'd have a relapse."

Anna started to speak, then bit her lower lip.

"Your mother's illness is not physical," she reminded him, nearly in a whisper. "Even if it is cold, a few minutes outside always raises her spirits."

Wesley melted.

"Yes, all right then. But only for a few minutes. And please make sure that she is properly covered."

He pushed away from the table.

"I must see about getting to work now."

"Do you want some help with the carriage, sir?" Simon asked, starting to get up.

"No, Simon, stay where you are. I'll not hook up the carriage today. I think it will be easier to just ride Smoke, and I can saddle him easy enough by myself."

Simon nodded, and Wesley stepped out the back door into the wintry day.

Anna clasped her hands together and hurried out of the room to tell Mrs. Smith the good news while Simon and Jenny rose to begin their daily chores. Trudy, however, poured another cup of coffee and sat down to enjoy it with her husband.

"Methinks, my love, that I now know why the young Mister broke it off with Miss Jessica," Trudy said, a smile on her face.

"Yes? Why?"

"Didn't you see the way he looked at our Anna? Why, when she came into the room you'd think the sun just burst through. And if I'm not missing my guess, she is feeling the same way."

Trudy smiled, and Ian contemplated his wife.

"You being sure about that?" he finally said. "You know that could cause quite a stir, them being from different . . . well, different backgrounds and all."

"Pshaw!" Trudy exclaimed. "Ian McNeil, you of all people should know, sometimes you don't choose love. It just comes all on its own, and there isn't a thing to be done about it!"

She rose from the table and began clearing the dishes.

"I only wonder if the two that's feeling it can recognize it when it comes."

Ian walked over to where Trudy was filling the sink and planted a kiss on the top of her head.

"If they be feeling it like I was when I met you, then they won't be able to ignore it for long," he whispered into her ear.

Anna did manage to get Patricia Smith outside for a few minutes that day, as well as most of the following days. With the exception of the early winter snow and a brief ice storm one week before Christmas, the winter, so far, proved to be mild.

Daily Patricia Smith grew stronger. Even more color had returned to her cheeks, and her eyes often appeared animated when she talked. Anna felt a cautious hope that her charge had turned the corner and was truly on the road to recovery. She even harbored a secret hope that one day soon she may convince Patricia Smith to try to walk. According to Patricia's doctor, to whom Anna had spoken many times, there was no physical reason the woman couldn't walk. Anna planned to broach the subject with Mrs. Smith after the holidays.

Yet, despite her improving health, Patricia Smith did not show any signs of coming closer to accepting God's will. Whenever Anna tried to introduce the topic, Patricia immediately changed the subject, or flatly informed Anna that she did not wish to discuss it. Mrs. Smith had, however, allowed Anna to read from the Bible on occasion during their daily reading time. She appeared to be especially fond of the Psalms that spoke to suffering, so Anna tried to choose those passages often.

So it was with new hope that Anna approached each day, encouraged by Patricia Smith's progress, and by her own toward finishing her lessons by the end of the spring term. Still, she missed her family desperately, and she continued to harbor strong feelings for Wesley, no matter how much she tried to ignore them.

On the first day Anna and Patricia were able to get outside following the December ice storm, Patricia surprised Anna with an unexpected question.

"Will you be returning home for the holidays?"

Anna stopped and turned around.

"Why, Mrs. Smith, I did not plan on it. It is so far, and I am needed here."

Patricia Smith closely studied the face of this girl that she had secretly come to admire, even love. She did not relish the thought of losing Anna's company for a time, but she knew how much the girl had been pining for her family. Why else would Anna be walking around with a dreamy look on her face?

"Well, I suppose that I could manage without you for a time. I managed to make it this far in my life without your constant company."

Anna suppressed a smile at Mrs. Smith's sharp tone, realizing that in her own way, Patricia Smith was attempting kindness.

"I would like to see my family."

"It is settled, then," Patricia said, tilting her chin in the air. "I will talk to Wesley about it tonight."

True to her promise, Patricia did speak to her son about giving Anna some time to return home. Wesley immediately frowned upon the idea.

"But Mother, you are doing so well. I really think Anna should stay and continue to care for you during the holidays."

"Nonsense, Wesley. Trudy and Jenny are perfectly able to take care of my needs for a week or so. Anna needs some time away. She has seemed rather distracted lately."

Wesley could not deny this. Every time he approached her, Anna seemed to have a far away look on her face, and she appeared to be making every attempt to avoid him. He had feared that she might be thinking about leaving her position and return home, possibly to that red-haired young man who had so wistfully watched the day they had left on the train. Wesley thought that maybe he didn't want Anna to return home for a visit because she might decide to stay. How could he stand it without her cheerful presence in the house?

Sighing, he paced over to the window and peered out. The stars sparkled brightly through the clear, cold air.

"That's not all, you know. I simply cannot take time away from the office right now to accompany her home, and I refuse to allow her to travel by herself. I have the Wainbridge trial coming up the first of the year, and I will need all the time between now and then to prepare."

Patricia looked at her son curiously, a spark of an idea beginning to form. Softly she spoke, "Wesley, if you truly believe that Anna must be escorted, then why not ask Simon to do so? I'm sure he would be glad to accompany her. He does seem rather fond of her."

A frown crossed Wesley's handsome face, providing confirmation to Patricia's cautious thoughts.

"Yes, I have noticed," he replied.

It was true. Simon seemed quite infatuated with his mother's companion to the point of finding excuses to enter the house at the times when Anna might be in the kitchen. Anna, however, seemed oblivious to Simon's admiration, treating him as she would treat an older brother.

Patricia threw out another comment intended to provoke further confirmation of her discovery.

"I think that Simon and Anna would make a nice couple, don't you? They are both kind and bright. It might be just a perfect match."

Wesley's jaw tightened and Patricia recognized the look. Was it true? Could her son be in love with Anna Svensen?

Suddenly Wesley turned and faced his mother.

"I will check with Simon tomorrow morning to see if he would be willing to spend Christmas accompanying Anna to West Bend. If he agrees, I will purchase tickets for them immediately."

He strode over and kissed his mother's forehead, then left the room.

"Oh Wesley," his mother breathed. "I do hope you will not find your heart broken."

Chapter Nineteen

Anna was thrilled at the prospect of visiting West Bend, if only for a few days. Simon had agreed to accompany her, and Wesley purchased the train tickets as he had promised his mother. It was decided that Anna and Simon would stay for two weeks before returning shortly after the start of the new year.

Before they left, Ian sat his son down to have a talk about Simon's feelings for Anna. Simon confessed that he fancied her, just as his parents had suspected. But after Ian had tactfully pointed out that it appeared that Wesley Smith might have feelings for Anna, Simon agreed that it would be best to seek a love interest elsewhere.

True, Simon had been disappointed at first, but he quickly remembered that young Katie McClure had been throwing him warm glances and friendly smiles after services each Sunday. In the good-natured way that he had, Simon shrugged off his disappointment, and decided to make a call at the McClure cottage as soon as he returned from West Bend.

The train ride to western Kansas seemed longer than Anna had remembered. Unlike the fear of the unknown she had felt on the way to Kansas City, this time Anna experienced great excitement and could hardly wait to see her family at the train station. During the trip, Anna told Simon about all of her family members, and about many of her West Bend friends as well, spending much time describing Tina Stevens.

It was nearly midnight when the train finally pulled into the station. Anna quickly scanned the platform and was disappointed to see no one waiting. However, as soon as she and Simon stepped out of the car carrying their small valises, Oscar and Christina opened the door of the station and embraced their daughter.

"Oh, Anna," Christina exclaimed, brushing her daughter's hair back from her face. "I am so happy to see you! You look so ... so grown up!"

Anna fought back the tears and hugged her mother and father again. Then, remembering her manners, she introduced Simon. The two men shook hands warmly, and Oscar led the family to the waiting wagon.

"Where are the others? I have been looking so forward to seeing them."

"My daughter, you are forgetting what time it is," Oscar replied, chuckling. "They had to go to sleep. But do not worry, they have many plans for you tomorrow."

Anna smiled, basking in her parents' love.

By the time they arrived at the homestead, Anna and Simon could barely keep their eyes open. Oscar unhitched the horses while Christina took the pair in and led Simon to the boys' room at the back of the shanty where a cot had been prepared for him.

Anna fell into bed beside Elsie, who had taken to sleeping in Anna's old spot in the main room. The small girl stirred, and Anna drew her close, reveling in the familiar scent of her sister's hair. Anna fell asleep with a smile on her face, thankful to be in the warm surroundings she had missed so much.

The next day dawned clear and bright, and Anna awoke to Elsie shaking her shoulders.

"Anna, Anna! Hurry and wake up! It's morning!"

Anna opened her eyes sleepily and smiled at her sister. Elsie quickly wrapped her arms around Anna's neck and gave her a tight squeeze.

"I am so glad you are home, Anna," Elsie said, drawing back. "The yellow barn cat, you remember her, well, she had kittens just last week. I can't wait until you see them, and Mama and I have been baking for days, and we have planned a big feast for Christmas Day. Miss Stevens is coming, and Papa said we could cut a Christmas tree today . . . ."

"Elsie, please! Wait until I sit up," Anna laughed at her sister's exuberance.

"Oh, Anna, I'm so glad you are home!'

Elsie threw her arms around Anna's shoulders again, bringing tears of joy to her sister's eyes.

"Well, I can see that the sleepy heads have finally decided to wake up."

From the stove across the room, Christina turned and smiled at her daughters.

"The boys have been awake for quite some time already. Simon left with them to help with the morning chores."

Christina turned back to the pot she was stirring at the stove. Anna took a deep breath and sighed contentedly as she savored the warm aromas emanating from the kitchen.

"That Simon does seem to be a nice young man," Christina said, continuing with her stirring. "So kind and willing to help."

"Yes," Anna nodded, rising and reaching for her clothes. "His whole family is that way. The McNeils have been so wonderful to me."

Anna reflected on this as she quickly changed into one of the simple dresses she had brought. Often, if it had not been for Trudy's reassurance or Jenny's friendly smile, Anna would have been tempted to give into her frustrations with Patricia Smith and leave the household. The McNeils prayed for her, too, Anna knew.

As she bustled about the kitchen, Christina listened for evidence that there was more to Anna's feelings for Simon McNeil than mere friendliness. Lately, in her daughter's weekly letters, Christina had noticed a certain wistfulness, a longing that did not become apparent until one had reread the letters several times. Was this longing associated with the young man who had accompanied Anna home?

Christina did not have time to ponder the question long because soon the Svensen men and Simon entered the small home, joking and laughing and hungry for breakfast. Christina was glad for Anna's quick hands while finishing up the simple meal.

After a short but heartfelt prayer by Oscar, the family and their guest devoured the porridge and warm muffins. Plans were soon made to harness the horses to the wagon so that the whole family could go in search of the perfect tree to decorate the family's home. The previous Christmas, due to Elsie's grave illness and the dangerous winter storm, the Svensens had gone without a tree or much of a celebration of any kind. Christina and Oscar had already spoken and decided that although money continued to be tight, they would find a way to celebrate the birth of God's son this year.

Dishes were quickly washed, dried, and put away, and the Svensens and Simon bundled up, looking forward to the adventure of finding a tree. Pine trees were not plentiful on the Kansas prairie, but a selection could be found by the river winding close to West Bend. The group sang Christmas carols all the way to the river, including many in their native language. Simon could not help but be impressed by the way the Svensens' voices harmonized naturally, especially Anna's and Christina's.

By the time the family returned home late that morning, tree in tow, everyone was chilled and ready for a hearty meal of venison stew and fresh bread. The rest of the afternoon was spent finding decorations for the tree among the bits of lace and paper Elsie, Bjorn, and Joseph had brought from school. Anna reveled in the warmth of her family. That night, before she fell asleep, she did not forget to ask God to shower extra blessings on Patricia Smith for encouraging this unexpected visit.

The next day, Christmas Eve, was spent feverishly finishing the baking and last minute gift wrapping. Anna had accompanied Trudy McNeil on her weekly shopping trip one Thursday afternoon to purchase a small gift for each of her family members. She had been awed by the selection of merchandise available in the Kansas City shops, but she was also shocked at the high prices. Finally, after much deliberation, she had made her purchases, and she now placed the wrapped articles under the tree.

The West Bend church had planned a special Christmas Eve service, so the Svensens and Simon ate an early supper and then loaded into the wagon. Upon arriving, Anna was thrilled to find her brother, Aaron, waiting for her by the door. She embraced him warmly, and then noticed that his friend, Minnie, hung back, waiting for him.

"I am sitting with her family tonight," Aaron whispered to his sister. "Then I will be taking her home after the service. We have something to discuss."

Aaron simply beamed as he smiled at his sister, and tears of joy filled Anna's eyes.

"Oh, Aaron," Anna breathed. "I'm so happy for you both! You will be at home tomorrow for Christmas dinner, won't you?"

Aaron assured her that he would, then hurried off to be seated with the Johannsens.

Soon the service began and Anna felt uplifted as she heard the words of the familiar and well-loved Christmas story. Candlelight threw a soft glow across the congregation as voices rose in song.

"This night is nearly perfect," Anna thought. "If only I could share this with . . . ."

Thoughts of her employer crowded into Anna's mind. Shaking her head slightly, she vowed to try to push such thoughts away. Wesley Smith would always be out of reach for someone like her. She needed to just concentrate on all the blessings she did have in her life. Anna lifted her face, closed her eyes, and joined in the singing.

Anna's few days at home flew by quickly. Christmas Day was joy-filled, with Aaron sharing the news that he and Minnie were planning to marry in June. Tina Stevens came for dinner, and she and Anna were able to sneak away that afternoon for a few hours of walking and shared confidences.

"It's only a few months now," Miss Stevens breathed, clutching Anna's arm tightly. "Samuel's letters are filled with plans."

The teacher stopped walking and looked into the distance.

"Samuel has received his assignment. As soon as we are married, we will be traveling to New Mexico. We are to start a new church on the reservation near Taos."

Anna turned to her teacher in surprise.

"But . . . that is so far . . . will it be safe?"

The young teacher chuckled. "We really had wanted to be sent overseas, to South America, or maybe even to China, but this will be a good start."

She looked wistfully into the distance.

"I have been given permission to start a school there, for the children. They had one a few years back, but it folded when the last minister and his wife left. Oh, Anna, I'll still get to teach!"

Anna hugged her friend and the pair turned to make their way back to the shanty. A thought struck Anna as they were walking.

"Who will be the teacher here, then?"

"Well," Miss Stevens began, "the board has been sending letters inquiring about replacements. So far, they haven't heard any news. I've been praying about the situation."

Anna nodded and mentally added this concern to her lengthy prayer list. Tina Stevens stopped walking and touched Anna's shoulder.

"Would you be interested, Anna? I mean, I know you still have this term to complete, and then you would need some further training, but I'm sure the board would be willing to waive some of that training upon my recommendation and that of some of the parents."

Anna paused and thought about the proposal. She had to admit that she had considered teaching as a possible career, but one that would be sometime in the future. She knew that she had work to finish with Mrs. Smith. In addition, there were her feelings for Wesley . . . .

"I would love to teach . . . but in the future. I have responsibilities to my employer now."

During the rest of their walk, Anna explained the progress that Patricia Smith had made. She shared the frustrations and joys she had experienced throughout the long fall. Before Tina Stevens had left that day, Anna had a new stack of lessons to complete as well a sense of peace about the choices she had made.

After Christmas Day, the rest of Anna's two-week visit seemed to fly. Although she did spend several hours helping her mother with chores, Anna also found time to visit some of her friends from school, including Mary Richards. Anna chose an afternoon when she knew that Michael would be busy with farm work so that the chance of seeing Mary's brother would be slim.

The bouncy redhead seemed a little cool at first, but soon the girls were talking and laughing much as they had during school breaks the year before. Just before Anna got ready to leave, Mary grew serious and confronted Anna.

"You broke Michael's heart, Anna, when you turned down his proposal."

Anna nodded and sympathized with her friend. She knew how she felt when any of her brothers were hurt.

"I love Michael as a friend, a dear friend," Anna said. "But my feelings . . . they are not any deeper than that. It would be wrong to make promises I did not believe were based on truth."

Mary looked down and wiped her eyes.

"It's just that he was so sad afterwards. And when you left, well, we didn't think he would ever start acting like himself again."

Anna felt a stab of pain as she sat with Mary, but then her friend brightened some.

"I think he is starting to feel better now."

She leaned forward, conspiratorially.

"He has been calling Esther Nelson. Her family homesteads by Leeds, north of West Bend? Well, it takes nearly two hours to get to her father's place, but Michael has visited her twice already."

Anna sighed with relief. She had been praying that Michael would find someone with whom to share his life. It came as a surprise, then, when Anna heard a familiar knock the evening before she and Simon were to return to Kansas City. She hesitated, and then opened the door to find Michael Richards.

She smiled at him, genuinely glad to see him, and she invited him inside. After a few moments of visiting with her parents and joking with Elsie, Michael turned to Anna and asked if she would like to go for a short walk.

Anna nodded and dressed warmly, throwing an extra shawl around her coat and winding a woolen muffler around her neck. The January night, while unusually mild, was still quite cool.

When she had seen Michael at the door, Anna had feared the worst. Would the young man be back to discuss marriage? But she soon felt comfortable in his presence as they chatted like old friends do, speaking of both his work and hers. They paused by the creek, close to where they had stopped the summer before when Michael had proposed.

Michael turned to look at Anna in the moonlight. Although he had tried hard to push her from his thoughts these last few months, he still found her achingly beautiful.

"I wanted to speak with you to see if you changed your mind any about . . . well, about what we talked about last summer."

"No, I have not, Michael." She took a breath and continued. "I still think of you as a dear friend. One whom I do love, but like a brother. I cannot see that my feelings on this will change."

It was the answer Michael had been expecting to hear, yet he still had to know.

"All right," he said, his jaw tightening. "You see, there is someone else I've been seeing. She's sweet and kind and . . . well, before I went any further with her, I had to know . . . ."

Anna touched his arm. "I am sorry, Michael."

Surprisingly, the young man turned to her and smiled.

Oh, it's all right. I've been expecting the answer you gave. I just thought I'd give it one more try."

The pair ambled back to the house chatting amicably the whole way. After tipping his hat to Anna and saying a quick goodnight to her parents, Michael rode off in the moonlight. Anna closed the door, glad that Michael would remain her friend, yet choose to seek love somewhere else.

She did not notice Simon, who was sitting in the corner reading to Elsie, as he examined her face when she returned. Had his father been wrong? Was Anna not in love with her employer, Wesley Smith, as they all suspected, but instead, actually pining over this red-haired young man?

Chapter Twenty

All too soon, Anna's parents again made the early morning trek to the train station. Once again she cried as she left her parents, but this time, she found herself looking forward to seeing Patricia Smith, and although she tried not to think about it, Wesley, too.

When they arrived at the Smith mansion late that evening, Anna expressed her gratefulness to Simon for accompanying her on her visit.

"It was my pleasure, Anna. You've got a good family. I enjoyed myself."

With a smile and a tip of his hat, the young Irishman swung off to join his family, and Anna entered the darkened mansion. Unlike the first time she arrived after a long train journey, this time Anna knew exactly how to navigate the darkened halls and find her bedroom. Exhausted from the journey, she fell into bed and immediately into a deep sleep.

She awoke with a calmness tinged with excitement the next morning. She had missed her daily time with Patricia Smith more than she had anticipated, and she harbored a slight hope that she might greet Wesley before he left for work.

During her time with her family in West Bend, Anna had not had much time to think of Wesley or her feelings for him. Before she left she had hoped to find a way to rid herself of what she had decided was a silly school girl crush. But arriving back at his home, she found her thoughts turning to the handsome attorney even more.

"Good morning, Mrs. Smith," Anna said cheerfully, entering the woman's room after getting dressed.

"Oh, Anna, how good to see you! Did you have a nice Christmas?"

Anna paused by the door and examined the woman reclining in the bed. Although still quite thin, Patricia Smith stood out in stark contrast to the woman Anna had seen in the bed several months earlier. This woman had a smile on her face and small spots of color in her cheeks. Joy caused tears to form behind Anna's eyes.

"It was quite wonderful, thank you, Mrs. Smith. It was good to see my family and my friends once again."

"I'm so glad to hear that. But I must say, I am glad you are back. I have some exciting news to share with you."

Anna walked forward and sat on the edge of the bed, looking at the older woman curiously. Never had she seen Patricia Smith in such high spirits. The older woman reached out and took Anna's two hands into her own.

"I've found your God, Anna. I asked his forgiveness for all of my sins, and I asked him to come into my life. I feel truly changed."

This time Anna let the tears fall unabatedly down her cheeks. After only a moment's hesitation, she gathered Patricia Smith in her arms.

"Oh, Mrs. Smith, I'm so happy for you. I have been praying about this!"

"So have I," a deep voice said from the doorway.

Anna released her hold on Patricia and turned to see Wesley leaning against the door.

"Well," said the older woman, resting her head back into the pillows, "I suppose it was bound to happen then. After all, how could the prayers of two such stubborn people be ignored?"

All three laughed. Wesley strode into the room and sat on the side of his mother's bed opposite Anna. Patricia Smith looked from one to the other.

"Seriously, I feel truly blessed to have the love of two such caring people."

Anna smiled at her, and then glanced at Wesley. She felt her cheeks grow warm as she saw him gazing intently at her.

After what seemed like only a moment longer, Wesley stood and said, "I must be getting to work. I have a trial starting tomorrow, and I have much to do to prepare today."

He stood and was gone. Anna breathed a quiet sigh, feeling relief that he had left, yet at the same time, feeling bereft. With a trial taking place during the next few weeks, she supposed Wesley would not be around the house very often. Shaking off these thoughts, she stood and remembered all that she had to be thankful for.

"I'll go and get our breakfast, Mrs. Smith, and you can tell me the story of when you decided to accept God's promise."

"Thank you, my dear," Patricia Smith responded as Anna left the room.

After Anna had closed the door, Patricia Smith smiled and murmured to herself, "I must get those two to recognize their feelings for one another. Somehow, there must be a way."

Although Anna continued to be busy during the next several weeks, it was a different kind of activity that occupied her time. Instead of following a series of commands given by her employer, Anna now spent many hours a day just talking with her, listening to stories of Patricia's earlier life. They also continued to read the Bible together, and both women discussed the passages freely. Every day Patricia seemed to grow stronger and more animated, and every day Anna gave thanks for the change in the older woman.

True to his word, Wesley was absent from his home often during January. When Anna did catch glimpses of him, he seemed preoccupied, poring over papers on his desk or silently eating in the kitchen. Anna continued to try to push thoughts of Wesley from her mind, but she often found her thoughts turning in just his direction, especially when Patricia would tell stories of his childhood.

Anna and Patricia were housebound most of the month. Heavy snows and a bitter cold snap kept most Kansas City residents behind doors that winter. By the time February arrived, both women restlessly longed to spend some time outside.

Finally, in the middle of the month, a warm front passed through and melted nearly all of the snow. Temperatures rose to a bearable degree, and Anna and Patricia bundled up and resumed going outside for a few minutes each day.

Patricia had begun taking small steps around her room at the end of January, although she still needed help climbing and descending the stairs. Her legs were unsteady at first, due to their long disuse, but with help, she learned to navigate the room. The doctor said if she continued to exercise daily, she should be able to regain full use of her legs.

With Mrs. Smith making few demands on her time, Anna quickly completed her final lessons toward earning her high school diploma. In the middle of March, Anna received a letter from Tina Stevens stating that all requirements had been completed. Much to her surprise, Anna felt a heavy sadness when she read the letter. Although excited to have finished school and met a long-term goal, she enjoyed her studies and wondered how she would fill her time.

A growing and disturbing thought began to blossom in her mind. With Mrs. Smith's newfound independence and faith, there really was no need for Anna to remain in the Smith household. Trudy and Jenny could easily handle the domestic chores. When spring came, she would return home. She could no longer continue to take money from the Smiths when her services were obviously not needed any more.

By the end of March, the remaining snows had melted and a few brave crocuses poked their heads through the damp soil in the Smith's garden. Ian and Simon were kept busy during the day turning the soil and planning the plantings for the coming year, in addition to tending the horses and making repairs to the house.

Inside the house, Trudy and Jenny had begun the spring cleaning early. The unexpectedly severe winter had everyone yearning for spring and warmer temperatures.

With her studies finished and Mrs. Smith beginning to take over more of her personal care, Anna had much time to lend a hand to Jenny and Trudy's efforts. Together the three laughed and shared many a story as they swept down walls, scrubbed cabinets and beat rugs in the fresh but still chilly air.

One day, when Jenny had been sent to the market to pick up a few supplies, Anna helped Trudy clean the pantry. Trudy handed the many jars of preserves and canned fruits and vegetables to Anna who carefully dusted and then stacked them on the kitchen counter. It was during a break that afternoon that Anna decided to confide in her friend.

"Trudy, I think that it is time for me to return home," she said, stirring her cup of tea.

Trudy set down her own mug and looked at Anna thoughtfully.

"The missus does seem to be better," she said. "She doesn't need much tending any more."

Anna nodded, then added, "Mrs. Smith told me yesterday that she would like to begin coming downstairs to take her meals as soon as she can climb the stairs by herself."

Trudy smiled at Anna.

"You have been so good for her, my dear. And these past few days you have been such a help to Jenny and I. I would so hate to see you leave."

Anna smiled back, feeling tears press against her eyes.

"I will hate to go," she said. "But I do not feel it is right to stay longer."

She paused and took a deep breath.

"Mr. Smith brought me here to care for his mother. This is why I earn my salary. His mother does not need my care anymore, so I should not keep accepting his money."

Trudy nodded her understanding, yet she could not help but notice the pain in Anna's face. How much of that pain was due to leaving Wesley Smith?

"You must do what your heart tells you is right," Trudy said. If you pray about it, and you still believe that you should leave, then you must. But you should talk it over with Wesley first."

"Yes," Anna nodded her agreement. The idea of speaking directly to Wesley brought butterflies to her stomach, but she knew it must be done. She would look for the first opportunity to speak to him.

Much to Anna's surprise, she didn't have to look for an opportunity after all. That evening, as she shared dinner with Patricia in her room, Wesley entered after knocking softly.

"Good evening, Mother, Miss Svensen," he said, nodding his head in Anna's direction.

"Good evening, Wesley," Patricia said, motioning for Wesley to sit beside her on the bed. "Can you join us for dinner?"

Wesley smiled and Anna could not help but notice how tired he looked. Dark circles formed under his eyes, and he seemed a bit paler than usual. She felt a surge of concern, but attempted to not let her feelings show.

"Thank you, but I already ate with Trudy and Ian. I've spoken with Dr. Bronson, and he says you are making wonderful progress."

"Yes," Patricia said, leaning back and pushing away her now-empty tray. "I am going to attempt the stairs tomorrow. I just have to work up a little bit more nerve."

She glanced at Anna.

"I would like to put it off another few weeks, but Anna won't rest until she sees me up and about and walking in the garden."

Anna smiled fondly at Patricia, knowing now that her stern manner was all in jest.

Wesley regarded the two women with love. How often he had hoped, as he became aware of his feelings, that his mother could grow to love Anna as much as he did. Now, it seemed as though his wishes had come true. If only . . . if only he could tell Anna how he felt.

He watched as she lifted the tray from his mother's lap and brushed a few crumbs from the blankets. He noted the care she exhibited with his mother, and an idea began to form in his mind. Deciding he had nothing to lose, Wesley reached out his hand and brushed Anna's shoulder.

Startled by the warmth of his hand, Anna nearly dropped the tray. She turned and looked into his eyes.

"Yes?" The word came out as more of a gasp.

"I was wondering . . . ."

Wesley dropped his hand looked at the carpet, and then back at Anna. "I was wondering if you would accompany me to dinner tomorrow night. That is . . . I mean . . . if Mother can spare you ... the trial is over . . . and . . . and . . . there are some issues we should discuss."

"Of course, I can spare her," Patricia inserted. "Tomorrow night I will eat in the kitchen, with the McNeils. It will be a fitting tribute to celebrate my first attempt at managing the stairs."

"Fine, then," Wesley said, his gaze not breaking away from Anna's face. "Shall you be ready at say, six-thirty? We'll take the buggy so as not to inconvenience Simon."

Dumbly, Anna could only nod. Was Wesley Smith asking her for a date?

"All right. I'll see you tomorrow night. Goodnight, Mother."

He leaned down and kissed Patricia's cheek.

"Goodnight, Wesley," she replied, not missing the visible tension between the two young people in her presence.

Anna floated through the rest of her duties that evening without really realizing what she was doing. She returned the tray to the kitchen, nodding and smiling when Ian said something to her that she didn't even hear. She listened attentively as Mrs. Smith read a chapter of a novel they had started earlier in the week. As she had improved, Patricia had begun to read on her own again, and often she and Anna would take turns reading in the evenings.

Finally, after forty-five minutes of reading, Patricia laid the book aside and regarded the younger woman. Anna had sat almost silent during the entire evening, staring into the distance. Patricia had little doubt that Anna was thinking about Wesley's abrupt invitation. Wanting to be kind, Patricia feigned a fatigue she did not feel, and sent Anna to her room early.

Back in her room, however, Anna was unable to sleep. She paced the floor restlessly, occasionally stopping to glance out the window at the full moon outside.

Anna's thoughts troubled her. Why had Wesley invited her to dinner? Would he ask her to leave now that his mother was well on her way to recovery? Is that why he had been looking so tired and worn lately? Could he no longer afford her salary, a salary which Anna had always believed to be more than generous?

After several hours of pacing the room and worrying, Anna made a decision. She would not force Wesley Smith into the position of asking her to leave. After all, that would surely hurt his pride as well as her own. Before he had a chance to let her go, she would tell him that she planned to leave. Commencement exercises in West Bend would be taking placed in three weeks. Anna would ask to be released from employment in time to attend the ceremonies. Exhausted and sad, she finally drifted into a troubled sleep.

Down the hall, Wesley Smith, too, had difficulty trying to sleep. He had surprised himself by inviting Anna to dinner, yet he felt relieved to have done so. He had seen the way Anna had been watching his mother lately, with joy at Patricia's progress, yet sadness in her own eyes.

"She is planning to leave," Wesley thought. "I must tell her of my feelings before she goes. As ridiculous as it may seem to her, I must tell her."

On impulse, he had invited Anna to dinner, and now he had to make sure that every detail was perfect. Soon after issuing the invitation, Wesley had decided to make reservations at the Caldridge Hotel, one of the nicest places to eat in the city. He wanted to treat Anna like royalty, to tell her how much she had brought into the life of his mother and into his own. To ask her to stay, not because Patricia needed her any longer, but because he needed her. Maybe even to ask her to be his wife. Finally, towards dawn, Wesley felt sleep coming on, and he laid down, still mulling over the plans for that evening.

Chapter Twenty-One

Anna awoke with a strange energy considering the small amount of sleep she had gotten. She believed the energy came from the decision she had made. Tonight, she would tell Wesley Smith that she would be leaving his employment. As hard as it would be to leave Patricia Smith and the McNeils, Anna felt certain her decision was the right one. She could no longer, in good conscience, accept money for completing a job that didn't need to be done.

When Anna entered Patricia's bedroom that morning she found Patricia already awake and gazing in her closet. Patricia had made her own bed and was dressed. Several colorful dresses lay draped across the bed, and Anna wondered what had gotten into the woman.

"Oh, there you are," Patricia exclaimed, turning as she heard Anna's soft knock and then footsteps entering the bedroom. "I've just been going through my closet. I . . . ."

At a sudden loss for words, she stopped. Anna waited expectantly.

"Well," the older woman continued, "I thought maybe you might want to borrow a dress for this evening. Wesley mentioned this morning that he planned to take you to the Caldridge, and it's frightfully fancy. I just thought that maybe you might like to wear something . . . something new."

Anna blushed and looked down at the plain calico dress she had on. Although Wesley did pay her a handsome salary, she had spent little of it on clothing, choosing instead to send most of her paycheck home. It bothered Anna to think that Patricia thought Wesley might be embarrassed by her appearance.

"I planned on wearing my gray wool," Anna muttered softly. "You know, the one I wear to services on Sunday."

"Yes . . . yes," Patricia said, a slight frown crossing her face.

"That dress is quite nice and serviceable. I just thought it might be fun to try something new. There isn't time to go shopping, and you are close to my size, or the size I used to be...."

She let her voice trail off as she noticed Anna's embarrassment. She stepped to her bed and sat down, pushing the dresses aside and patting the mattress beside her to indicate that Anna, too, should sit.

"I don't for a minute want you to think that your clothes aren't acceptable, Anna," Patricia said. "I just wanted this to be a special time for you and Wesley. I thought a different dress might just make the occasion that much more meaningful."

Anna looked into the face she had grown to love and gave Patricia a hug. She was going to miss her dreadfully.

"Oh, thank you. I was afraid you might think that I would embarrass Mr. Smith if I wore my own clothes."

Patricia pulled back and looked intently into Anna's eyes.

"My dear," she said, brushing the wisps of hair away from Anna's face, much as Christina would do. "Never be afraid to be who you are. Nothing you do would embarrass me or, I suspect, Wesley. You have brought light and a tremendous joy into this house. I cannot tell you what that means to me."

The two women hugged tightly again, each one quietly praising God for the gift of the other.

Later that day, Patricia descended the stairs without aid for the noon meal. She didn't even appear breathless, but instead, greeted the waiting Anna, Trudy, and Jenny with a wide smile.

Although Anna rejoiced with her employer over the accomplishments, Patricia's ease in handling the stairs just strengthened Anna's resolve to leave.

After lunch, Patricia retired to her bedroom for a nap, and Anna also rested. Although she had slept little the previous night, Anna found she could not close her eyes. She spent most of the afternoon in prayer, asking God to help her find the words to announce her resignation to Wesley without breaking down and crying in front of him. Being convinced that Wesley planned to tell her that she was no longer needed in the Smith household, Anna also prayed for the ability to save him the embarrassment of having to fire her.

She owed him much, Anna thought, and she thanked God for what the Smith family had provided. Due to her position and her regular paychecks, Anna's family had been able to hold on to their farm another year. Her parents had added an extra room onto their house, and her father had replaced all of the remaining livestock that had been lost in the blizzard. Also, Aaron had saved enough to marry Minnie, and their wedding was planned for the first Sunday in July.

"Yes," Anna thought, rising from her knees to prepare for her evening, "God has been good. I need to be thankful."

Yet, as she rose, Anna couldn't help but feel the tears press heavy against her eyes. How was she to leave these people whom she had come to love? And most of all, how was she going to leave Wesley when her heart cried out to have him hold her in his arms?

By 5:30 p.m., Anna had dressed, and she knocked softly on Patricia's door.

"Anna? Come in."

As the young woman entered the room, Patricia set down the book she had been reading and gasped.

"Oh, Anna! You are simply a vision!"

"Thank you, Mrs. Smith. It is surely the dress . . . such a beautiful color."

She smoothed the soft skirt with her hands. Made of royal blue silk brocade, the dress was the most elegant piece of clothing that Anna had ever worn. When Patricia had pulled it out of her closet that morning, both women had agreed upon the selection at once. Upon slipping into it, Anna had been surprised at the near perfect fit.

"Yes, the dress is lovely," Patricia said, standing up, "but so is the person wearing it. Look."

She guided Anna to the full-length mirror next to the closet. Anna gazed in surprise at her reflection. Was that truly her?

Surely the person staring back at her was another woman, more sophisticated and refined.

"I think these will do nicely," Patricia said, stepping behind Anna and holding up a pair of pearl drop earrings.

"Oh, I have borrowed enough already, Mrs. Smith," Anna protested.

"Nonsense. I always put these on when I wore that dress. They complement each other nicely."

Patricia clipped the earrings to Anna's lobes. Anna moved her head slightly from side to side, feeling the earrings sway.

"I have never worn earrings before," she said, giggling a little. "They feel so heavy."

"Oh, you'll get used to them soon enough."

Patricia turned and walked back to the table where her book lay. Anna looked so beautiful in the blue dress. She couldn't help remembering the last time she had worn it, just a few weeks before her husband had . . . .

There was no sense in thinking of that now. Patricia Smith shook her head a little. Yes, she had many lovely memories of the past, but there would be much to look forward too, also. Patricia closed her eyes and said a quick prayer, thanking God once again for sending Anna, and asking Him to be her strength when the sadness crept in.

"Mrs. Smith? Are you feeling all right?"

The older woman smiled at the younger one.

"I'm fine, dear, just fine. As a matter of fact, I'm feeling quite hungry. I think I am ready to go downstairs and see what Trudy has conjured up for dinner."

Anna smiled and the two women traveled down the stairs. Patricia seemed even more confident with the staircase than she had earlier in the day.

When they entered the kitchen, Trudy was bent over the oven, peering into intently.

"Something smells wonderful in here," Patricia said, closing her eyes.

"Oh, my! You startled me!"

Trudy turned, then dropped her jaw in surprise upon seeing Anna.

"Could this be our little Anna?" she asked, drawing closer.

Anna smiled and turned in a circle for inspection.

"Simply beautiful!" Trudy exclaimed. "I am certain that Wesley will have the most beautiful date in the restaurant tonight."

Again, Anna flushed under her friend's compliment.

"Did I hear my name? Surely you ladies aren't talking about me?"

In unison, the women turned to see Wesley enter the kitchen with a teasing glint in his eyes. He took in Anna's appearance appreciatively.

"We were just speaking about how Anna will turn the heads of everyone in the room tonight," Patricia said, moving to stand by her son and then reaching up to kiss his cheek. "Although I must admit, you look quite handsome yourself."

Anna had been having the same thought. Decked out in a black suit that set off his dark hair and eyes, Anna thought Wesley had never looked more attractive. When he smiled at his mother's compliment, Anna thought her heart would melt.

"Thank you, Mother," Wesley said, kissing her in return. "Are you ready, Anna? It's a little early, but I thought we might ride through the park on the way to the restaurant. It is a lovely evening."

Anna nodded, not trusting her voice.

"Fine. I'll bring the buggy around to the front. Goodnight, Mother," he said, and then vanished out the kitchen door.

"Well, have a wonderful time, my dear," Patricia said, selecting a chair from those placed around the kitchen table. "I believe I'll stay right here and visit with Trudy."

Anna nodded again.

"Do you want me to check on you when I return?"

"Oh, no. That won't be necessary. Stay out as late as you want. I'm sure Trudy or Jenny can help me back up the stairs, if I need help, that is."

On an impulse, Anna rushed over and pecked her employer's cheek. She then turned, and practically ran from the room.

After she had left and Trudy had turned back to her dishes on the stove, Patricia said thoughtfully, "I wonder if those two young people will have any news for us tomorrow."

Trudy turned and smiled at her employer and friend.

"I was a wonderin' if only I had noticed the sparks flyin' between those two."

"Oh, they've been apparent to me for a while now," Patricia said, then softly added, "I only wonder if they are aware of the feelings themselves."

Chapter Twenty-Two

Anna had not been waiting long on the side steps in front of the house when Wesley pulled the buggy up. Unlike the carriage, the buggy held only two people, and Anna was keenly aware of Wesley's presence after he helped settle her beside him.

"Are you warm enough?" he asked. "I have a lap blanket here if you need it."

"Oh, no, I am fine. It is a lovely evening."

"Yes," Wesley paused for a moment gazing at the evening sky, and then gently snapped the reins. The horses seemed to respond to his smallest gesture, and Anna noticed how at ease Wesley seemed to be with guiding the buggy. She remembered when she first saw him riding a horse, trotting briskly up to her parents' shanty to discuss plans for her employment.

"May I inquire about your thoughts?" Wesley said, guiding the horses down the long drive and onto the city street.

Anna flushed and became flustered. She couldn't tell him that she had been remembering how fine he looked on a horse.

"I was just thinking . . . about how many good horses you have."

She pointed at the bay pulling the buggy.

"That is a beautiful horse, so large and strong. My father would say he comes from good stock."

Wesley chuckled.

"My father would say the same thing. He probably did, in fact, say it many times. That is Rex, one of my father's favorite horses."

Anna worked up enough nerve to glance sideways at her companion, who seemed lost in thought.

"My father loved horses. I've sold many of his horses in the past few months because . . . well, because I simply haven't had enough time to ride them all, and Mother, well . . . you know."

Anna nodded.

"But I've kept a few. Rex, here, and my saddle horse, and Tessie and Claire, the two that pull the carriage and the wagon when Trudy and Ian go for supplies."

Wesley paused again, thoughtfully.

"I just haven't seemed to have enough time to enjoy the horses like Father used too."

Anna nodded again, and turned her gaze outside the buggy. The pair rode in companionable silence through the tree-lined streets. Anna soaked in the sights. Having been pretty much restricted to the Smith household and the church she attended with the McNeils during her stay in Kansas City, Anna enjoyed seeing more of the city than she had since she arrived.

"Would you mind if we take a turn through Swope Park?" Wesley asked, breaking into her thoughts.

"Oh, could we? I'd love to see it!"

Wesley felt a stab of guilt. The young woman beside him had been dreadfully cooped up since coming into his employment. Why hadn't he thought about seeing that she got out more often to take in some of the beauty of this city he loved so much? Of course, Wesley knew the answer to his question. He hadn't trusted himself around Anna; he was afraid his feelings for her might become obvious, and it would surely have been inappropriate to let her explore the city on her own. Although, he realized, Simon would have been glad to accompany her.

Wesley smiled wryly to himself. Of course, that would have been unacceptable, too. No, he had been too selfish where Anna was concerned. He had not wanted to share her with anyone else, yet he hadn't see to it that she had been properly exposed to the city while under his care either. Well, that was about to change.

Anna's contented sigh broke into Wesley's thoughts.

"It is so lovely here," she murmured, her gaze soaking in the trees and the flower beds where daffodils were blooming in the rain-softened ground.

"Yes, I've always loved the park. We had many picnics here when I was a child."

He proceeded to tell her about the park's history. Anna listened intently, becoming so engrossed in the story that she hardly noticed when they left the park and turned onto a street no longer containing houses, but lined instead with stores and offices. She loved to hear the cadences in Wesley' voice, to watch his strong jaw move.

She had allowed herself to relax, just a little, when she felt the buggy stop. They had pulled up in front of a hotel with wide glass doors and smart brick walls. A man wearing a gray flannel coat and hat trimmed with red braid and gold buttons stepped forward.

"May I take your buggy, sir?" he asked.

"Yes, please," Wesley replied.

The doorman approached Anna's side of the buggy and held out his hand. It took her only a moment to realize that he was waiting to help her step down.

Blushing, she accepted his help, and stepped onto the wide wooden sidewalk. Gas lamps lit the front of the building, and Anna was admiring them when she sensed, rather than felt, Wesley's presence at her side.

"Shall we?"

Wesley offered his arm and Anna shyly placed her hand though it. Together they stepped through the hotel's wide doors. Once inside, Anna blinked her eyes rapidly. It was not overly bright outside, but the only light inside the hotel came from the soft glow of the candles setting on the tables.

"Welcome, Mr. Smith."

Anna saw a man dressed in a neat black suit approach from the middle of the room.

"Good evening, Gerald, I have a reservation."

"Very good, sir. Right this way."

Wesley stood and let Anna follow the maitre d' past several tables to a small alcove near a fireplace.

"Will this suffice, Mr. Smith?"

"Yes, this will be fine."

Gerald stepped to one side and pulled a chair away from the table. Only after Wesley motion to her to sit did Anna realize that he had pulled the chair out for her. Embarrassed, she sat quickly and smiled her thanks.

"Thomas will be with you soon, Mr. Smith. Would you like anything to drink while you wait?"

Wesley glanced at Anna, then replied. "I believe we'll just have water, thank you, Gerald."

The man nodded slightly, and then disappeared.

Anna let her gaze trail around the room. Although she had, on occasion, been in hotels and restaurants before, including the one in Salina when she first came to Kansas City, never had she witnessed such finery. From their table she could catch a glimpse of the lobby where smartly dressed guests were checking in for the evening underneath crystal chandeliers. In one corner of the room, a string trio played soft music. And their own table was covered by a while linen cloth with a single red rose in a crystal vase serving as a centerpiece. Everywhere candlelight glowed, casting soft shadows on the luxurious scene.

After spending several minutes contemplating her surroundings, Anna became aware of Wesley's gaze.

"Is it to your liking?" he asked, a smile in his voice.

"Oh, very much so. I have never seen any place so . . . so beautiful before."

Wesley's eyes traveled around the room.

"Yes, it is beautiful. But not nearly as beautiful as my guest this evening."

Anna lowered her eyes.

"Thank you," she murmured, then busied herself spreading the linen napkin on her lap.

At that moment, much to Anna's relief, the waiter came. Wesley, having evidently frequented the restaurant before, suggested that she try the prime rib. Because she had been overwhelmed by the number of choices available on the menu, Anna gratefully accepted his suggestion.

After the waiter left, Wesley continued to talk, relating humorous stories about his mother and father and his own early years. Anna warmed to the stories, not telling Wesley that she had heard many of them before from his mother and from the McNeils.

Soon their food arrived and Anna ate with relish, thinking that she had never tasted anything so delicious. As she smiled at the man across from her, she wished that the evening could continue, that she would not have to find a way to tell him that she was leaving.

As they neared the end of their meal, Anna noticed that the string trio had been joined by a pianist. Several of the tables near the musicians had been removed, and three or four couples were dancing.

Wesley followed her gaze to the dance floor. He, too, had been enjoying the evening tremendously, even to the point of eating slowly as to make his time alone with Anna last. An idea formed in his head.

"Would you care to dance?" he asked, turning his gaze back to the young woman sitting across from him.

Anna looked in wonder at his question.

"Me? I would not know how. I have not learned to dance . . . not in that manner."

"Oh, it's easy, really."

Wesley stood and came around the table to stand next to her, offering his hand.

"All you have to do is follow me. I dance tolerably well, at least so I've been told."

Anna felt flustered. She did not want to embarrass herself in front of Wesley, nor in front of the well-dressed crowd in the restaurant. Still, they had been having such a nice time, and one dance couldn't hurt.

"All right then," she said, rising and flashing a smile. "But do not blame me if your toes are sore tomorrow."

Wesley chuckled as he led Anna across to the dance floor. After only a few minutes of awkward stumbling, Anna felt that she had the rhythm, and she and Wesley glided across the floor without too much trouble.

She relaxed into the dancing, feeling secure with Wesley's hand touching the small of her back, and her hand resting lightly on his shoulder. They danced three numbers straight, talking little.

After the third song ended, the musicians announced that they were taking a short break, and Wesley led Anna back to their table. Their plates had been cleared and fresh cups of coffee awaited them.

Feeling confident with the way the evening had progressed, Wesley decided the time had come to speak frankly with Anna about his feelings. Before beginning, he looked deeply into the eyes of the young woman across from him.

"There's something I must tell you, Anna," he began, his voice husky.

"Yes, I know," Anna interrupted. She had promised herself that she would not make Wesley Smith fire her, and she meant to keep that promise.

"You do?"

Wesley leaned back, blinking rapidly.

"Yes. I know that my services are no longer needed now that your mother is feeling so much better. There is no longer any reason for me to stay and continue taking your money. I have decided to leave at the end of this month."

Wesley felt a sharp pain in his temple.

"Well, there is no real reason to rush . . . ."

"It is all right," Anna set her chin firmly. "I have sent word to my parents that I will be home in time for graduation exercises at school."

"I see," Wesley said. "Have you discussed this with my mother?"

"No."

Anna bowed her head for a moment.

"I thought," she continued, "that because you had hired me that I should let you know first."

She paused, look at the man across from her. His face had grown dark and serious. Maybe he had wanted her to leave earlier, possibly as early as this week?

"Of course," she continued. "I could always leave sooner if you wanted me too. I could leave whenever the train schedule allows."

"That won't be necessary," Wesley responded. "Not unless you want to, of course. I think it will be important to Mother to get used to the idea of you being gone. She has come to enjoy your company so much."

His voice dropped to almost a whisper.

"As I have hers."

"What will you do when you return home?"

"Oh, there is plenty to do on the farm. There is always more work than there are hands to complete it. And our school teacher, Tina Stevens, is getting married soon. She won't be returning next year. I have thought . . . ."

Anna let her voice trail off.

"Yes?"

"I have thought of applying for her position. I don't have my teaching certificate, of course, but I think they might overlook that. It is often difficult to get teachers in rural Kansas."

"I see."

Wesley looked away for a moment, then forced his gaze back to hers.

"Will you get married?" It was a rude question, Wesley realized, and also quite brave, but he very much wanted to hear the answer.

Anna flushed deeply.

"I do not know . . . I hope to, someday."

Wesley nodded his head. So that was it. There was someone at home, waiting for her. Possibly it was the young man with red hair who had so forlornly watched the train leave West Bend last fall. Well, he couldn't stand between Anna and the man she loved.

"Well, if you are finished with your coffee, we should be getting home," he said, abruptly standing up.

Anna quickly followed him as he strode out of the restaurant, stopping only briefly at the entrance to pay their bill. They rode in silence most of the way back to the Smith mansion. Only when Wesley guided the buggy up the long driveway toward the house did he speak again.

"I'd appreciate it if you would inform Mother soon of your plans to leave."

"Yes, of course."

"It will be difficult for her, letting you go."

Wesley stopped the buggy at the front of the house and wrapped the reins around the hitching post. He stepped across and helped Anna down, and then walked her up the stairs, opening the door with a key produced from his coat pocket.

Anna began to enter the house, and then turned suddenly and looked into Wesley's face.

"Thank you so much, Mr. Smith, for this evening. It was quite lovely. I'll never forget it."

She turned and ran inside, blinking back the tears.

"Nor will I, my love. Nor will I."

With a sigh, Wesley turned and walked back down the stairs. He needed to stable the horse before retiring to his room.

Chapter Twenty-Three

Patricia Smith tried to fall asleep but found herself unable. Despite her best intentions, she stayed awake, straining to hear the sounds of Wesley's and Anna's return.

"Oh, I do hope he tells her," she thought. "I do hope he does not let her leave without letting her know how he feels."

Patricia was keenly aware that Anna had been considering leaving the Smiths' employment. It wasn't anything she had said, but more in the way she watched Patricia as they moved about their daily activities. Patricia knew that Anna, in her own way, was quite practical. She never would want to take a salary from someone if she felt her services unnecessary.

The thought of Anna leaving made Patricia feel sad, of course, yet she felt such great peace within herself as she daily improved in both physical and spiritual health. As she realized how much she came to enjoy Anna's company, she harbored hopes that she could continue their relationship, but now in the form of a mother-daughter one.

In the midst of these thoughts, Patricia heard the door open to Anna's room. She listened closely as she heard Anna enter and begin to undress. It was the sound of sobbing that confirmed Patricia's worst fears.

"Did he not tell her?" Patricia thought, wanting to go in and comfort Anna, yet aware that the girl needed her privacy.

Was it possible that, perhaps, Wesley was not interested in a relationship with Anna? Or maybe it was Anna herself? Maybe Patricia had misinterpreted the glances the two shot each other when each thought the other wasn't looking.

"Dear Lord," Patricia breathed, "Please offer comfort to Anna. She is sorrowing, Lord, and I don't know why. Please bring peace to her as she has done to me."

Patricia continued her prayer long into the night. Finally, she fell into a deep sleep, confident that the God she had come to wholly trust would care for the two people she had grown to love most in the world.

Patricia could tell by the slant of the sun coming through the windows that she awoke late the next morning. She had heard a soft knocking at her door, and now, as she watched, Anna padded into the room, concern on her face.

"Are you feeling all right, Mrs. Smith?"

The older woman smiled her reassurance.

"Yes, I'm fine, fine. I just had trouble falling asleep last night, and I think I was making up for lost time this morning."

Anna returned her smile, and hurried to her bedside with a tray full of tea and thickly buttered toast.

"Well, because I was not sure of your health, I thought I'd bring your breakfast to you this morning, instead of making you walk those stairs again."

Patricia chuckled.

"Oh, those stairs are no problem for me now. In fact, I rather enjoy making the long trek. Although, if it was to be done over, I think I'd design this house so the bedrooms and the kitchen would not be quite so far apart."

Anna smiled, but Patricia could not help but notice how drawn and pale the girl looked this morning. Patricia's stomach sank as she anticipated that there would be no news to share from the previous night's dinner.

"Is everything all right, Anna?"

Anna smiled again, yet this time, Patricia could see the wetness near her eyes.

"Have you been crying?"

Anna put down the tray and sat on Patricia's bed, burying her face in her hands.

"Oh, Mrs. Smith, I'm so sorry. This is not the manner in which I wanted to tell you."

Patricia patted the girl's shoulder in an attempt to comfort her. "There, there, Anna. Slow down. I'm sure it will be all right."

Finally, when Anna seemed to regain some of her composure, she spoke. "I must tell you that I will be leaving, Mrs. Smith. I believe that you are healthy, now, and you have no more need for me here."

Anna managed a weak smile.

"I am so pleased with your health, and your faith. I feel it is time for me to go and be with my family now."

Much to Anna's surprise, Patricia nodded her head in agreement.

"As much as I hate to see you leave, I agree that you must," the older woman said, adding wryly. "I have learned through these months that we have spent together that you need to be kept busy. Now that I can and want to do so many of the daily chores myself, you must go somewhere else where you can feel needed."

Anna blinked rapidly. Because Patricia Smith was, on many levels, a practical woman, Anna had expected her to accept the decision eventually. She would have liked it, however, if Patricia had seemed a little more sorrowful at her leaving.

"Oh, Anna," Patricia patted the girl's hand. "Don't worry. I'm sure the moment you leave I'll find a hundred reasons to need you back immediately."

Patricia paused.

"But knowing you, I'll bet you have prayed about this decision. You must follow your heart on this."

Anna nodded and rose to bring the tea tray.

She had prayed about the decision. Anna poured the steaming tea into the china cup. Yet somehow, her heart did not feel at peace. In fact, with every minute that passed, her heart felt just one step closer to breaking.

Plans were made for Anna to leave in two weeks, and the days passed quickly. A letter was sent to the Svensens explaining when they should plan to meet Anna's train. Anna and Patricia passed much time in the garden, enjoying the spring air and even helping Ian and Simon tend to some of the smaller flower beds.

Patricia did confront Wesley about Anna's decision to leave. The day after the fateful dinner date, Wesley knocked on his mother's door in the evening, after he was sure that Anna would have gone to her own room for the night.

"Mother, may I come in?"

Patricia was sitting at the table near the window, reading. She put down her book as her son strode into the room.

"You're still up?"

"I was waiting for you? Why weren't you at dinner tonight?"

Wesley sighed.

"I had some business that couldn't wait. What is it that you need?"

He drew near and sat on the edge of her bed.

"Son, I just cannot believe it. I cannot believe that you are letting that girl go without telling her how you feel."

Wesley blinked at his mother. What was she talking about? Surely she didn't know about his feelings for Anna. He had never confided in her about his feelings . . . not concerning Anna, at least.

"Mother, what are you talking about?"

"You know perfectly well what I mean."

As Patricia glared at her son, Wesley could not help but feel like he was seven years old and had just been caught with his hand in the cookie jar right before dinner.

Patricia's voice and face grew gentler.

"Son, you're in love with Anna Svensen. Everyone around you can see that, except, perhaps, Anna herself. You must tell her. You must not let her leave without telling her."

Wesley looked at his mother, wanting to be comforted, and felt the tears press against the back of his eyes. He would not cry! He had not cried for years, not even at his own father's funeral. He swallowed hard.

"I planned to, Mother, really I did. But Anna saved me from the embarrassment of expressing my feelings. You see, she has a young man at home who is waiting for her."

Patricia looked at her son, confusion evident on her face.

"What do you mean?"

"Just what I said. There is someone at home waiting for Anna. I gathered that she wanted to help her family so desperately that she left her young man behind so that she might make a salary."

Wesley paused and shuffled his feet.

"I guess we must consider ourselves thankful that she did come to us. Her prayers helped bring you to the Lord, and your health is so much improved."

Troubled, Patricia got up and walked to her bureau. She looked deeply into the mirror hanging over it, as if to find the answers she was looking for in the face staring back at her.

"Yes," she said, finally, her voice quiet and reserved. "Anna's presence has been a blessing. But I know, that with you praying for me daily, I would have eventually found the Lord anyway, or He would have found me."

She turned to Wesley and smiled.

"As soon as I opened my heart to him, even just a little, He was right there with open arms, waiting for me."

Wesley smiled back at his mother. Yes, for this he was truly grateful.

"But," Patricia continued, a frown crossing her face. "I just cannot believe that Anna has a young man at home. I mean, she has never mentioned him, and, to my knowledge, she has never received any mail from anyone other than her family members and her teacher.

"Son," Patricia crossed the room and sat next to Wesley on the bed. "Perhaps you misunderstood her. Although she speaks English quite well, hardly with an accent even, sometimes she does have difficulty understanding the language completely."

"I don't think so. Not this time, at least," Wesley said wryly.

Patricia took Wesley's hands into her own and stroked them gently.

"Just consider that maybe you did misunderstand her. Just think about giving her a chance to know your true feelings. That's all I ask."

Wesley looked into his mother's eyes and saw the compassion and tenderness there that he had always loved. How could he say no to this woman?

"All right, Mother. I will think about it."

In truth, during Anna's remaining few days in the Smith household, Wesley thought of little else. Several times he attempted to speak to Anna, but she always seemed to avoid situations in which they might be alone.

Finally, Anna's last night in the Smith household arrived. Anna had spent the day packing her belongings and carefully cleaning the room she had called home the last ten months. As she shut the final bag lying on the bed, she looked around and sighed. She would miss this room with its airy curtains and ruffled bedspread. She would miss the view of the garden from her bedroom window, and her daily chats and walks with Patricia Smith. She would miss Jenny, Trudy, Ian and Simon.

But she knew, in her heart, that she would miss Wesley Smith most of all.

Trudy had prepared a special feast for Anna's final meal in the household. It was served, as Anna had requested, in the kitchen, and everyone, including Wesley and Patricia, were already seated when Anna came down.

"Well now, Missy, I don't know what we're to be a'doing without you," Ian said, throwing Anna one of his special smiles.

"Oh, Ian McNeil, you stop that this instant or you'll wind up with tears in your soup!"

Trudy stood up and went to the stove. Anna could see by her red-rimmed eyes that the gentle woman she had quickly grown to love as a second mother had already been crying.

"Here, let me help you," Anna said, stepping to the stove.

"Nonsense. This meal is to honor you. You just sit down now, with the others."

Trudy pushed Anna toward the table where she reluctantly sat, directly across from Wesley. Jenny rose and helped her mother with the final preparations, and soon after Wesley delivered the blessing and all were partaking in Trudy's fine cooking.

Anna found that she didn't have much of an appetite, even though Trudy had prepared her favorite dishes, including a rich chocolate cake for dessert. Anna tried to force herself to eat anyway, because she knew that cooking was one way Trudy showed love, and she didn't want to disappoint her friend.

As if she knew how hard the evening was for Anna, Patricia tried her best to keep everyone's spirits light. She related stories about her own cooking, in the days before the family hired the McNeils, and soon everyone was laughing over tales of burnt pudding and rock-hard bread.

Everyone, including Wesley, lingered at the table long after the last cup of coffee was drained. Anna couldn't help but be pleased that Wesley had managed to squeeze time out of his schedule to spend the evening with his mother. In fact, she had noticed that he seemed to be around quite a bit more than usual during the last two weeks. She assumed that he was trying to spend more time with Patricia because she herself was leaving.

Finally, as the hour grew late, Wesley stood and said, "Well, I imagine it is time to retire for the night. Anna and I must get an early start in the morning."

Anna looked up in surprise.

"You are going with me?"

Wesley turned and met her eyes.

"Why, yes. I thought you knew. I cannot allow you to make such a long journey alone, and I would like to see Uncle again. I will stop in Salina for some business on the way back, anyway."

"I see," Anna said, her cheeks flushing under his direct gaze. She had assumed that this time she would be making the trip to West Bend alone, because the journey was so familiar to her now. She couldn't help but be pleased that Wesley would be accompanying her.

"Yes, well, both of you had better be rested for your trip, then," Patricia said, breaking the sudden silence that had fallen on the room.

Anna looked blankly at her, and then nodded. Turning to Trudy, who had risen to stand by the sink with her back turned, Anna walked softly towards her.

At the sound of Anna's shoes tapping across the floor, Trudy turned, her eyes brimming. Silently Anna threw her arms around the woman who had been so much more than a co-worker during her stay in Kansas City.

"I'll miss you," Trudy whispered in Anna's hair.

"And I'll miss you," Anna responded. "Thank you for . . . well, for just everything."

The two hugged a moment longer, and then Anna turned to Jenny and gave her a warm squeeze. By the time she finished hugging both Ian and Simon, Anna realized that Wesley and Patricia had left the room. With one quick backwards glance, she fled upstairs. Before entering her own room, however, she stopped in front of Patricia's. Tentatively she knocked.

"Come in."

Anna found Patricia standing by the fireplace, holding a framed photograph in her hands. As she walked closer, she saw that the photograph was of a girl, the same young girl Anna had seen in the Smith family photograph all those many months ago on her first day of work.

"This was my Alison," Patricia said, not looking up. "She was a lovely child. When she died, I thought my world would end."

Patricia set the photograph down and continued.

"But then, Wesley grew and consumed my attention, and Arthur, my husband, was so full of life, I tried to push all thoughts of Alison from my mind."

Patricia walked over and stood close to Anna, grasping her hands. Anna could smell the soft floral scent of her perfume, and she felt the tears come.

"You have been as a daughter to me this past year, Anna. I couldn't have asked for any more from a child of my own."

Patricia hugged her, and then, letting go, pressed a small black box into her hands.

Anna turned it over, feeling the smoothness of the velvet.

"Go on, open it."

Tentatively lifting the lid, Anna caught her breath as she lifted out a heart-shaped locket dangling from a gold chain.

"You have helped me learn to love again, Anna. I wanted to give you something to remind you that you will always be in my heart."

"Oh, thank you," Anna said, hugging her employer one final time. "I will never forget you."

She darted into her own room.

Patricia stood, watching the door close behind her.

"Nor I you, Anna. Nor I you."

Chapter Twenty-Four

Wesley and Anna left before dawn the next morning. Neither had slept well, yet both seemed quite awake and prepared for the journey they faced. However, neither spoke much on the ride to the train station.

When they arrived, Simon once again helped Anna out of the carriage and lifted down her bags. Anna couldn't help but remember the evening when she first met Simon. She had grown to love him like a brother.

After securing her bags, Wesley reappeared and guided Anna to their seats on the train. Again, Anna remembered their first journey alone together and how silent Wesley Smith was. Would he be equally as quiet on this journey?

Again they sat alone in a small compartment separated from the narrow hall of the train by heavy curtains. Again, the seats they sat on were covered by plush, red velvet. And again, as soon as the train pulled out from the station, Wesley opened the briefcase he carried and retrieved a thick sheaf of papers which he promptly began reading.

It was close to one p.m. before the train pulled into the Salina station. Anna's stomach had been reminding her that it was lunch time for nearly two hours. However, when Wesley suggested that they dine again at the hotel where they had eaten on their first journey, Anna politely declined.

"Trudy made some sandwiches," she explained. "I think I'll take a short walk, and then eat while sitting on that bench, over there."

Wesley looked in the direction Anna pointed and saw an uninhabited wooden bench across the street from the dry goods store. He determined that it would be safe, and then nodded and turned in the direction of the hotel.

Anna had hoped that he would join her, but she didn't feel surprised when he chose not too. Still, she felt disappointment as she walked toward the bench.

After lunch, they boarded the train together and followed the same routine they had in the morning. Wesley buried himself in his reading, and Anna, after attempting to finish a book she had borrowed from the Smith's library, laid her head back against the high seat and dozed.

After she had been soundly asleep for a few minutes, Wesley laid down his papers and gazed at her. In truth, he had not been reading at all during the long ride, but rather, he had been trying to read; trying desperately to focus on anything other than counting the few hours he had left in Anna's presence.

He looked at Anna, examining the way her features, while pretty when she was awake, softened into a deep beauty while she slept. He wanted to reach over and brush back the wisps of blonde hair that grazed her forehead, but he knew an intimate gesture like that might cause her to awaken.

He turned his gaze to the window, his heart crying out. Why, oh why, must he have such strong feelings for a woman whose heart belonged to another?

Quietly, in the security of the train sitting beside a sleeping Anna, Wesley Smith finally let the tears come.

Once again Oscar and Christina were waiting for Anna when the train pulled into West Bend lat that evening. They showed some surprise at seeing Wesley. Anna had not mentioned anything about his arrival in her letter. Christina harbored a small hope that maybe Anna and Wesley would have some news for them, but one look at Wesley's drawn face told her otherwise.

After securing the bags in her father's wagon, Wesley turned and faced Anna.

"Well, I guess that will be all then. I'll be staying at Uncle Heggarty's a few days if you happen to remember anything you left, or if you have a message for Mother."

He tipped his hat and turned to leave.

"Wesley?"

He turned back at the sound of his name. Never could he remember her using his given name before, even though he had asked her to many times.

Suddenly shy, Anna glanced down at her feet.

"Will you be coming to commencement exercises? They are scheduled for Saturday afternoon."

Wesley quickly counted the days. Saturday was five days off, and he had planned to leave after only three. Plans could be changed, however.

"Yes . . . yes, of course. I'll be there."

"We would like it if you and Pastor Heggarty could join us for supper following the ceremony," Christina said, stepping forward.

"Yes . . . well, I don't know Uncle's plans, but I would love to, Mrs. Svensen," Wesley said.

"We will see you on Saturday, then," Oscar said, smiling.

"Yes, yes. See you then."

Wesley tipped his hat to Anna, holding her gaze for just a moment. Then he turned and walked towards his uncle's house, a sudden spring to his tired step.

Anna's eyes followed Wesley's dark form until she could no longer see him, and then she turned to her mother, a small smile on her face.

"Thank you for inviting him, Mother," she whispered as the two women made their way toward the wagon, their arms wrapped tightly around each other.

"Of course, my darling," Christina whispered back.

In the morning, Anna awoke to see Elsie sitting on the side of her bed, staring at her. Instantly, Anna noticed how tall the girl had become, and how her face had begun to lose many of its childish traits.

"I thought you were never going to wake up!"

Elsie bounced on the edge of the bed with excitement. "You've missed all of the early chores, and you almost missed breakfast."

Anna smiled and pulled her sister into a hug.

"It is so good to see you, Elsie. You will have to tell me about everything that has been happening at school."

"Oh, there won't be much to say," Elsie said, frowning slightly and leaning forward. "But I would really like to hear what it is like in Kansas City."

Anna laughed and promised to tell her sister the little she had learned about the city she had lived in for nearly a year.

At breakfast, Oscar prayed thankfully for his daughter's safe return, and Anna felt the warmth of her family fill her pained heart. She answered questions from each of her parents and siblings as fast as they could ask them, and she marveled at the improvements in Elsie's, Bjorn's and Joseph's language skills.

Aaron did not eat with the family that morning as his job at the hardware store had turned into a full-time position as manager. With Aaron's capable assistance, the hardware store owner had decided he could take a much-needed break and turn over the daily responsibilities. Aaron's new position offered a noticeable raise, and he was able to purchase a small cottage in West Bend. He and his soon-to-be bride had been busying themselves filling the house with homemade furniture, curtains, and rugs.

Anna looked forward to visiting with Aaron and Minnie on Saturday, after the commencement ceremony. Their wedding was scheduled in three weeks.

All-in-all, Anna's homecoming would soon be overshadowed by the commotion surrounding the end of school and the wedding, and she felt relief. She needed to keep her hands and her mind busy, so she would quit thinking about the McNeils and Patricia Smith in Kansas City, and Wesley in West Bend, so close and yet soon to be so very far away.

As soon as the breakfast dishes were dried and put away, Anna joined Elsie, Joseph, and Bjorn on the familiar walk to the country school. Only three days remained in the spring term, and Anna could not wait to see Tina Stevens.

As she walked, Anna breathed deeply of the fresh spring air. Already in early May, the air held a touch of heaviness that Anna knew would soon turn to the typical summer humidity. Yet as they walked, the sun shone, and Anna thanked God for the chance to experience nature which she had desperately missed during the long winter months in the city.

At last they arrived at the school. Conspiring with her brothers and sister, Anna decided to wait outside, behind the building, until the students completed the day's opening exercises. Once the morning recitation had begun, Anna would sneak in and sit in her old seat, which had remained unoccupied, according to Elsie.

The plan worked perfectly. With her attention focused, Tina Stevens listened while two young boys took turns reading. Anna padded quietly to her old seat, slipping in next to Mary Richards who seemed surprised, and then genuinely happy to see her.

Motioning with her eyes in Miss Stevens' direction, Anna faced Mary, placing one finger in front of her lips. Smiling, Mary nodded, then reached over and squeezed Anna's hand. A look passed between the two young women then that filled Anna's heart with peace. Mary had forgiven her for not marrying her brother, Michael. Anna squeezed Mary's hand back, and shook silently with excitement.

"Very good, Benjamin," Miss Stevens said, rising and coming toward the center of the one-room school house. "Now, I'd like to hear from . . . ."

The teacher's voice trailed off as she saw Anna. Tina Stevens blinked once, and then twice, and then a wide smile broke across her face.

"Anna," she said, rushing forward and grabbing her friend's hands in her own. "You surprised me! I didn't realize you would already be home!"

Anna laughed with delight, as did Elsie on the second row.

Finally remembering the other students in the class, Miss Stevens turned and scanned the room. All eyes seemed to be on the reunion between her and Anna, and no one appeared to be studying.

"All right students. It is time to get back to your work. We will have time this afternoon, after closing ceremony exercises, to welcome Anna back properly."

That said, the young teacher resumed her duties, but only after throwing Anna a brilliant smile. The smile warmed Anna and distracted her, at least for a time, from her thoughts of Wesley.

The day flew by. Anna picked up right where she had left off the previous spring, helping the youngest students with math and reading. Mary had proven to be an able teacher, filling in with the younger students, but she had confided to Anna during lunch that she had plans to marry soon.

"His name is Hank Breckridge, and he has only lived in West Bend a few months," Mary had gushed, her bright eyes sparkling at the mention of his name. "He is a few years older than us, and he has actually traveled."

Mary clapped her hands together on the last word, expelling air as she did so.

"How much . . . older?"

Mary played with the slice of bread lying in her lap.

"Oh, not too much, I suppose."

She raised her head and continued. "He was most recently in California. He rode by horseback all the way here to purchase the Zeilinger place. His aunt and uncle farm the homestead next to it, and they had written him about it. He had been looking for some land to settle on, and this was the perfect opportunity."

Anna smiled and nodded, hoping that this Hank Breckridge was worthy of her friend's devotion. She also hoped that if the two did marry, that Hank wouldn't tire of Mary's enthusiasm and seemingly endless desire for conversation.

When the school day ended, Anna waited while the other children packed their homework and left, so she and Tina Stevens could have a much-anticipated talk. In only a few short days, the schoolteacher would be leaving West Bend for good to marry her Samuel.

"He graduates from seminary in one month," Miss Stevens said, the excitement evident in her eyes. "We will get married the following weekend. Oh Anna, after waiting all of this time, I can't believe it is so close!"

Happy for her friend, Anna listened as she described the wedding plans in great detail. It was to be a simple ceremony, followed by a potluck dinner in the churchyard.

"I wish you could be there, Anna. You, and so many other people I've met here."

Miss Stevens looked wistfully at the books neatly stacked on her desk. Carefully she ran her right hand along the edge of one's brown cover, tattered from daily use.

"I'll miss teaching here, of course. I wouldn't want to give up the people I've met or the experiences I've had the past two years."

"Not even meeting Jed Dennison on your first day?"

The teacher looked at Anna and chuckled.

"Not even that!"

The memory launched the two women into other stories of Miss Steven's teaching career. Finally, after Anna realized she needed to get home or she would miss dinner, the two prepared to leave.

"Will Samuel be coming for the commencement?"

"No, he's busy with exams. I'll take the train on Monday to Kansas City. My parents will meet me there, and then we'll travel together to St. Louis."

Anna pondered this for a moment.

"Are you worried? About riding the train by yourself, I mean."

"Oh, goodness no! I feel quite secure in the coach section. The conductors really seem to look out for women like me who are traveling alone. If you remember, I came alone to West Bend."

Anna nodded without speaking. She remembered quite well her friend's arrival in town.

When their paths diverged, Anna gave Miss Stevens a hug, and the two promised to find more time to spend together before Tina had to leave on Monday. As Anna set off for home, she couldn't help but wonder why Wesley Smith had insisted on accompanying her on the train when clearly, women traveling alone were not such a rarity.

Saturday dawned sunny but unusually cool for May. Intermittent rain had plagued the area on Friday, and Anna had hoped the rain wouldn't linger and spoil the plans for commencement. When she awoke and saw the sun streaming through the front window of the shanty, she murmured a quick word of thanks.

Anna had not returned to school for the final two days, but rather had stayed at home and helped her mother bake and clean. The end-of-school ceremony was scheduled to be a day-long event, beginning with recitation by the younger students in the morning. After a hearty covered dish meal, the older grades would recite followed by the first commencement ceremony West Bend had held in nearly five years. In addition to Anna and Mary Richards, a new student, Tom Blanca, would be graduating.

Soon all members of the Svensen household bustled through their morning chores in a hurry to reach the schoolhouse grounds. After a hasty breakfast, Anna washed the dishes and changed into the dress her mother had surprised her with the day before.

"I made it off of one of your old patterns," Christina had said as Anna lovingly stroked the embroidered bodice of the cornflower blue dress. "I hoped that you size was the same as when you left."

"It's perfect Mama," Anna said, holding it up to her shoulders. "Where did you find this material?"

Obviously pleased, Christina smiled proudly.

"It was at the dry goods store. Mrs. Harkness had just gotten it in. The minute I saw it I knew it would be perfect for you."

Anna made no attempt to brush away the tears that rolled down her cheek. She knew how her mother struggled with placing orders in English. Usually, Christina just wrote down what she needed and Oscar would request the items. The fact that Christina had chosen the material and had it measured herself made the dress all the more special.

"Thank you, Mama," Anna whispered.

"It is not every day that I have a daughter who is graduating," Christina said, pulling Anna into an embrace. "I am so proud of you."

As Anna pulled the beautiful dress over her head, her thoughts wound back over the last two years. For so long, she had held the goal of completing her education. Then, last year, when her parents struggled to keep the farm, her goal had changed to being able to help them financially. Now, both goals had been realized; she was graduating from school and the farm seemed to be secure with the promise of productive crops this year.

"What will I work on next?" Anna mused, brushing her hair and tying it securely in a knot on the top of her head.

Although her plans loomed uncertain, Anna felt peace as she placed her future in God's hands and turned to join her family in the wagon.

Chapter Twenty-Five

A crowd had already gathered in the school yard by the time the Svensens arrived. The family piled out of the wagon and went to greet their many friends. Anna looked around discreetly for Wesley, but she did not see him or Pastor Heggarty. Her heart gave a sudden lurch as she wondered if his plans had changed, and if he had already returned to Kansas City.

She pushed such thoughts aside, and helped her mother unload the many dishes they had brought to contribute to the midday meal. The tables, already laden with the best dishes the West Bend families could offer, would soon be groaning under the weight of even more delicacies.

After setting down the dishes, Anna joined Tina Stevens near the door to the school. The teacher was counting heads, making sure that all of her young pupils were present, clean, and ready to perform.

As soon as she saw Anna, the teacher stopped counting and smiled widely.

"The weather turned out beautifully, didn't it? I love your dress! Elsie had mentioned that your mother was working on a surprise."

"Thank you," Anna replied, pulling her skirt wide with both hands and making a mock curtsey. "This dress is so elaborate, I feel like royalty."

"And may I say, you look like royalty, also."

Anna froze at the sound of his voice. Her face flushed hotly as she turned around.

"Good morning Miss Svensen," Wesley said, tipping his hat. "Good morning Miss Stevens. It is nice to see you again."

"Good morning, Mr. Smith," Tina said, rescuing her friend from her speechlessness. "It is nice to see you again, also. I was so please to hear of your mother's return to health."

Wesley's face softened.

"It was truly an answer to prayer," he replied. "Although I do credit Miss Svensen with having much to do with it."

Recovering her voice, Anna responded, "Thank you, Mr. Smith. Your mother is a special woman. I already miss her."

"As she does you, I'm sure."

Wesley turned to Anna and looked intently into her eyes.

"This is a special day for you. I am quite proud of you."

Trying hard not to drop her eyes and break his gaze, Anna whispered, "Thank you."

After a long pause, Wesley spoke again to Tina Stevens. "Thank you for including me in today's festivities. I was honored to receive your letter inviting me to such a special event. I wasn't sure that I'd be able to make it, but . . . ."

Anna flinched. Had her teacher written to Wesley? Why would she do such a thing?

"You're welcome, of course, Mr. Smith. I wanted as many friends of Anna's as possible to join her today. I'm just sorry it was too long of a trip for your mother."

"So am I. Well," Wesley said, tipping his hat again, "I will be seeing both of you ladies at lunch."

Anna watched as he sauntered away, and then turned quickly toward her teacher.

"Did you invite him to come to my commencement?" she demanded, her voice strained.

"Yes, I did," Tina Stevens replied calmly.

"How dare you do such a thing without my knowledge! I feel so . . . so foolish having people make plans all around me. I am not a child, you know!"

If Tina Stevens had not expected such a reaction from her friend, she would have been hurt. But the teacher, wise beyond her years, had anticipated Anna's less-than-enthusiastic reaction to the knowledge that she had corresponded with Wesley Smith. Briefly, she wondered how Anna would feel if she knew that her teacher had written to Patricia Smith, also.

"Anna," Tina began, reaching out her hand and touching her friend's shoulder. "I didn't mean to hurt your feelings. I just wanted to include Mr. Smith today because I could tell, through your letters, that he was your friend. I only wanted to make this day special for you."

Anna stood silent for a moment; fighting back the anger she knew was irrational. If only she could tell Tina just how special Wesley was.

"It is all right," Anna said, forcing herself to smile. "Please forgive my anger."

"Of course," Tina Stevens hugged Anna gently. "Now can you help me line up these children? It is almost time to start."

A short time later the youngest students stood fidgeting, waiting for their turn to perform. After a few comments by Tom Allen, school board president, five students marched to the front and began reciting. Family and friends of the school children filled the benches that had been brought in wagons from the church for this special occasion. In addition, many people sat on quilts that had been spread out beside the benches. It seemed as if the entire community of West Bend was there.

Scheduled to perform third, Elsie patiently waited while the two children ahead of her recited the state capitals from memory. In contrast, Elsie had selected a poem by Walt Whitman to memorize. As she waited, Elsie rehearsed the poem silently.

Anna watched her sister. Just the previous evening she had listed to Elsie practice the poem. Anna knew she could do it, but still, standing in front of such a large crowd was daunting.

With her eyes fixed to Elsie's small form, Anna didn't notice that Wesley Smith, sitting two rows behind her, had his own eyes fixed on her. Wesley had spent many hours during the past few days in deep conversation with his uncle. Under the pastor's guidance, Wesley had come to realize that no matter what Anna's reaction would be, he must tell her of his feelings before he left for Kansas City. If he did not do so, he would never be able to fully give his heart to another woman.

"It will be today, dear Anna," Wesley thought to himself. "It has to be today."

Elsie performed impeccably as did most of the children who followed her. Soon the festivities broke for lunch, and Anna found herself surrounded by several family friends she had not seen since the previous spring. She filled a plate with food, all the while watching for Wesley. She finally saw him conversing with Aaron, but she felt a hand on her elbow before she could make her way towards them.

"Hello, Anna."

She turned to look into the face of Michael Richards. Although surprised, she felt genuine pleasure as she returned his warm smile.

"How are you, Michael?"

"I'm fine. Wonderful actually. And you?"

"I am well."

"Do you have a few moments?"

Anna cast a quick glance towards Wesley but saw that he had moved away from Aaron and was now speaking with his uncle.

"Of course."

Anna followed Michael toward a bench. She thought that Michael looked much the same, although he walked with more confidence than she had remembered.

They saw on a vacant bench in the shade of the school house. Anna noticed that Michael did not have a plate of food.

"Have you eaten, Michael?"

"Not yet. I will in a minute."

"You better hurry, or there might not be anything left," Anna teased.

Michael smiled and then turned quickly somber.

"I'm getting married, Anna."

Anna's stomach jumped quickly, and she felt a flash of jealousy. Then, just as quickly, a feeling of warmth passed through her.

"It is the girl I mentioned at Christmas."

"Oh, Michael, I'm so happy for you! When will the wedding be?"

Anna reached out and patted her friend's hand. Michael's face broke into its familiar smile.

"It is the week after Aaron and Minnie's wedding. I wanted to tell you myself before you heard it from anyone else."

"I'm glad that you did."

The two continued talking for a few more minutes, and then Mary Richards joined them and introduced her friend to Anna.

Across the schoolyard, Wesley watched as Anna reached out and touched the red-haired man's hand. When the man smiled at Anna, Wesley's heart clutched. Could this man have been waiting for Anna? Wesley was positive that it had been this man who had looked longingly at the train last fall as it pulled away from the station.

He felt a sudden surge of doubt at his decision to confront Anna with his feelings. Maybe it wasn't too late to catch the evening train for Salina tonight.

After everyone in the crowd had eaten his or her fill, the tables were pushed back and the families gathered again to continue closing exercises. Two more groups of students had to recite, and then it would be time to honor the three students who were graduating.

Anna's palms grew moist and her heart raced. To an outside observer, she appeared to be listening attentively to the performances on the makeshift stage, but in actuality, she didn't hear a word that was spoken.

After the final group of students sat down, Tina Stevens made her way to the front of the crowd. Anna marveled again at how such a small woman could command the attention of nearly everyone in West Bend. The audience quieted as the teacher spoke.

"It is with great pride that I stand before you today," Miss Stevens began. "The three students that I am about to present represent the first high school graduating class in West Bend in five years. All three of these students have worked diligently to achieve this honor, and I hope neither they, nor the community, takes this lightly. It is with great pleasure that I present to you Tom Blanca, Mary Richards, and Anna Svensen."

The crowd broke into thunderous applause as the three graduates stood and made their way to the front. Upon their arrival, each was presented with a certificate stating that they had met the requirements for graduation from West Bend

Community School. Anna stared at the scripted lettering, and a surge of joy passed through her.

As they began to leave to take their seats, Anna felt Tina Steven's hand on her arm.

"Wait a moment," the teacher whispered into her ear.

After Mary and Tom had sat, Miss Stevens spoke again.

"I have the honor of beginning a new tradition here in West Bend," she said.

Anna's heart pounded rapidly as she scanned the crowd.

"Many schools in the east are now honoring their graduates who score the highest marks in the class. At a meeting last month, the West Bend Board of Education decided to do the same. It is with great pride that I present to you West Bend's first valedictorian, Anna Svensen."

Anna caught her breath in surprise. In front of the entire crowd, Miss Stevens pinned a small gold broach in the shape of a lit torch to Anna's collar. The teacher then hugged Anna, and motioned for her to return to her seat.

Although she felt the eyes of the entire community upon her, Anna fairly floated back to her seat. As she sat and listened to the closing remarks from Miss Stevens and Tom Allen, Anna breathed a prayer of thankfulness. How glad she was that the Lord had led her family to this place, this prairie full of strong and loving people. God was so good.

There was much noise and confusion at the close of the day's events. Mothers scrambled to retrieve their best dishes and round up their children. Fathers went to hitch up the teams, glad to have sacrificed a precious day in the fields for such a noteworthy event.

Anna seemed surrounded by people as soon as she stood up. Well-wishers congratulated her, shaking her hand and patting her back.

"I hear you just might be our new school mistress, Anna," Tom Allen said.

Anna lifted her head to speak to him.

"Yes, I am considering that, Mr. Allen. Of course, I will not be able to complete the teacher training program by this fall, but Miss Stevens said you may be able to make an exception."

"Given the high recommendation from Miss Stevens, we just might consider such a thing."

He winked at Anna and turned to join his family.

Standing nearby, Wesley Smith's jaw dropped at the news. Anna a schoolteacher? He had been sure that Anna had wanted to return to West Bend to be married. Wasn't that why she had been speaking to that red-haired man?

Wesley turned and strode towards his horse. He had been prepared to speak to Anna, to congratulate her on her accomplishments and make his excuses for missing her party, and then, to turn bravely away and return to Kansas City. But that was when he had made up his mind that Anna was in love with someone else. He would have to take some time to assimilate the fact that she wasn't going to get married, that instead, she was planning on teaching.

Wesley decided that he would keep his promise to Christina Svensen to attend Anna's celebration. But first, he would spend some time in his uncle's church. He desperately needed to talk with God.

Chapter Twenty-Six

Carefully Anna sliced thick pieces of chocolate cake that she had baked the previous day. Wesley loved chocolate cake, which she knew from living in his house the past year. Trudy had made this exact recipe for all the special occasions throughout the year. Anna first tasted it on Wesley's birthday, in September. The rich icing melted on her tongue, and she had immediately asked for the recipe.

Her mother's kitchen did not have all the supplies needed for the cake, but Anna had tasted a nibble and was pleased with the substitutions.

If only Wesley would arrive!

Anna surveyed the Svensens' home with a critical eye. Compared to the opulence found in the Smith's Kansas City mansion, the shanty seemed terribly small, even primitive. But Anna knew that her parents' home was filled with warmth and love, and she could never be ashamed of something her mother and father worked so hard to maintain.

Lost in her thoughts, Anna did not hear the horses' hooves outside the door. Only when Elsie burst into the kitchen did Anna turn.

"Look who's here, Anna! Pastor Heggarty and Mr. Smith!"

Anna turned as Wesley and his uncle stepped into the room. For a moment, no one spoke, and Wesley and Anna stared deeply into each other's eyes.

Sensitive to the wordless exchange between his nephew and Anna, the pastor waited quietly until Christina came into the house. She had been setting up the table outside.

"Welcome, Pastor, Mr. Smith!" Christina said, a wide smile on her face. "We are so happy that you could be here to share this special evening with us."

Anna broke free from Wesley's strong gaze to glance at her mother. When had her mother learned to speak so well in English?

"Come, Anna," Christina said. "Bring the cake. We are ready to eat!"

"Yes, Mama," Anna said quietly.

Christina turned and Pastor Heggarty and Elsie followed her outside. Anna lifted the cake and made to follow also, keenly conscious that aside from stepping back to let his uncle pass, Wesley hadn't moved at all. She waited for him to leave the room, and when it became obvious he had no such plans to do so, she stepped in front of him.

"Anna."

Wesley spoke softly, reaching out and touching her arm as she passed. Anna looked up into his face, trying to read the intensity of feelings she found there.

"I must speak with you. Can we take a walk after we eat? Alone, I mean?"

Anna didn't hesitate.

"Yes, of course."

Wesley smiled and then nodded, releasing her arm.

"I'll look forward to it," he said, huskily.

Anna brushed past him, her heart pounding wildly. Whatever could he want?

Still full from the noon meal and the excitement of the day, Anna barely ate. Although Christina had saved many of Anna's favorites for the evening picnic, Anna only pushed the food around on her plate.

Christina noticed, of course, but refrained from speaking about it, and gently shook her head at Oscar when he began to mention his daughter's lack of appetite. The young lawyer did not seem to have much of an appetite, either, Christina noticed.

Wesley thought the meal drug on forever. Of course, he always enjoyed spending time with his uncle, and the Svensens were a special family. But his desire to be alone with Anna, to once and for all pour out his feelings, overwhelmed him.

Finally the meal ended. Anna helped Christina carry the dishes into the kitchen, while Joseph and Bjorn brought the table inside. At the basin, Christina surprised her daughter by stating that they would just let the dishes soak instead of washing them right away.

"But Mama," Anna protested.

"Hush, Anna. We must not leave your guests outside to enjoy the evening without the pleasure of your company."

Anna grinned quickly and gave her mother a hug. She patted her hair and rushed outside.

The men had gathered near the front of the home. Oscar and Pastor Heggarty rested on the bench that the boys had left outside, while Joseph and Bjorn squatted nearby. Elsie sat on her father's lap, enthralled by the story Pastor Heggarty was telling.

"But how could he live inside a fish?"

"Well, Elsie, that's a good question . . . ."

Anna tuned out the good pastor's words as she noticed Wesley leaning against the front of the house. Their eyes locked, and Anna caught her breath. Reaching out to brush her arm, Wesley lifted his eyebrows in an unspoken question. Anna nodded, and turned to her mother, standing in the doorway.

"Mr. Smith and I will be taking a short walk," Anna began, searching for an excuse to explain why she needed to spend time alone with Wesley.

Christina lifted an index finger and touched Anna's lips, silencing her from any further explanation.

"Go ahead. We will be here, waiting for you."

Anna smiled, and then turned to join Wesley who had stepped away from the house.

The pair walked in silence in the growing dusk, unaware that the story of Jonah had stopped as soon as they left the gathering.

"Mama, where are they going?' Elsie spoke in a loud voice. "Can I go too?"

"Hush, Elsie," Oscar said, pulling his daughter further onto his lap. "Mr. Smith and Anna have some business to discuss. We will stay here and finish the story."

"It is more than business on their minds, I hope," Pastor Heggarty said, a smile in his voice. "Now, where were we? Oh, yes, inside the great fish . . . ."

Anna and Wesley walked in silence for several minutes. They headed toward the creek, toward the same outcropping of rocks where Anna and Michael Richards had sat. Anna shivered slightly as they walked.

"Are you cold?"

"A little."

Wesley removed his jacket and wrapped it around Anna's shoulders. Anna shivered again, but suspected that this time it was due to Wesley's nearness. She breathed in his smell through his jacket, and smiled slightly.

"Thank you."

They walked until they reached the creek. Due to the abundance of spring rains, it bubbled merrily and loudly. Anna led Wesley to the rocks where, without speaking he brushed the loose dirt and helped Anna sit.

"It is beautiful, isn't it?" Anna said, gazing at the remnants of a spectacular gold and orange sunset.

"Yes. I was just thinking the same thing."

Anna turned to Wesley and found him staring at her. She averted her eyes.

"Anna," Wesley began, his voice just slightly shaking. "I have something I want to tell you."

Anna shook her head.

"Really, Mr. Smith, there is no need to . . . ."

Anna stopped abruptly as Wesley pressed two fingers to her lips.

"Not this time, Anna. This time, I want to speak first."

She noticed the way a slight smile played about his mouth as he let his fingers linger on her lips slightly longer than necessary.

Reluctantly, he drew his hand away. Then, on impulse, he picked up both of her hands in his. Anna sat expectantly, hearing the beat of her own heart over the sound of the gurgling creek. Time seemed to stand still as she felt her palms pressed into Wesley's large, warm hands, her face only inches from his.

"Anna," he began again, his voice almost a whisper. "I've wanted to tell you this for such a long time, but I couldn't find the words. I was so afraid of being rejected. But I love you, Anna, more than I've ever loved anyone in my life, except God and my parents. I love everything about you. The way the sunlight plays in your hair, the way your mouth turns down at the corners when you have your mind made up about something, the way your eyes shine when you are around the people you care about. But most of all, I love you for your convictions. Your faith, your honesty, ..."

He paused, stroking her hands.

"My love for you kept me from marrying Jessica. I don't know if you could find it in your heart to return my love, but even if you can't, it will never change my feelings for you."

Wesley paused again, and noticed the tears rolling down Anna's cheeks. He let go of her hands and wiped the tears away with his thumbs.

"Oh, Wesley," she said. "I never knew . . . I hoped of course ... but we're so different. We come from different . . . ."

With a gasp of surprise, Wesley smiled widely as he recognized the love shining on her face. He drew her near and brushed her lips slightly with his own.

"We're not so different, I think. In fact, we're more alike than either of us realize. We're both stubborn, aren't we?"

Anna chuckled, happiness flowing through her. Wesley brushed her lips again, and then laid her head against his broad chest, stroking her hair.

"I was afraid to love you," Anna whispered. "I couldn't stand the pain of not being loved in return."

"Shh, it's all right now. Everything is all right."

After several moments, Wesley pulled away and looked into her eyes again.

"You will marry me, then? Not immediately, of course, but you will consider it?"

Anna smiled, tears flowing again.

"Yes."

He hugged her tightly.

"Then let's return and let them know. I think they are waiting on us."

Anna nodded, not wanting to lose their time together, but instinctively knowing that the years ahead would bring many more moments to share.

They rose together, brushing off their clothes, and hanging on to each other's hands as they made their way back to the shanty to share their good news.

Epilogue
Two years later

Anna carefully lowered herself into the rocking chair by the window.

"Are you feeling okay? Any pains?"

Anna smiled and raised her head to meet the concerned gaze of her mother-in-law, Patricia Smith. The irony that they had exchanged places as caregiver and patient was not lost on Anna.

"I am fine, really. I am just feeling so heavy."

Patricia chuckled as she gently patted Anna's rounded belly.

"Well, I have to say you are looking rather large. I think this little one might just be a bit bigger than we were expecting."

"I think so too."

Both women turned their heads to see Wesley stride into the room. He kissed his mother on the check, and then leaned down to look into his wife's face.

"I am glad you are home," Anna said, gently running her hand down her husband's strong jaw.

He smiled and brushed her lips.

"I've brought you a surprise."

Wesley straightened and stepped aside just as Christina and Elsie came into the room.

"Mama! Elsie!" Anna struggled to stand.

"Now you just sit, daughter. You must rest! Soon it will be time to bring this baby into the world, and you need your strength."

Anna smiled and let herself be hugged by first her mother and then her sister, now a tall girl of nine.

"Oh, thank you so much for coming! I couldn't bear to think of going through this without you. I didn't think you could come. Wesley didn't tell me. . . ."

Anna glanced at her husband, smiling in a corner of the room. He strode over and planted another kiss on the top of his wife's head, and then turned to his own mother.

"I think we should leave the three of them to catch up, don't you?"

"Yes, of course, dear. You have a good visit now, and we'll talk more during dinner."

While Christina thanked Patricia and Wesley for their hospitality, Anna silently thanked God. Surrounded by people she loved and expecting a baby she wanted dearly, Anna's heart was full. She sighed with contentment, closing her eyes. With the anxiety of giving birth to her first child close at hand, Anna was often tempted to give in to worrisome thoughts.

Anna smiled. There was no need to worry. She followed a God she could trust.

Printed in the United States
108213LV00004B/16/P